adobeDreams

A Novel of Santa Fe

by Robert Burke

Acknowledgements

I thank God for the words; Mondaine for teaching me to read before I started school (the best education I ever received); Julia and Marcus for the most precious years of my life; Alice for editorial suggestions that sparked an amazing transformation of the manuscript; and Mary Rose for her unconditional support and patience.

Dedication

For light workers everywhere
who empower life, human life, and
quality of life on this planet.

Burro Alley

"I've been waiting for someone to show me the way."

Abigail Regan stood on a street corner in Santa Fe, New Mexico, waiting for a man. She turned from the light and caught her reflection in the window of a small café facing Water Street. Even as a young girl mirrors held a special fascination for her, and she often imagined their surfaces as portals to other worlds. For that reason she constantly checked to see if the image held the Abigail she knew, or if some alternate self stared back from a mirrored universe.

In the café window she saw a young woman with a brunette ponytail and large sunglasses. The dark lenses concealed a scar underneath her right eye, but she knew it was there all the same. A weathered fishing vest over a short sleeve plum blouse and khaki shorts completed her attire. The fishing vest carried filters and memory cards, while over one shoulder a non-descript canvas bag held cameras and flash.

Satisfied that she was still herself, she opened a city map to look one last time for adobeDreams, an exclusive bed and breakfast she knew only through obscure Internet references. Finding the unlisted B&B was crucial to the success of a travel guide she planned to publish in the spring, and she'd contacted a guide to lead the way.

"If I were a mystery hotel, where would I be?" she asked.

"You look lost," a man said.

She turned toward the voice. The morning sun blinded her for a moment until she made out the silhouette of a man with his back to the light. The glare created a halo around his blond hair, and obscured his face.

"My apologies," he said, and stepped to the front so that he could be seen without the glare.

Well, hello, handsome stranger. The man was six feet tall, mid-thirties and lean, with unruly curls behind his ears. He had green eyes with facets that caught the light and shone with an inner glow. He wore a white sports coat over a dark grey pullover, with pressed jeans and scuffed brown loafers. Abigail judged him to be a professional of some sort, perhaps a lawyer, or a civil servant. He appeared ten years older than someone with whom she'd normally find an attraction, but unlike boys her own age, at least this one knew how to shave.

"I am Raphael Mendoza, at your service," the handsome stranger said. "Can I help you find something?"

His fair skin, green eyes, and blond hair didn't seem congruent with a Hispanic surname. It was a little like meeting an Asian person with the last name of "Washington." She wondered if he could have been adopted.

He apparently noticed her confusion and explained, "From the Scandinavian Mendozas."

She laughed. She hadn't realized she'd been staring. This could be a new record for offending a complete stranger.

"I'm sorry," she said, "that was rude. I don't know what I was thinking!"

"You are lost, or looking for something?" he said.

"Yes, yes," she stammered. Oh this is going well, now I can't even talk correctly.

"I'm looking for a B&B that's not on the map. It's called adobeDreams. Have you heard of it?"

"Yes, I know of it. It is a little difficult to find. Which way were you going?"

"I was waiting for someone to show me the way, but it looks like I've been stood up. I thought I'd go to the Plaza and start from there."

Raphael looked up and down the street. A few tourists window-shopped in the distance, but no one approached.

"Actually, it is closer to Burro Alley," he said, "I am walking that way. May I accompany you, Miss...?" He raised his eyebrow and cocked his head to reinforce the question.

"Abby! Abigail, actually, but my friends call me Abby." Of course they call you Abby, you dork, that's what people call you when your name is, "Abigail."

She stepped back and scanned the empty street, and then read Raphael's face. He seemed trustworthy enough, and who could say whether her alleged guide would ever show up?

"That's very kind of you. Are you sure it's not an inconvenience?"

"It is no problem at all. I am glad to have the company."

The two walked north on Don Gaspar Street. The New Mexico light had been exquisite earlier that morning, but now the combination of the intense sun and low humidity threatened to broil Abigail's skin. She retrieved a small water bottle from her bag and took a large drink.

"Is this your first visit to Santa Fe?" Raphael asked.

"Yes, it is," she replied. "I've wanted to come here for years! I love the adobe architecture and the light."

"Welcome to the 'City Different,'" he replied. "Are you here for the Indian Market?"

"Yes, but I came a few days early to see the city before the market begins. Do you have any recommendations for places I should visit? Besides adobeDreams, I mean."

He looked at her bag and vest. "You are a photographer? Have you visited the galleries along Canyon Road?"

"Actually, I'm a travel journalist. I try to find the unusual attractions that other guides miss."

"That explains your interest in adobeDreams. How did you hear of it?" he asked.

"I saw it mentioned a few times in chat rooms. The writers said it was a special place that changed their lives. Do you know anything about it?"

"It as you say," he said, "but I suspect if you are ready for something to change your life, that something will find you."

"'When the student is ready, the teacher will appear,' or at least, that's the cliché. Is that what you're saying?"

Raphael laughed, and gave her a warm smile. His easy-going confidence put her at ease. She noticed he didn't wear a ring, and she wondered if he had anyone special in his life.

"I like to think that teachers are around us all the time, in many forms. From a certain point of view, everything that happens is simply feedback from the environment. The question is, are the students listening?"

"That's rather deep," she said.

"The trick," he replied, "is that any experience capable of teaching you something new is also by definition a challenging experience."

He paused for a moment, and then explained further, "If it does not make you uncomfortable, then it is not really anything new."

Abigail stopped to look at him.

"You're one of those thinking types, aren't you?"

He laughed.

"I suppose I am. I plead guilty to too much people watching."

"And what else has 'people watching' taught you?" she asked.

He thought for a moment before responding.

"I see people who want to change their lives, but never leave the comfort zone. They trick themselves into believing they're on a different course, but the truth is, they just keep doing different versions of the same thing, and their lives remain the same."

"Is that so bad, for most people?"

"It depends," he responded. "It depends on whether you want your epitaph to read, 'She watched a lot of great television.'"

Abigail laughed with a snort and then quickly covered her mouth with embarrassment. She couldn't remember ever doing that before. What was wrong with her?

"No, that wouldn't be much of an epitaph, would it?" she said, after regaining her composure.

"No, it would not, but I think you walk a different path."

His reply crossed an invisible line in her head. A line crossed so many times by overbearing males who tried to tell her what to think or how to feel, or worse, *not* to think or feel anything at all. She was done with all that. *Who are you to tell me what path I'm walking?* We've known each other for what, five minutes, and you're already trying to define my experience?

She tried to pull her mind back into the moment, but silence filled the space between them. Support posts of the building overhang cast vertical shadows on the walls. Abigail feigned interest in the display windows of small art galleries and shops as they passed. At the intersection with San Francisco Street, they strolled west toward Burro Alley.

"So what do you do, Raphael?" she at last thought to ask.

"I am an arbitrator... for select clients."

She wondered if his careful phrasing of "select clients" meant "the rich and famous," but didn't know if she should press it. She did anyway.

"That sounds mysterious," she said. "Can you give me any hints about the people you work with?"

He smiled.

"No one that you would recognize, Abigail. I can only say that they are among the best, and the worst, and sometimes even entities at such extremes must find a way to work together."

"And that's what you do?"

"Yes, that is what I do," he said as they turned into Burro Alley.

A statue of a burro with a load of firewood stood at the entrance, and Abigail allowed her fingers to float across its rear flank. The bronze felt hot to the touch. In earlier times, Burro Alley was Santa Fe's "red light" district, and got its name from the sturdy pack animals that brought firewood down from the mountains. It took more than body heat to keep those cantinas warm in the cold New Mexico winters.

As they approached Palace Avenue, a blue door appeared along one wall. Abigail paused to admire the play of light across its weathered surface. Chips and cracks in the paint exposed older, faded streaks underneath. She ran her fingertips over the rough texture and raised her sunglasses to obtain a better view. The streaks were actually long scratches in the wood, as though animals had clawed at the door.

"This must be hundreds of years old," she said.

"The blue represents running water, a barrier that evil spirits may not cross."

He turned the knob and opened the door inward. The doorway opened to a long, narrow path between tall adobe walls.

"For purposes of Feng Shui, blue doors also represent abundance," he said.

Two thoughts immediately occurred to Abigail. One, this is the part of the movie where the handsome stranger shoves you through the door where his henchmen lie in wait. Two, never accompany a perpetrator to the secondary crime scene, because that's where the sexual assaults and murders occur.

"Never go where the bad guy wants to go," an instructor in a rape awareness class had said. She advised students to run for their lives, grab the steering wheel and crash the car, or do whatever they had to do to avoid going to a more secluded location.

The class included self-defense training against an instructor in a heavy protective suit. Abigail thought of Edgar, her ex-boyfriend, as she kneed the mock assailant in the groin, and tore into him with elbows and palm heels. Edgar outweighed her by almost twice her bodyweight, and he hit her! *He hit her!* That outrage fueled an interest in martial arts, and she took additional kickboxing classes to learn the proper way to punch and kick.

She looked at Raphael and wondered, why couldn't I remember all this stuff before I walk away with a complete stranger, someone with whom I've hardly had five minutes of conversation? Raphael, I'm keeping my eye on you!

A breeze touched the sweat on her forehead. She pulled the sides of her vest together to cover her breasts and stepped through the doorway, enticed by the coolness and the unknown. Perhaps it wasn't a smart thing to do, but she felt compelled to move forward.

Brown adobe bricks lined the path between the walls, with narrow drains running along either side. The bricks were uneven in spots with shallow craters where weeds had been pulled from the joints. Abigail couldn't see the other end of the path, although she knew it could not be more than a block long. She turned to look at Raphael. He stepped inside the door and closed it.

"Where are we going?" she asked.

"Only as far as the path takes you."

Warning bells should have rung in her head. In a secluded area with a strange man she didn't know, anything could happen. The sincerity of his voice overruled any concerns, and she felt safe in his presence even though she couldn't say why.

She admired the texture of the adobe, and floated her fingertips across the rough surface as they walked. The walls stood two stories tall, with the sky a blue river between them. Soft light reflected back-and-forth between the walls, and gave the path a glow like warm caramel. She looked up at the sky and vertigo twisted her stomach. The narrow path created a sense of isolation and her frame of reference involuntarily inverted with that of the sky. For a moment she couldn't tell if she stood on the ground, looking up, or if she peered from some great height at a river far below. The air chilled her skin, and gooseflesh popped up on her exposed arms.

A little girl with brown skin walked out of an intersecting path. She wore a dark grey tunic under a black shawl over her shoulders, with red flowers embroidered at either end. Two long braids of black hair fastened with silver barrettes framed her face. Her brown eyes sparkled at Abigail.

The girl looked back in the direction she'd come, and said, "Tenga cuidado con los demonios."

Abigail didn't understand her words, but she understood the meaning. "Demonios" sounded like "demons" in English, and she'd warned Abigail not to walk that way.

"Are you okay? Where is your mother?" Abigail asked.

The little girl smiled, and then continued down the intersecting path. Her small body disappeared into darkness.

"Little girl? Little girl?" Abigail called. She wondered if she should go after her, but the whole thing had been so strange. What if it was a trick? She looked at Raphael. He maintained a respectful distance behind, neither too close nor too far.

Abigail removed her sunglasses and looked down the opposite path. It too dimmed to complete darkness. She turned to walk away and heard the shuffle of something in the dark. Her eyes strained to see the source of the noise. Large, indistinct shapes moved within the darkness, or perhaps some trick of her vision suggested movement?

"We should keep walking," Raphael said.

Abigail stepped away and low, angry snarls erupted from the shadows. Stealthy footsteps approached the intersection. She imagined feral dogs creeping forward to attack. The hair stood up on the back of her neck and she stumbled away, not knowing what to do. In a flash, Raphael stood in the intersection, and faced the approaching beasts.

"Stop!" he shouted.

A blue flame in his right hand illuminated the walls with a bright glow, and he stood firmly rooted as a tree. The flame pulsed with energy and an unseen force pressed against Abigail's body. Her equilibrium tilted, and she stiffened an arm against a wall for support. The snarls stopped, and the darkness fell silent.

"What are you? A magician?" she asked.

Raphael closed his hand, extinguishing the flame.

"Keep walking, Abigail. Your way is secure."

Onward she walked, much further than she believed possible for this short block within the city. She looked back. Raphael maintained his vigil in the intersection, safeguarding her passage. The air currents turned chill and flowed across her skin as thick as fog. She turned her palms up. Every crease and line flowed with blue light. Even the swirls of her fingertips pulsed with a radiating glow.

Have I been drugged? The effect mesmerized her and she couldn't resist the urge to watch. Her hands felt electric. She held them up, palms out, and made small circles in the air. Rippling wakes followed her movements like fish swimming through heavy liquid. She looked at the dial of her sports watch and saw the second hand frozen at one second past nine. Something was very wrong here, but the thought slipped away.

She collapsed to her knees, hands splayed in front, supported by the bricks of the path. Her canvas bag slid drunkenly to her side. A wave of nausea washed over her and she struggled to hold the contents of her stomach.

A red wasp landed in her field of vision, and groomed a foreleg with its mandible. Abigail focused on the insect in an effort to control the nausea. The wasp displayed no concern for the giant human looming over it, and acted as though time had no consequence.

The insect first groomed one foreleg, and then the other. The wasp, she saw, simply acted according to its nature. Nature does what it does, without doubt, without hesitation, and without deliberation. It can do nothing else. Few humans achieve such a connection to the universe, and perhaps then only in the flow of creativity, or acts of selfless love, or the abandonment of sexual ecstasy. Something inverted in Abigail's brain, and she struggled to make the distinction between the human looking at the wasp, and the wasp looking at the human.

The edges of her vision collapsed and she woke standing upright, looking at the night sky with the Milky Way above her.

"My God, that is beautiful," she said to no one in particular.

She felt the rotation of the Earth beneath her feet and watched the stars. The same strange thoughts she experienced with the wasp came back. Am I the human, looking up at the galaxy, or am I the galaxy looking at the human? Perhaps in this place, there is no distinction between the molecule and the mass.

She inhaled cool air through her nose and expanded her diaphragm to fill her lungs with oxygen. She exhaled through her mouth and lowered her head. Calmed by the deep breath, Abigail assessed her circumstances. She stood in a small clearing, with an adobe archway and wall in front of her. The wall reached over a story high, and stretched into darkness in both directions.

A wood gate with two doors stood closed under the arch. Candles burned in small sconces on either side. A small placard hung below one of the candles. She strained to read it in the dim light: adobeDreams.

A braided pull-string of fibrous plant material hung between the gate and the placard, passing through the wall. A pull of the string would ring a bell on the other side. Abigail grabbed the string, hesitated, and then tugged.

adobeDreams

"You are here, the time is now, and that is
sufficient."

Abigail debated whether to ring the bell again
when footsteps approached from the other
side of the wall. The gate opened and a young
Hispanic woman stood in the doorway. She wore an
ankle-length white gown that took on a gossamer glow
from lamps in the background. Long black hair fell
over her shoulders and her brown eyes sparkled in the
night. For a brief moment she looked like an angel.
Abigail liked her immediately.

"Welcome," brown eyes said, "I am Caroline, and
this is adobeDreams."

Abigail stumbled forward and forgot to introduce
herself. Her legs wobbled and her head felt too heavy
to lift. Caroline caught her arm and guided her toward
a structure.

"You've come a long way to visit us," Caroline
said. "We've looked forward to your arrival for some
time."

Abigail wondered whom she meant by "we," but
couldn't formulate the question. Tunnel vision
obscured everything but their footsteps across a
bricked path. She thought of the night she drank too
much at a neighborhood bar and friends escorted her
home amidst giggles and laughter.

The giggles morphed into birdsong. The birds sang of dawn and their hunger for the warmth of the sun, and of air currents stirring through the leaves. *Nice birdies.*

Abigail woke beneath a down-filled comforter in a large adobe room. Morning light cast a vanilla glow through sheer curtains. Coarse wooden beams crossed the ceiling above. She didn't want to move. Ever.

She snapped awake and sat up with her brain doing quick math. She was in a strange bed in a strange room and didn't have any clothes on! She grabbed the comforter with her fists and pulled it over her chest. Wide-eyed, she scanned the room and extended her hearing to detect any threats. At first she heard nothing at all, but at last the melody of the birds returned.

She lifted the sheets and performed a quick inspection. Her body appeared intact, and her panties hadn't been removed, so she retained some dignity regardless of what happened the night before.

A black robe with jagged red and white striping lay across the back of a chair with her clothes folded on the seat. Her vest and canvas bag rested on a small table against a wall, below a silver-framed mirror. She reached for the robe, looked around, and then stepped out of bed to put it on. Square brown tiles on the floor warmed the soles of her feet.

She inspected the contents of the canvas bag. The camera gear rested inside exactly as she'd left it. She fished a cell phone out of a front pocket of the vest, and flipped open the clamshell. The signal strength indicated, "No service." *No kidding, service is really lousy when you wake up on Mars!* She looked around the room and saw no phone, no clock, and no television.

Abigail dropped the phone back in the vest pocket and looked into the mirror above the table. Why is it when you first see your reflection, it takes a moment to realize that it is you? She studied the dark haired woman in the mirror. Her mother's blue eyes stared back, but her focus went to the scar beneath her right eye.

Her fingertips traced the scar in the reflection. It was a permanent reminder of bad decisions and her own shame. If an alternate Abigail existed on the other side of the mirror, she hoped she'd had a better life.

She moved aside a curtain to look out. A small table and two chairs sat on a balcony above a magnificent garden. The arch of a circular moon gate rose above beds of multi-colored flowers. *So that's how I got here, I beamed in through the moon gate!*

She hugged the belt of the robe, looked left and right to ensure that no one could see, and stepped out. Her room sat on the second story of the building, at one end of a long rectangular garden. The long sides of the rectangle had only ground floors. Solar panels and raised flowerbeds sat on top of the lower roofs. The moon gate faced her room and had an outer band of deep fuchsia with an inner ring of light blue. Strange symbols inscribed the inner circle, but were too far away to decipher. Japanese maple trees framed either side of the gate. That is going to be beautiful in the fall, she noted for future reference, as photographers sometimes do.

A circular path curved through the garden to the gate. The path straightened after it went through, and then curved away and disappeared into more foliage. Black-eyed Susans and white-petaled coneflowers grew thick underneath the balconies. Bees buzzed from one blossom to the next. Blue flax and yellow-tipped red blanket flowers lined the edge of the path nearest Abigail's room. Further away she saw pink prairie roses, hummingbird mint, and stands of ornamental grass. The gardens covered as much ground as a public park, and she wondered how this much real estate could be hidden in Santa Fe.

Two balconies lay on either side of Abigail's room, while additional balconies extended along ground floors on both sides of the rectangle. High vegetation along the far edges of the garden blocked her view of how far those rooms extended.

She stepped back inside and dressed. She slung the canvas bag over one shoulder, put on her sunglasses, and checked the mirror one last time.

In the hall she followed a staircase that curved to a lower floor. The stairway opened to a large dining area where small groups of people chatted at tables. Columns separated the area into two sides and supported exposed ceiling beams. The far wall opened to the outside air with a balcony that overlooked the garden.

Morning light suffused the entire room and the aroma of food made her stomach rumble. She hadn't eaten since the previous morning, or at least, she assumed it'd been the previous morning. Truthfully she couldn't say whether more than twenty-four hours passed since she met Raphael on the street corner in Santa Fe.

Raphael? She hadn't seen him since he scared away the dogs in the alley, but what did he do to her? Somehow she'd ingested a hallucinogen and been led here against her will. It was the only thing that made sense, and somebody had some explaining to do.

Hungry or not she intended to walk out and go straight to the police. Then she saw Caroline, sitting alone at a table. Caroline with the sparkling eyes, she recalled with a blush. Caroline smiled and waved her over. Abigail hesitated, then went to the table and sat down.

Caroline wore a black, cap sleeve blouse with large red poppies printed diagonally across the front, and black shorts with cargo pockets. Abigail felt an unexpected attraction and didn't understand why or how to handle it. She remembered the warmth of Caroline's hand on her arm and tried not to notice how lovely the other woman looked. She kept the sunglasses on to hide her scar.

"Good morning, Abigail. You must be hungry," Caroline said.

Fresh apples and other fruit sat on the table, with open containers of granola, water, and juice. A waitperson reached over Abigail's shoulder and sat an empty bowl and spoon in front of her, then disappeared.

"The granola is good, but perhaps you would like a breakfast burrito, with eggs and salsa verde?"

Abigail looked to either side, then leaned close to Caroline and asked, "Where am I, and how did I get here?"

A subtle smile crossed Caroline's expression.

"This place is adobeDreams, and you walked through the gate."

"I know I walked through the gate, but that's not what I'm asking. How do I get here, now, to this place? How did I get to adobeDreams?"

"You asked for a guide, and one was provided."

"Raphael? Raphael was my guide? Then why didn't he just say so?"

"You asked for a guide, and the universe provided one. Rather than question circumstances, perhaps simple gratitude is a better response."

Whoa, there, Missy! Who are you to tell me how I should respond?

"I want to speak to the manager, before I decide whether to call the police."

Caroline stood up, straightened her blouse, and sat back down.

"How may I help you?" she asked.

"*You* are the manager?" Abigail blurted.

"At your service. Ask me anything you want to know."

Abigail sat back in her chair. She wanted to feel annoyed but lost focus every time she made fleeting contact with Caroline's eyes. The perfect symmetry of Caroline's lips vexed her. She looked away. She needed to do something to regain control, to get the momentum of the conversation going her way as the aggrieved party. She stared Caroline in the face and for dramatic effect took off the sunglasses to reveal her scar.

"Who drugged me, and why?" she demanded.

Caroline showed no reaction to the scar.

"I understand why you might feel that way, but no drugs were involved. The disorientation you experienced occurs at the boundary of the veil. The first time is the worst."

Veil? What veil? What kind of scam are you people running?

"Cut the crap," Abigail replied. "What are you trying to sell? Club memberships? Timeshares? Exotic cruises?"

Caroline grasped Abigail's hand and looked into her eyes. Abigail had seen similar expressions of sincerity before.

"Oh, god, it's not insurance, is it?"

Caroline chuckled.

"No, we sell no insurance. The mission of adobeDreams is to provide *discovery*."

Oh, boy, here it comes! First get the sucker's trust, and then spring the trap.

"And how much does that cost?" Abigail asked.

Caroline gave Abigail's hand a gentle squeeze.

"You didn't allow me to finish. The mission of adobeDreams is to provide discovery, and that process is unique for each individual. What *you* came here to discover is the person on the other side of the mirror."

The air went out of Abigail's lungs and the edges of her vision went dim. She gasped to catch her breath. How could Caroline know about the mirror?

"Are you for real?" Abigail asked.

"Look at me," Caroline answered.

Abigail looked into the other woman's eyes and recognized selfless concern, someone who had only her best interests at heart. No one had looked at her that way in a very long time, not since her mother.

"You are a guest here, and may stay as long as you wish. It's that simple."

"But who's footing the bill?"

"We are beneficiaries of a private trust."

"Let me guess, the same people Raphael works for?"

"That's very intuitive. Some of the same entities, yes."

"What about my luggage at the hotel?"

"It has been handled and will be there when you return."

"I can't have my luggage?"

"Everything you need is in your room."

"Don't tell me what I need. Is there some reason I can't have my own stuff?" Abigail demanded.

"You may have your 'stuff' anytime you wish. Simply walk out the door and turn left," Caroline said matter-of-factly.

Abigail expected a "we-can't-do-that" excuse. Caroline's response took an unexpected turn and put her off balance. She thought about the journey to get here, with Raphael, the blue door, the strange vertigo, and the red wasp.

"If I leave, I can't come back, can I?"

"You are here, the time is now, and that is sufficient."

Brown eyes or not, that pushed Abigail's patience over the edge. Nothing got her attention like someone telling her how to think or feel, and

Caroline had just crossed that line one too many times.

"Don't tell me what is 'sufficient.' And don't try to define my experience," Abigail snapped.

"As you wish," Caroline said, as she stood up and walked away.

Her abrupt departure threw Abigail off. "That went well," she said under her breath.

The fruit on the table mocked her empty bowl. Should she stay or should she go? There was more here than what she'd been told. It didn't add up. She eavesdropped on her parents once as a young girl, and she knew from that conversation that when something didn't make sense, it was time to walk away. Her father's explanations didn't add up, and her mother didn't listen to her own intuition. That hadn't work out so well. She pushed the bowl away.

Then again, she came to Santa Fe to find adobeDreams, and here she sat in the dining room. The mystery was a little bigger than she supposed, but so what? The hotel provided the perfect "hook" to set her travel guide apart from any other. She needed the story and her editor expected her to come back with the full scoop.

What better opportunity for a journalist than one that puts a table full of food right in front of her face? She pulled the bowl back and reached for an apple. Besides, she wanted to see Caroline again.

The Grotto of Hearts

"Why shouldn't the Earth be the best possible
place it can be?"

After breakfast Abigail decided to explore the
hacienda. She'd only walked a short distance
when a young woman with short, cropped blond hair
approached from the opposite direction. The woman
wore a black spaghetti strap top that hung loosely over
black athletic pants and dark grey running shoes
without socks.

Even from a distance she looked tall, six feet or
more, with muscular arms and no hips. Abigail surveyed
her build and took her for a volleyball player, German
perhaps, or maybe Norwegian. Her athletic pants had a
small red hummingbird embroidered above the pocket.

"Excuse me, are you a staff member?" Abigail asked.

"No, I am a guest. You are...?"

"Abigail," she replied while extending her hand.
"Abigail from the planet Earth."

The woman shook Abigail's hand and chuckled.

"I understand. It does seem like we landed on
another planet. I am Rayna, and I, too, hail from planet
Earth."

Rayna carried herself with a toughness of
character that matched the strength of her
handshake. She sounded Israeli and Abigail
speculated that she'd served in the Israeli Defense
Forces.

"Good morning," a familiar voice spoke before Abigail could continue the conversation. Raphael walked towards them wearing a purple short-sleeve shirt tucked into light-colored trousers. Thick veins covered the muscles of his forearms, which appeared strangely hairless.

"So, it's the alleged arbitrator," Abigail said. "What's going on here?"

"The answer to that question is best experienced, rather than explained, but we shall do both. Would you come with me, please?"

He walked away as though he expected the women to follow. Well, Abigail thought, I guess the one with the penis is in charge. Imagine that!

Raphael looked back and smiled as if he'd heard. His pace slowed when he turned his head, and Abigail saw the details of his shirt. What she presumed to be random patterns were actually symbols, only a shade lighter than the eggplant fabric itself. Abigail thought they might be the same characters she'd seen on the moon gate.

With each step the cheeks of Raphael's butt moved with muscular fluidity inside his form-fitting trousers. You gotta like a man with a nice butt, Abigail mused, while looking over at Rayna. Rayna seemed to have been thinking the same thing and they both smirked and giggled. Raphael paid no attention. They walked toward the front of the hacienda, then veered off down a flight of stairs between stone walls. The steps curved in a spiral as they went down, down, down into the earth. Strip lighting at knee height along both sides of the walls created two long ribbons of light that illuminated the path and curved out of sight.

"You have questions, and I will explain as best I can," Rafael said as they walked. "I told you that I am an arbitrator, and that is the truth. I arbitrate agreements."

That's what arbitrators usually do, Abigail thought; now tell me something I don't know!

"What you may not expect," he continued, looking back at her, "is that agreements take many forms. There are agreements among events, and there are agreements among paths we take through life. Your arrival at adobeDreams is just such an agreement. You wanted to come, and the hacienda stood ready to welcome you."

The circular path troubled her equilibrium, and so did Raphael's words. Abigail steadied herself with one arm against the wall. How many floors they descended, she didn't know, perhaps six or more. Near the bottom she saw that Caroline, beautiful brown-eyed Caroline, waited at the landing. Abigail smiled and her heart beat a little faster.

What was happening here? She'd felt passing attractions to other women before, but always interpreted it as admiration for the way they carried themselves, their accomplishments, or their choice of wardrobe for the day. Abigail felt drawn to Caroline like opposite poles of a magnet.

They all stood together at the bottom of the stairs, with Rayna next to Caroline. Abigail wished Rayna were somewhere else for fear that Caroline might like her more. Then she realized they hadn't bothered to introduce themselves, which meant they already knew each other. Abigail reprimanded herself for the jealousy. What are you, in grade school?

The stairway opened into a massive domed chamber. Pinkish stone slabs rose in arched columns to the top of the dome; others fit together in long diamond shapes or triangles with broad bases. The top of the dome had four dark concentric bands suspended from the ceiling, with a massive seven-pointed star hanging beneath. Each arm of the star had a silver gash pointing from its base to the center of the star. Seven heart-shaped planters hung from the walls of the dome with flowering plants. Each plant bore red bell-shaped flowers.

Finely crushed stone covered the floor of the dome, compacted and smooth as concrete. A light grey outline crossed the floor in a complex pattern of interconnecting lines and whirlpools. The diameter of the floor exceeded twice the dome's height, too far across to see the entire pattern from ground level. No detectable source illuminated the space, yet everything received even light. The chamber appeared to be thousands of years old.

"Whoa," Abigail said, as her jaw dropped. Rayna mumbled something in Hebrew that seemed to express the same sentiment.

"What is this place?" Abigail asked.

"This," Raphael said, "is the Grotto of Hearts."

He led the group to the center of the floor. The height of the dome left Abigail wide-eyed in awe, and she marveled at the precise fitting of the stone joints. Looking up at the heart-shaped planters, Abigail understood how the chamber got its name.

"This place is insane. How can you keep something like this a secret?" Abigail asked.

"The Grotto," Raphael explained, "is a portal. A portal that takes you where you need to go, to see what you need to see."

Abigail started to ask another question and Raphael held up his hand to urge patience.

"Now is the time when experience provides what words cannot," he said. Something shifted the moment Raphael finished his sentence. A wave traveled through the air and spun through the chamber like a whirlwind, but stirred no dust. Abigail and Rayna wobbled on their feet, but Caroline held steady.

"I'll take your things," Raphael said, as he reached for Abigail's camera bag.

She gave him the bag, then removed her vest and handed that over, too. "What's happening?" she asked.

"Something marvelous," Caroline answered as she stepped between Abigail and Rayna. The three of them locked hands and looked up. Abigail felt reassured to once again hold Caroline's hand. Have two human hands ever fit together so perfectly? She wanted to apologize for being aggressive at the breakfast table, but now was not the time.

"I have one question for you, and one question only," Raphael said, as he looked at each of them in turn.

"Why shouldn't the Earth be the best possible place it can be?"

He didn't expect an answer. Abigail repeated his words to herself: Why shouldn't the Earth be the best possible place it can be?

"Focus on the center of the star," Caroline said.

Abigail concentrated on the seven-pointed star at the top of the chamber. The star pulsed and seemed to pull her closer. An unseen force tugged her body upwards. Vertigo swept over her and she struggled to hold onto her breakfast. She closed her eyes to regain composure.

When she re-opened her eyes, the three of them stood in a pocket of stillness. The dizziness faded. Abigail realized that she now looked *down* at the center of the star, instead of up, as though gravity had somehow reversed itself. The three held hands in a circle as their feet hovered above the surface of the star. The floor of the Grotto lay far below their heads. Raphael watched for a moment, and then walked up the spiral stairs, out of sight.

"*Holy crap,*" Abigail exclaimed.

"Don't be afraid," Caroline said, as she squeezed Abigail's hand.

Abigail looked up, sideways, and down. Her legs trembled as she struggled to calm her fear. Look, ma, no hands! No ropes or safety nets, either!

The glowing spokes of the star grew bright and surrounded them with a wall of light. The surface of the star seemed to move. Blue streaks of light filled the micro fissures within the stone, became liquid and traveled in rivulets across the surface like mercury. The rivulets joined together in small puddles of blue light and grew larger. The grain patterns within the surface of the stone oscillated in a vibrational pattern that formed interconnected whirlpools of energy.

The vortices reminded Abigail of the vibrational pattern of atomic nuclei as recorded by an electron microscope. The patterns of the stone appeared the same, except the oscillations she now saw moved and vibrated with a life of their own. The puddles of blue light grew larger and filled the area beneath their feet. The surface rippled with whirlpools of energy.

The stone vaults shook with a rumble of thunder. Abigail looked for the source and two of the triangular shapes in the roof opened. A flash fell through each of these openings, one light, and one dark. The flashes were shaped like men, with luminous wings lifted above their heads and folded back. She followed the shapes as they accelerated toward the floor of the dome. The figures impacted the floor with booms of thunder that echoed off the walls. She expected the floor to crack and burst into fragments, but it did not. A figure stood calmly at each impact point, arms raised in the air. The figures lowered their arms and the illusion of wings went away.

Angels! The darker of the two looked at her in that moment, and Abigail sensed a smile. The angels walked toward the sides of the dome beyond her field of vision. From this vantage point she saw that the designs on the floor of the dome appeared to form a huge mandala, although the protective wall of light obscured the outer edges.

Abigail looked down. Her body sank toward the vibrating blue liquid. The pool embraced her as her feet slipped below the surface. The liquid felt warm and comforting as a tub of bath water. She looked at Caroline.

"Water is life," Caroline said.

Abigail nodded her head, "yes," as she struggled to embrace the moment and simply trust Caroline.

Their legs sank into the warm blue pool. The liquid rose up their lower legs and knees. As it rose to Abigail's thighs the feeling became almost sexual; a warm caress that involuntarily caused her to spasm. The liquid connected the women in an embrace that their clenched hands could not. They were lovers. They were sisters. They were children cuddled together in the same mother, waiting to be born. The pool rose above their waists and enveloped their clenched hands. It rose to their chests and kept rising. They would sink below the surface at any moment!

Caroline looked at Abigail and whispered, "It's okay."

Abigail wondered how "okay" was defined on her planet. In what way could upside-down submersion in a blue pool of liquid at the top of a dome equal "okay?" Abigail caught a slight smile on Caroline's face a fraction of a second before the pool rose above Caroline's mouth. The liquid hadn't yet reached Rayna's chin, another advantage of her height.

Once more she heard Raphael's voice, "Why shouldn't the Earth be the best possible place it can be?"

And then she went under.

Earth Paradise

"How many clawed the earth to survive, so that
we might be?"

A large blue globe blinded Abigail with its
intensity. Shapes of blue, white, brown, and
green coalesced as her vision adjusted to the light. The
shapes of Africa and the Middle East, the cradle of
humanity, became recognizable. *Earth.* Earth as it is
seen from space. *Oh, momma, we are so very, very
far away from home!*

The Moon appeared much smaller than Abigail
expected. She sensed Caroline and Rayna, but saw
only the blackness of space. The women existed as
bundles of consciousness in the dark, connected by
a nebulous sense of presence in the void.

If she had eyes in the moment, Abigail would
have wept for the beauty of the Earth. She
understood what astronauts meant about seeing our
planet from space. How beautiful and how fragile it
appeared in the darkness.

From the bleakness of space Earth emerged as
humanity's bright, shiny paradise in the void, the
only known planet capable of nurturing human life.
There was nowhere else to go and no other place for
human beings to reside. Earth was it, and it was the
only "it" there was, or that there may ever be. Earth
was a treasure, a gift from God beyond
comprehension.

God? Abigail did not think of herself as religious. She took a critical look at religions during her college years, and saw institutions designed to perpetuate patriarchal domination through guilt, condemnation, and a belief in magic. Even if intellectually she did not believe those criticisms to be true, she dismissed the idea of any man telling her what to believe. The question she asked herself was, "Who died and made men the masters of the Earth?" Because you know what? That isn't working out so well for the rest of us!

Looking at the beautiful blue Earth, she realized that the real magic was that life, and intelligent life, exists on the planet. You want miracles? We, the children of the Earth, are the true miracles.

She focused on Africa, and felt drawn to an area along the eastern edge where the continent forms a massive peninsula jutting up into the Arabian Sea, the Horn of Africa. She had no stomach with which to experiences queasiness, but familiar feelings of nausea and vertigo rose within her. She had not planned on an African vacation, but sensed that she was about to get one, ready or not.

Abigail suddenly stood on the ground amidst knee-high grass. The sun beat down on her head and shoulders with her shadow directly beneath. Nothing moved in the heat but the smell of the baked earth, not even insects. She looked down and saw a body covered with coarse hair. She screamed and heard a bestial bark. Panicked, she jumped from the sound and tried to brush the hair off her skin. She flailed her arms trying to push the beast away and pounded her feet until dust rose above her knees. She shook and gasped, then hugged herself in an attempt to restore calm.

"Oh, my God! What's happened to me?" she screamed, but heard only guttural huffs.

She examined her face with both hands and felt fine hair over its surface. Her eyes receded under heavy brows with wide cheekbones and a small chin. In a flash she understood what she had become. If it hadn't meant eating dust, she would have fallen to her knees. Instead she held her feet and grasped the tattered remnants of her sanity. *I am Abigail the Australopithecus, ape girl of the savannah!*

Dark lumps moved in the shade of nearby trees. Underneath the limbs, Abigail's troop of early hominids escaped the mid-day sun. She walked to them through walls of heat. The troop looked on with curiosity, no doubt wondering why she ventured out into the broiling sun. Abigail squatted and peed. *There, now you know all about it!*

She lay down in the shade, her head supported by one arm. The troop numbered less than a dozen animals with three males, six females, and two babies. The babies had large eyes and fat cheeks with tiny fingers that grasped the fur of their mothers. A baby suckled at the breast of the lead female, while the alpha male looked on with apparent indifference.

Abigail was a young female in the group, not yet of childbearing age. She sensed Caroline and Rayna, but didn't know if they shared her experience, or lived their own.

The males were half-again larger than the females. Somehow she knew that one of the lieutenants had tried to mate with her, but the older, alpha male chased him away. Afterwards the alpha sniffed her private parts and then left her alone, but someday she knew he would have her. All the females belonged to the alpha.

Perhaps big alpha was the long, lost ancestor of her father? Except, Abigail's father never tried to use her for sex. He tried to pork everything else that moved, but he hardly ever touched her, for any reason. She suddenly envisioned a big rock in big alpha's future, when he least expected it.

The troop dozed in the shade all afternoon. One of the females approached and groomed Abigail's fur in the manner of chimpanzees. She plucked debris from Abigail's coat and ate the insects. "Thank you, Rayna," Abigail wanted to say, hoping that Caroline was one of the other, prettier females, if "pretty" is a word that could be used for ape-girls of the savannah!

Abigail sat up and groomed the female's coat. The other female smelled familiar, and Abigail wondered if she could be a sibling. The grooming activity eased her nerves, and Abigail felt a primal connection to the troop.

In the late afternoon lightning popped across clouds on the horizon. The alpha male stood up and grunted, followed by his lieutenants. They barked at the rest of the troop and everyone assembled. They needed water, food, and shelter before nightfall. The big male and his lieutenants led the way, each carrying a stick with a crude point. Some of the females carried sharp-edged pieces of stone and other small objects wrapped in tattered pieces of hide. The first purses! *Just wait until they cost three thousand dollars.*

The troop followed animal trails through the savannah until at last they descended into a wide gulch. A thicket of trees marked an area where dense vegetation suggested they might find water. The males moved into the thicket, looked and sniffed, took a few more steps, and then looked and sniffed again.

The troop followed the males. They picked berries from the bushes and ate leaves from select plants. Light shone through gaps in the trees and illuminated the blossoms of fragrant flowers. The females snatched insects that crawled through the brush, tore off the legs and wings, and dispatched them down the gullet. *Yummy!* One of the male lieutenants squatted and defecated on the ground, passing very loose stool. Now, that's not sanitary, Abigail thought, as she avoided the spot.

The troop moved on through the thicket, and paused ever so often to eat, sniff the air, and listen for anything untoward. They scooped water from an ankle-deep stream. The current created small cascades that flowed over smooth stones.

The gulch deepened to a canyon, and the troop broke free of the thicket to bed down for the night. The walls narrowed further down, but the slope of this location, though steep, would allow escape if the need arose. The males located an overhang of sedimentary rock a short distance from the stream, with bushes on either side that provided some amount of wind protection. The males cleared the area of small rocks, and the females snapped off branches and swept away smaller debris.

The troop huddled close under the overhang and watched the sunset. The distant storm moved away. There was no moon, and Abigail speculated whether that had something to do with their choice of campsite. The stars popped into view a few at a time and she wondered if her companions had any appreciation for the lights in the sky. Millions of years separated these early hominids from an accurate comprehension of what those lights were, how they formed, and how many of them there really were. How could you explain the concept of "billions upon billions" to someone who cannot count their toes?

Then she realized these creatures felt the Earth and the cosmos in their bones. Regardless of whether all of them added together couldn't form a complex thought in their brains, they belonged to the universe as much as any homo sapiens that would ever evolve from them. Eat, screw, poop; it was life at its most elemental and direct.

These hominids were more alive than anyone she ever met. No higher brain functions generated an endless stream of drivel to separate them from their experience with the environment. They lived in the moment, every moment, and lived with power and grace beyond anything she'd ever known. At least when their time passed on this Earth, they would leave behind only bones, not plastic water bottles and foam packaging. Abigail's modern technological arrogance skittered away in shame, and she wept silently for what human beings lost so very long ago.

Warmed by collective body heat, the troop slept soundly until a strong wind blasted through the area. In a dream Abigail saw the face of a dark-haired human who frightened her. He had the look of a predatory bird that wanted to eat her flesh.

She woke staring up into the Milky Way as the dream faded into the night sky. She tried to identify the few constellations she knew, but saw nothing familiar. She supposed the position of the stars appeared differently millions of years ago.

The wind died down and she became aware that the entire troop was awake and alert. She heard soft steps on rock, little more than a whisper of noise. The steps stopped on the ledge above, accompanied by faint breathing. Something big lurked up there. Something with claws, and teeth, and hunger for meat. Abigail wanted to run but knew it was pointless. She wondered if the morning headlines would read, "Night Monster Massacres Proto-Humans – Ten Dead." Where is a flamethrower when you absolutely, positively, MUST have one?

The troop listened to the breathing for a long time. It began to sprinkle. Big raindrops struck the earth. Thunder boomed somewhere above the rim of the cliff. The creature took off with a violent scattering of rocks. Stones showered down from above and they cowered in fear of an attack, but afterwards heard only the sound of approaching rain. The troop huddled together in silence and did not move, though some continued to tremble with fright.

Snapping noises came from further up the gulch, and gathered to a continuous rumble. Unlike thunder the rumble did not dissipate but continued to grow in volume. Stone struck stone and tumbled together to hit more stone. Cracks boomed and echoed off the cliffs. *Flash flood,* she realized. No flamethrower could stop the monster that was about to attack!

Abigail stood up, undecided which way to run. The lieutenant who had tried to mate with her barked a command. She looked at the alpha and he crouched poised for action, though apparently also uncertain about what to do. "So hard to think with so little to work with," she wanted to tell him.

A huge black mass moved toward them from further up the gulch. These poor, dumb brutes would be dead in minutes if Abigail didn't do something. She grunted with her ape-girl voice and motioned with her ape-girl hands, and scooped the air as they'd drank water from the stream, urging the others to come with her. It was no use. They didn't understand. She scrambled for the edge of the overhang, where she could walk around the bushes and gain higher ground. The lieutenant barked at her. "Come back," he seemed to say. *Not happening.*

Abigail moved as fast as her ape-girl legs could carry her. Big alpha finally sprung to action. He charged Abigail with blind fury in his eyes and she expected to be struck down with a mighty blow. Instead he charged past in complete panic. His rage turned to fear a microsecond after he stood up and saw the black mass of water bearing down. Apparently "ladies first" was an unknown concept in the Pleistocene!

Abigail was stunned by how fast big alpha could move. He reverted to all fours and scrambled up the edge of the slope tearing clods of turf in his wake as he hauled his big alpha hairy butt out of there. In less dire circumstances Abigail would have burst out laughing, or grunting, or whatever it was that ape-girls do. Instead she hurried after him, and heard the others get up to follow. Then the black waters were upon them.

The lieutenant that barked at her stood on the far side of the overhang. He stepped down to run past the others who were bunched up to reach the edge. The floodwaters hit his ankles and swept his feet from underneath him. He howled with his ape-lieutenant voice and tore at the ground with his ape-lieutenant arms as the waters bore him away. His eyes went wide with panic. Abigail saw his mouth gape open in mid howl when he went under. He didn't come back up. Goodbye, barky boy, have fun mating with that!

She reached the edge and ascended the slope on the trail of the big alpha. The others were right behind. She thought to reach out and help but the fear in her guts pulled her up the slope, beyond any hope of reasoning.

She looked back after she escaped immediate danger. One of the mothers held onto the bush at the edge of the overhang. Her other arm lay outstretched in the flood with her baby in its grasp. She couldn't keep the child's head above water, and its limp body flopped in the current. Abigail recognized the soul behind the anguished eyes of the mother. *Caroline. Oh, Caroline!*

The bush gave way and the mother and the baby were swept away. The last Abigail saw of them the mother held the bush with one hand and the baby with the other. The bush popped to the surface and floated free in the distance.

The troop struggled up the slope and into the rocks as the waters continued to swell. Rain swept over them in thrashing sheets. Abigail gasped for breath and stopped to look back. The female who had groomed her, the one whom she jokingly thought of as

Rayna, was gone. It looked like all of the others made it into the rocks. The alpha female lay below, one hand dug into the slope while the other held her infant to her chest. The baby trembled with fear and cold, but lived. The alpha female's eyes blazed with a ferocity Abigail could not hold. She would attack the ground itself to defend her child. *Rayna.* The alpha female had to be Rayna. The alpha male was nowhere to be seen. Abigail imagined he was still running, somewhere over the horizon. That wasn't a bad idea!

Abigail turned and scrambled up the rocks. She wanted out of the canyon, and she wanted out now. Her body began to transform as she climbed through the storm. The rain beat down and washed away the dark, coarse hair on her arms. Her torso lengthened and the bones of her legs grew long with smooth muscles. Lightning flashed and she saw the pale flesh of her hands. Her fingernails were pink and thin. Wet strands of hair clung to her shoulders. Her ape-girl self fell away as she climbed up out of the past, up out of the dark fury of the flood, and away from the monsters of the night.

At the top of the cliff a spider web of lightning exploded across the sky. Abigail counted the seconds, "one-thousand-one, one-thousand-two, one-thousand-three," and then the thunder exploded. She reeled at the concussion.

Lightning struck the plains with little delay between the flash and the boom of thunder. Shockwaves traveled through the ground, and brought her to her knees. She knew she should seek shelter but was too exhausted to move and too traumatized to care. No one followed her above the rim. Maybe they were all dead. Maybe they still cowered in the rocks below.

The full fury of the storm fell upon her, and random death struck from every angle. She could hardly open her eyes in the pounding rain. *She'd had just about enough of this.* Her blood burned hot and her hands clenched into tight fists.

She stood up with her arms raised as tall as her exhausted body could make her and screamed, "Come and get me," into the storm.

This, she understood, was the essence of life on Earth. Fight for your life to survive. Live long enough to reproduce. Stare death and defeat in the face and curse the darkness. The Earth offered opportunities for survival, but no guarantees.

Why shouldn't the Earth be the best possible place it can be? Abigail had her answer. The Earth should be the best possible place it can be because our ancestors fought and died for the right to be here. They earned that right by surviving long enough to produce the next generation. By virtue of their survival we are here. By virtue of all the ape-girls, the alpha males, and all the mothers who clutched dead babies in their arms to the last breath, all the way back through the eons of history, we are here. How many clawed at the earth to survive, so that we might be?

We owe them our survival. We owe our survival, and the survival of the human race, to the next generation. In the memory of all the ancestors who ever struggled and died to push humanity further up the evolutionary chain, it's up to us to ensure that the people who follow inherit a better Earth. We fight wars and we wage revolutions to ensure these things.

We fight to the end of our lives to make the world a better place, and such has it always been.

Why shouldn't the Earth be the best possible place it can be? It can be and it must be because that's what is in our genes, our bones, and the very force of life that we carry from one generation to another. It's who we are and what we do. "Come and get me," we shout into the storm and stand defiant.

Abigail collapsed on the ground, and leaned forward with her palms supporting the weight of her torso. The storm fell heavy upon her. She thought to shield her head with her hands but was too tired to move, too tired to do anything but to keep breathing and survive. The rain pounded and she felt the water rise on her collapsed thighs. She squinted and focused on the space between her hands. Her forearms extended into muddy water above the wrists. Small bits of flotsam danced in a symphony of kinetic energy. Her scraggly hair hung in tangles, little more than a conduit for the rain that poured off her head.

The air turned chill. Her body trembled from the pounding and shivered from the cold. She now understood the expression, "Pain is the body's way of letting you know that you are still alive." She wanted to pass out and escape this agony, but could only close her eyes and hold on.

Water drops dripped from overhead branches and plopped the wet earth. Trembles rolled through Abigail in shuddering waves. Fear gripped her chest and clenched the back of her throat. She was too depleted to move and did not want to open her eyes, fearful of what she might see. She struggled to push herself to her feet but her arms would not hold. She relaxed and gathered strength. She inhaled deeply through her nose, and then exhaled loudly through her mouth. Here goes everything!

She opened her eyes. The floodwaters were gone and she sat in pinkish-brown mud. A water drop fell from somewhere above and shattered in a small puddle.

She looked up. A few tenuous clouds drifted along in a sky of deep blue. A large circular shape in the form of a ring confronted her, backlit by the sun. She struggled a moment to see. It was fuchsia with an inner band of light blue. Dark grey symbols lined the inner band. It was the moon gate. She realized she was in the gardens of adobeDreams.

"Whoa," she said.

Girl Love

"Why do women waste so much time on the
wrong men?"

Caroline grasped Abigail's hand and pulled her
up. Abigail's stiff muscles protested with
agony as she rose. Rayna stood nearby, her head down
with apparent exhaustion. Naked and splattered with
mud, the feet and lower legs of the women were thick
with it. Splotches clung to their forearms and chests.
Their hair lay dirty and tangled. Rayna stumbled
toward the hacienda as if by force of will alone.

Abigail wrapped her arm around Caroline's waist
and held on. The nudity didn't bother her, but her
soiled condition was an embarrassment. She didn't
want her dirty body to touch Caroline, but the mud
equally soiled them both, and she supposed it didn't
matter. In that moment they were sisters of the mud
and Caroline's warmth comforted her. The women
took a few uncertain steps, found their balance, and
walked forward.

Caroline pulled Abigail through the gardens up a
stone stairway to the second story of the hacienda,
and then down the hallway to Abigail's room. It's just
a human body, folks, Abigail would have said to any
onlookers. We all have one, so grow up and get over it.

Caroline led her to the bathroom and turned on
the water in the shower. She tested the temperature
with one hand, while she supported Abigail with the

other. Abigail saw a wild version of herself in the mirror with tangled hair and skin peppered with mud. Her pupils were asymmetrical in shape and covered almost the entire area of her irises. Mud outlined the outer edges of her scar and looked like a leech attached to her face. Her arms were too tired to brush the mud away. In some alternate universe, did another Abigail look into the mirror and see the same mess?

Caroline helped her into the tub, and entered after her. The warm water brought immediate comfort. Abigail could do without many of the comforts of civilization, but not a hot shower. She washed her face with both hands and scrubbed the mud off. Caroline produced a small bottle of shampoo and washed Abigail's hair. After a moment, Caroline's soapy hands moved across Abigail's shoulders, and then under her arms and down her sides. No one had washed Abigail like that, or touched her like that, since her earliest years as a toddler.

She remembered standing in the tub at the age of three or thereabouts. Her little round butt glistened with suds as momma washed her. She stood dutifully while her mother's hands slid across her skin, so smooth. She giggled as her mother washed the round protuberance of her belly. Little Abigail stumbled a bit, and held her balance while her mother washed her chubby thighs.

In truth, her mother washed her not with soap and water, but with love. Her mother worshiped little Abigail with her hands in a celebration of life and a mother's bond with her child. Mother was the brightest star in Abigail's universe, and she had wanted nothing more than to be exactly like her. But that changed.

Caroline reached around and rested both hands on top of Abigail's *dan tien*, the abdominal area three-finger widths below the navel that is the seat of the body's energy field in Chinese medicine. Abigail knew the location from tai chi classes she'd taken years earlier. Caroline rested her head against Abigail's shoulder and pressed her pubic mound into Abigail's glutes. Caroline's hands and groin radiated heat and flushed Abigail's pelvis with warm blood. She placed her hands over Caroline's and squeezed.

When Abigail thought about the people to whom she'd been attracted over the course of her life, she'd always been drawn more to personality than parts. Even so, her only intimate, sexual relationship had been with a man. Caroline affected her differently from the moment Abigail first saw her. She wanted to lose herself in Caroline's eyes. She tried to ignore Caroline's lips, lest she kiss them without thinking. Abigail reprimanded herself for the thoughts, but the reproach held no conviction.

Caroline kissed Abigail through the water running down her shoulder; then kissed her twice more as she moved to the center of Abigail's back. Caroline sucked gently at the flesh on either side of Abigail's spine and then turned her head sideways and pressed her face against Abigail.

Abigail's heart drummed in her chest and her lungs seemed devoid of air. *Are we going to do this? Are we really going to do this?*

Abigail thought to slide Caroline's hands down her belly and press them against her mound, but hesitated. She didn't know how this should work without a penis in the party, so she held Caroline's hands while she tried to figure out what to do next. Caroline stood motionless.

Abigail turned her head to look back, but Caroline did not move. Abigail rotated her entire body in Caroline's arms so that they faced one another. Tears reddened Caroline's eyes.

Abigail first thought to ask, "What's wrong," but instead said, "I saw you."

"Yes, I...," Caroline struggled to speak, then swallowed her nerves and blustered, "...I was the mother with the dead baby!"

The dam of tears broke with the words and she burst with body-racking sobs. Her knees buckled and Abigail held her up. Abigail guided her to a sitting position in the tub, and held Caroline's head on her shoulder while she sobbed. Caroline seemed to feel that the loss happened directly to her. That child was her baby, and it died in her arms, and nothing could be done about it. Caroline pushed her head off Abigail's shoulder, arms outstretched, hands on top of Abigail's shoulders. Then she began a mournful howl, deep from her belly. The howl sounded primal, animalistic, and though it contained no words, Abigail's guts knew what it meant.

"Too much, too much," Caroline grieved. "Too much for me to bear!"

Abigail sensed that in this moment Caroline grieved all the losses of her lifetime. Whether those losses were her parents, her grandparents, or whoever else, they all spilled out of her guts. The baby had only been the catalyst that brought all else to the bursting point.

The water steamed the tub and Caroline howled in the mist and choked on tears for her loss. Abigail held Caroline's head in her hands and kept her from falling over. At last Caroline rested her head on Abigail's thighs and the wailing stopped. Water ran down the vertebrae of Caroline's curving spine. The sobbing passed. Caroline looked up at Abigail, her face swollen from tears, her long hair plastered against her collarbones and chest.

Abigail loved Caroline's eyes. She had loved them even before they met, and before Abigail's mother birthed her into this world. Caroline's lips were plump and wet. Once again Abigail wondered, are we really going to do this?

Well, I want it. She leaned forward and kissed Caroline. Caroline kissed her back. Their lips parted and they looked in each other's eyes with noses that almost touched. Abigail wanted Caroline and Caroline wanted her and their flesh ached with the heat of their need.

Caroline leaned forward and kissed Abigail full on, her tongue in Abigail's mouth. Her hand pulled the back of Abigail's neck and pressed them together. Abigail held her tight and accepted every kiss, every probe of the tongue, and every caress of her face, neck, and shoulders. They were yin and yang, spun together in harmony, simultaneous cause and effect. Their hunger was the hunger for life after death passes over you.

Abigail's heart pounded in her throat and heat flashed across her chest. The areola of her breasts expanded and her nipples hardened. Then the water turned cold.

Caroline put her arms on either side of the tub and pushed herself up with a groan. "Let's go to bed," she said. Abigail focused on Caroline's pubic mound as she rose. A comb of black hair feathered out from Caroline's cleft of Venus like the wings of a bird. Abigail grasped her hand and stood up. The women stepped out of the tub and toweled off, helping one another dry their backs. The bathroom hung thick with steam.

Caroline led Abigail to the bedroom. The towels slid to the floor. Soft light entered through the curtains and created a vanilla glow. Caroline sat Abigail on the edge of the bed, then held her face and kissed her full on, her tongue deep in Abigail's mouth. Then she pushed Abigail back onto her elbows and kissed her neck and shoulders. She picked up Abigail's legs and laid them on the bed. Abigail instinctively pressed her thighs together but Caroline spread them apart, exposing Abigail's vulva. Then Caroline mounted her. *Oh, momma, this ship is about to sail.*

Abigail still didn't know how this should work and wasn't sure if she was ready for female-on-female cunnilingus. Oh sure, Edgar tried it a few times, but he'd made terrible slurping noises like a thirsty dog lapping at a bowl of water. It was probably something he saw in a porn movie. Regardless of the inspiration, it wasn't attractive, and Abigail preferred to endure the mindless pounding of his penis rather than pretend to enjoy the oral stimulation. *Why do women waste so much time on the wrong men?*

Caroline brought her back to the present. She pushed Abigail's arms over her head and held them down while she leaned over and loved Abigail's mouth with her tongue. Caroline seemed to want to suck the soul out of her body and Abigail surrendered everything. Caroline kissed the side of Abigail's neck, and then crossed the collarbone to kiss the suprasternal notch between Abigail's clavicles, and licked the depression with the tip of her tongue.

Abigail's chest flushed with heat and warm blood rushed to her groin. Caroline planted a trail of kisses halfway across Abigail's other collarbone before moving down to her breast in a large circular motion. Caroline kissed and sucked the flesh in ever-smaller circles. She found the areola and traced the outline of the hardened nipple. She drew circles with her tongue, once…twice…three times, and then sucked the nipple with long, loving, demanding strokes. Abigail gasped. Her vagina flushed with anticipation.

Caroline moved to the space between Abigail's breasts, and sucked at the breastbone, before moving to the other breast. She repeated the circular pattern in the opposite direction until her mouth smothered the areola and playfully tugged at the nipple.

Caroline lay down beside Abigail and sucked while her hand caressed the other breast. She pinched the nipple between her middle and ring fingers, pulled gently, and then kneaded the breast with her fingertips. She continued to suck while her hand traced the outline of Abigail's ribs to the hipbone and then stroked the mound between Abigail's legs. A storm swelled in Abigail's pelvis and she rocked with the waves. *More please,* her body demanded, *much, much more!*

Caroline sat up and placed her free arm on Abigail's other side with her back to Abigail. Her fingertips teased and stroked the cavity between Abigail's legs. She looked over her shoulder with lustful intent, smiled, and returned to her play. Her fingers loved Abigail with long, firm strokes. Abigail heard the moan of the wind growing in the distance and her hips rocked with each rolling wave.

Caroline put her mouth on Abigail, and sucked. Her fingertips worked in short, curving strokes. Abigail gasped for air as the storm overtook her, and she placed her hands on Caroline's back and pushed her down. Abigail's clitoris retracted but Caroline's mouth pursued it. Waves swelled through Abigail's pelvis and torso. Abigail's body contracted around Caroline's fingers and sucked them deep inside. Still Caroline stroked and worked the flesh with her mouth. Abigail screamed and bucked without control. Caroline rode the waves with her through the storm, matched every contraction, and nuzzled every spasm until they both lay spent.

Abigail gasped for breath as her body continued to quiver with aftershocks. Her legs felt weak. Sweat beaded her collarbones and the space between her breasts. She put her right hand on the center of her chest as if to bring herself back together.

The clitoris, Abigail recalled from a sex education class, contains twice the nerve endings as the male penis and its sole anatomical purpose is sexual pleasure. *God must surely be a woman.*

Water ran in the bathroom sink as Caroline washed up. She came back to bed and lay beside Abigail with a contented smile. Woman, Abigail thought, I will kill for you. I will die for you. I will have your children. I will stand by you in sickness and health, from now into eternity. I will do whatever is necessary to keep you in my life!

Abigail felt so much that she had no words. She looked at Caroline's brown eyes, and the curve of her eyebrows. She followed her nose down to her lips, open with invitation. It was Abigail's turn to please Caroline.

All Goodness and Light

"...deceptions have a tendency to accumulate."

The women slept all morning, cuddled together like kittens. Abigail woke at mid-day and watched Caroline place a small pile of clothes on the table under the mirror.

Oh, honey, Abigail thought, as her eyes adjusted and she got a good look at the other woman. Caroline wore black shorts with a black cap-sleeve blouse. The blouse had a small red poppy printed on the front, above the left breast. The shorts were much shorter than the cargo shorts she'd worn in the dining room, and showed off her lean thighs to scintillating effect. Abigail liked the way the muscles moved under Caroline's skin. Caroline looked as luscious as a ripe peach, and Abigail's mouth watered.

What does it mean, when you desire someone so much that you want to somehow consume them, take them into your soul, and hold them there forever?

"Hey, sleepy head," Caroline said. "I brought some clothes for you if you're ready to get up."

"All I really want to do is lay here and watch you move, for hours," Abigail replied.

Caroline cocked her head and smiled, then said, "Breakfast is on the patio."

Okay, time to face the day, as lesbian Abby, or whatever she was now. She swung her legs out of bed and stood up, naked as the day she passed between her mother's legs. She had no shame in front of Caroline.

Abigail wobbled on her feet and looked down. Everything moved, and she thought, *earthquake!* A surge of power rolled upwards from the floor and flowed through her body like a giant wave. She stumbled a bit, and then regained her balance. The veins on her forearms popped out in sharp detail like the arms of a muscular man. She felt powerful, as though her hands could crush stone. She looked at Caroline and said, "Whoa!"

"What you just experienced is the *quickening*," Caroline explained. "Your body needed time to recover from the challenges you faced on primitive Earth."

She paused, with just a moment of sadness in her eyes. Abigail knew she recalled the loss of the baby. "Now that your body has recovered, your spirit may catch up.

"You also need sustenance," she said, "and clothes." She held up a black cap-sleeve blouse, similar to her own, except this one had the imprint of a red wasp on the left front, above the breast. "The red wasp is your totem," she explained, "and the red poppy is mine. It depends on what you experience during the vision quest that brings you here."

"You mean the path behind the blue door?" Abigail asked.

"Yes," she said. "You have many questions, and some will be answered, but now is the time for clothing and food."

"Only some of my questions will be answered?"

Caroline shook the blouse at Abigail to say, "Enough talk." Power rippled through Abigail's body as she crossed the floor. She could tear down the walls if she wanted, or run for hours and not stop. Abigail put on the blouse, without a bra, and it fit perfectly.

Caroline handed her a pair of black panties with two small red poppies printed at hip level on the left, and Abigail blushed. Her panties carried Caroline's totem!

Next, Caroline handed Abigail a pair of black shorts and Abigail gushed, "We're twins!" Caroline chuckled. A pair of black sneakers with short white socks completed the package.

For a moment Abigail wondered if they weren't secretly being placed in one of those restaurants designed to attract men who want to ogle the waitresses. Well, if they want legs, we got 'em, but if they're looking for hooters, they picked the wrong girls!

Abigail studied herself in the mirror, and saw the same woman she'd always seen in the reflection. Lesbian or not, her appearance had not changed and she had the scar to prove it. Her hair hung in a tangled mess and had that, "just been screwed, and slept half the day," look. Abigail liked it, and decided not to change a thing. She joined Caroline on the patio.

The sun smiled on multi-colored blossoms that flowed through the gardens like streams. They sat and ate granola with almonds and golden raisins, and plucked chopped fruit from bowls. Water and fresh juice sat in pitchers.

Abigail's earthenware mug had bands of brown, blue, yellow, and orange that flowed like mountains and clouds across its surface. A thumb groove dimpled one side and allowed for a better grip. She turned the mug in her hand and it was like watching a sunset. Caroline's mug was similar, yet different.

"These are handmade, aren't they?" Abigail asked.

"Raphael bought them from a craftsman in Arroyo Seco, just below Taos Mountain."

Abigail laughed. "I can't imagine Raphael shopping for stoneware!"

"He likes them because there are no two alike. He says they are just like people that way."

Light played across Caroline's face as she spoke. Abigail's heart swelled with love, and yet, she realized, they hardly knew anything about one another. They'd joined their bodies with incredible passion, shared the wailing depths of grief, and faced death together, but as incredible as it seemed, they'd only known each other for two days.

A week ago Abigail thought of herself as a straight girl and wouldn't have considered coupling with another woman. Well, that was not quite true; she'd always felt attracted to the emotional depth of a woman's character, but never expected to find herself going down on the muffin! Where would they be a month from now? Should they shift this relationship into a lower gear and slow down? What were they doing?

Caroline caught the change in Abigail's expression and asked, "What?"

It was one simple word, one simple question. How Abigail responded would affect the quality of their relationship from this point forward, or really, whether their relationship survived. Should she simply answer, "Nothing," and allow the moment to pass? Should she stuff her feelings under her heart and pretend they didn't exist? She knew from her experience with Edgar that little deceptions have a tendency to accumulate. Then they multiply. One moment you have a pair of furry, cuddly bunnies and you think they're under control, and then the next moment you have eight of them, all laying pellets and stinking up the cage. That's how deceptions work.

"Who are you?" Abigail asked.

Caroline was taken back for a moment. She looked at Abigail with curiosity, as though trying to read her intent. Finally, she held Abigail's eyes and responded, "I am the woman you love, and the woman who loves you. What is it that you wish to know?"

Abigail smiled and laughed a little with embarrassment, then spoke, "I was just thinking that I don't know..." she corrected herself, "...that we don't know that much about each other. Where were you born? Who are your parents? What were you like as a kid?"

Maybe those questions were too broad, so she narrowed it down. "Have you always been, you know, ...gay?"

Caroline laughed, "That's like asking, 'Have you always been a girl?' Yes, I've always been gay, but for a long time I didn't know what that meant. I didn't have a girlfriend until I was in college."

She thought a bit more and then added, "I had to get away from home before I felt free to think for myself. My parents are devout Catholics."

A hint of sadness crossed her face.

"Did they accept you? Your family, I mean?" The words caught in Abigail's throat because she feared the answer.

Caroline's eyes moistened with tears. Abigail reached out and held her hand.

"No, ...they didn't accept me," she said, covering her mouth with her hand as she fought to hold back the pain. She shuddered a few times and cried, then shook her head, "No," at the memories.

She had more to say; getting the words out would be difficult, but what else are girlfriends for? Caroline came with baggage, and so did Abigail. Abigail decided to look at the contents, dirty laundry and all.

"What happened?" she asked.

Caroline breathed in and out, and placed her hand over the top of her chest, before she spoke. "My father was the worst. He didn't mind that I never brought boys home or dated when I was in high school. At least that way he knew I wasn't out somewhere getting pregnant.

"That changed when I introduced my girlfriend. He saw what was up straight away and went ballistic. He screamed at me. 'Caroline,' he kept asking, 'What's wrong with you? What are you thinking? You can't do this!'

"Then he..." she started to say something, then covered her mouth and shook with tears. Abigail hugged her until the shaking stopped, then kissed her lips.

"Then he slapped me," Caroline continued. "He slapped me! I put my arms up to protect my face and he started beating me! I turned away and he hit my arms and shoulders. I couldn't get away from him and he kept hitting me!"

Blood rushed to Abigail's face. She made a mental note to some day have a *personal conversation* with Caroline's father.

"Mother pulled him off. He raised his hand to slap her, too, but she stood in his face and wouldn't budge. He stomped away and never looked at me again."

"Jesus," Abigail exclaimed, "that's awful! How did your mother take it?"

Caroline chuckled, "Jesus had nothing to do with it. Mother? She laid the big guilt trip on me. 'I'll never have grandchildren,' she said, and then she kept trying to fix me up with one guy after another."

"How did that work?" Abigail asked.

"It's funny. I'd go home to visit her when my father wasn't around, and there'd be some guy that she invited over for lunch. She'd pick guys that she thought were good husband material and came from good gene pools, but I knew those guys. I went to high school with them. They were all a bunch of jerks. All they wanted was to get between my legs...or a blowjob."

"So," Abigail asked with some jealousy, "did you ever sleep with any of them?"

"No, it was just too gross. It was like high school all over again. They were hairy and smelled bad, and only had one thing on their minds."

"How about you?" Caroline asked, meaning, what's your story? "I was your first, wasn't I?"

Abigail blushed. "Yes, you were my first." And you're my last, and my always. Oh, slow down, Abigail cautioned herself.

Caroline held her fingertips to her upper chest, and said, "You mean, I had the honor of bringing you over to the side of all goodness and light, ...little old me?" She stood up, her arms raised triumphant, and did a little turning dance.

"I'm the one, I'm the one," she sang as she danced and pumped her arms in the air. Then she suddenly stopped and pointed at Abigail, while holding her other hand up to her mouth, as though she grasped an invisible microphone.

"It is I, Caroline Flores..." she began. Abigail loved the way her tongue rolled the name "Flores" off the top of her mouth, and suddenly realized they'd never exchanged last names! The same revelation must have struck Caroline because she repeated her name. She wanted Abigail to know exactly who she was. "I, *Caroline Flores*, who seduced this beautiful young girl, this virgin of *girl love*, and inducted her into the legion of lesbian womanhood!" While continuing to hold her imaginary microphone, she folded her free arm over her waist and took a bow. She then stood up with a start, as though a marvelous idea had just occurred to her.

"Tell me, beautiful young girl," she continued, as though conducting an interview. "Have you had your muffin today?" Holding her pretend microphone in one hand, she rested her other hand on her hip, and waited for Abigail's response with mock consternation. "Well, have you?"

Abigail laughed and blushed. Her heart smiled at Caroline's playful spirit. She wanted to lick that spirit up one side of Caroline's face and down the other.

"I had my muffin last night, and I ate the whole thing," Abigail replied. "I am now officially muffinless," she added with mock sadness.

They laughed and leaned forward to kiss one another. Abigail wanted to feel herself inside Caroline and suck Caroline's body into her own, all at the same time. Their energy wrapped together like strands of a rope. Abigail felt faint when they finally broke the embrace to come up for air. She took a few deep breaths to re-oxygenate and pull away from the heat.

"What *is* this place?" she asked, waving her hand to indicate the hacienda, as she tried to calm her heart.

"This place," Caroline responded, "is literally adobeDreams, a place where realities open to you that could not be experienced any other way."

"Realities?" Abigail asked. "Is that we experienced as proto-humans, or whatever we were, in Africa?"

"Think of the Grotto of Hearts as a radio receiver, capable of capturing a wide band of frequencies. When the receiver and the frequency are in tune, magic happens."

Caroline leaned forward and kissed Abigail's lips, then licked them tenderly as she withdrew.

"Besides, perhaps reality is a dream, from a different point of view," she said.

The look on Abigail's face communicated that she had no idea what Caroline meant.

Caroline laughed gently and smiled, then started to say something but stopped. She turned her head toward the gardens and said, "They're waiting for you in the garden."

"*They?*" Abigail asked.

Caroline tilted up Abigail's chin and kissed her forehead. Caroline then looked in Abigail's eyes, and kissed her full on the lips. Abigail didn't want the kissing to stop. The quickening had not only juiced up her energy levels, but also her hunger for life. Caroline walked away without answering. Ordinarily Caroline's lack of response would have angered her, but Abigail couldn't be angry with Caroline, not about anything, not ever. Well, not just now anyway!

Abigail realized she still had not properly introduced herself. She'd wait for the right moment.

Trinity

"...human beings evolve in response to demands from the environment."

Abigail walked down the stone stairway to the garden. Bees hummed among blue cornflowers and red snapdragons along the path, and she stopped to look at the strange symbols inscribed into the inner band of the moon gate. The letters seemed somehow familiar, yet remained elusive. They reminded her of angelic script that she'd seen in a book, or perhaps it was Norse runes. She couldn't remember which. She followed the path for what seemed like an impossible distance, and again asked herself, how could anything this big be concealed in Santa Fe?

She rounded a corner and glimpsed Raphael at the far side of a circular clearing. The light figure and the dark figure she'd seen flash from the ceiling of the Grotto of Hearts stood behind him, one on either side. Both wore dark jeans with a pullover long-sleeve shirt. The clothing didn't seem to fit, as though they were unaccustomed to casual attire. The light figure was female and that surprised her.

The figures stood a head taller than Raphael and seemed bigger than life-size. All three held their palms together in prayer-like positions. Rafael lowered his hands to his sides, and then sank to his knees. He shifted his weight from side to side and then slowly raised his arms. He paused for a moment and then curved his arms downward as though rolling them over an invisible barrel. Abigail recognized it as the beginning movement of the *Yang* short form. She'd taken a few tai chi classes but never got the hang of it.

It seemed Raphael became one with the ground as the *chi*, the universal life force, expressed itself through him. She'd never witnessed such complete and effortless movement as one position flowed seamlessly into the next. Raphael completed the form and resumed the ready stance, hands at his sides.

"Good morning, Abigail," he said, "How are you?"

Well, I just had the most amazing sex of my life with a woman, and did things I never thought I'd do, and I can't wait to do them again if you really want to know the truth, and on a scale of from one-to-ten with ten being really, really good, the past twelve hours would rate about a twenty!

"Fine," she said, "just fine." *Oh, Abigail, you are such a chatterbox!*

"This is my brother, Michael," Raphael said, indicating the dark figure behind him. She wasn't sure if he meant "brother" literally or figuratively. Michael nodded, with the trace of a smirk on his face. His eyes sparkled with a deep blue that looked supernatural. His self-assured smirk reminded Abigail of every "bad boy" for whom she'd ever had an infatuation, and she felt attracted to him in a way she didn't like. She reminded herself that she'd switched teams and no longer had any interest in driving a stick shift!

"And this is Urielle," Raphael continued as he indicated the light figure. Urielle's bearing seemed almost manly, with long, straight blond hair tied behind her back in a single braid. She stood motionless, palms together over her chest, in an apparent state of indifference to Abigail's presence.

"You have questions," Raphael said, "and now is the time for answers."

"Are you angels?" she asked.

Raphael gave Michael a sideways glance, seeming to ask an unspoken question. Michael shrugged his shoulders as though to say, "Why not?" The subtle interaction suggested to Abigail that although Raphael did the talking, Michael was truly in charge.

"We are servants of creation. Our purpose is to defend the evolution of sentient life on this planet."

"That sounds like 'angels' to me. Why don't you just call yourself 'angels' and be done with it? Why don't you reveal yourselves to the world?"

"Revealing ourselves would be disastrous for the evolution of human beings on this planet. People want instant solutions. They want miracles. They'd rather believe in magic than work with the miraculous reality that is right in front of their faces.

"The fact is, human beings evolve in response to demands from the environment. In the absence of those demands, human beings adapt to a lower state of existence. If your body thinks it is no longer needed, then it declines, and so it is with hearts and minds.

"If human beings were certain of our existence, they would turn to us for miracles. They would turn to us for magic, and for instant solutions. And when those solutions were not forthcoming, they would turn against us."

Abigail hadn't thought of angels that way before, but what he said rang true. Nor had she ever considered that 'use it or lose it' might apply to the evolution of an entire species!

"Why am I here?"

"You are here because you came looking, and the agreements were correct."

He'd talked about "agreements" when he introduced her to the Grotto of Hearts. He said then that the hacienda "stood ready to welcome" her, but at the time she didn't understand what he meant well enough to phrase a question.

"An agreement," he continued, "can be thought of as a confluence of events. Think of it as two rivers that merge together at just the right moment. Together they form a greater outcome."

Abigail understood what he meant. She and Caroline had created a *confluence*, and she couldn't wait to be *confluent* again!

"But why me?" she asked. "I came here to write a story, that's all."

"Evolution," Raphael began, "sometimes makes a leap in one generation that otherwise requires thousands of years to complete. You could think of it as plucking an ace from a deck of cards, although the mutation is actually far more random than that."

"What are you saying? I'm some kind of mutant?" Abigail asked.

"I am saying that among a billion human beings on this planet you have a unique potential."

Abigail didn't feel unique. Her life had been about as crappy as anyone else's, and a little worse in some regards.

"So, am I going to sprout wings and fly, or what?" she asked.

Michael laughed, and then resumed his smirking countenance. Abigail found him annoying. Urielle remained aloof, and that, in Abigail's opinion, had become rude.

"Evolution," Raphael continued, "built the human brain in a series of layers. These are the reptilian, mammalian, and neocortex, roughly corresponding to actions, feeling, and thought. Each new structure evolved on top of the preceding layer and is thoroughly integrated with those that preceded it.

"A fourth evolutionary structure is the prefrontal cortex," he said, pointing to his forehead. "This area provides an executive function that allows control of impulses from other parts of the brain."

"Delayed gratification, morality, those sorts of things," Michael added, with a hint of boredom.

"*Your brain*," Raphael resumed, "contains an advanced structure, a specific bundle of neurons in the prefrontal cortex, that allows *tuning*."

"Tuning?"

"Tuning is the ability to experience an expanded range of frequencies. Think of it this way, human visual anatomy evolved to detect the wavelengths of light that are most useful for survival of your species. But this represents only a small portion of the electromagnetic spectrum. Each species adapts according to its needs. Bees, for example, detect ultraviolet wavelengths..."

"It's really kind of cool," Michael interjected.

"...but cannot see red," Raphael finished.

"Bummer," Michael commented.

"With proper stimulus and training, tuning allows you to experience more of what is out there. And more of what is in here," Raphael continued, pointing to his head. "Essentially, it allows you to master more of everything it means to be human."

"More bandwidth," Michael said.

"But why me? Why should I get involved with any of this? I'm just..." *I'm just a newborn lesbian girl who wants to sleep with her lover.* "...I'm just a journalist. I write travel guides for tourists who don't want to discover things for themselves."

"You have always been 'involved,'" Raphael answered, then touched the center of her forehead with the tips of two fingers.

A flash of light collapsed Abigail's vision and she saw herself as a young girl playing dress-up in front of a mirror in her parent's bedroom. Young Abigail wore her mother's black and white polka-dot dress with a pair of red pumps twice the size of her feet. The dress flowed to the floor and covered everything but the pointed toes of the shoes. Her cheeks glowed from an over-application of pink blush, and bright red lipstick covered her lips.

She pranced and curtsied in front of the mirror, and then lifted the folds of the dress to turn fast circles on one foot. If she spun fast enough, she hoped to catch a glimpse of herself before the reflection caught up with her. She turned again and again until at last she fell to her knees with the room spinning in circles.

She looked at the reflection, and the girl in the mirror looked back. Abigail sensed that something had changed, but couldn't figure out what. She reached to touch the mirror and the image hesitated, just a microsecond, and then also reached forward. As their fingertips made contact Abigail saw that the girl in the mirror wore no lipstick! An electric current rippled through her arm and she jerked her hand away from the mirror.

Both girls sat wide-eyed with amazement. Abigail jumped up and ran to the kitchen where her mother prepared a meal.

"Mommy! Mommy! Come quick!" Abigail shouted as the heels of the pumps clacked with each floppy footstep.

"Slow down, honey, or you're going to fall down," her mother called out.

"There's a girl in the mirror!" Abigail exclaimed as she entered the kitchen.

Her mother stirred batter in a large yellow mixing bowl on top of the kitchen island. A box of cornmeal sat alongside plastic containers of flour and sugar. Smudges of flour stained her checkered apron. She looked at Abigail and smiled.

"In the mirror? Is she playing dress up?"

"It's me, mommy! It's me! She looks just like me!"

Abigail's mother looked at a recipe on the kitchen island, then rested the spoon on the inside rim of the mixing bowl. She put her hands on her hips and smiled at Abigail.

"Does your friend have a name?" she asked.

"I told you, it's me! Her name is Abigail." *Haven't you been paying attention?*

"That's sweet, honey. Can you play awhile longer while mommy finishes cooking? We're having cornbread."

"But mommy, come see!"

"I can't right now, sweetie, but I'll come in a few minutes, okay?"

Abigail pouted, crossed her arms, and stomped back to the bedroom. The girl in the mirror waited for her, smiled, and then opened her mouth and pulled her eyes open with both hands to make a silly face. Abigail laughed. The girl smiled one more time and then disappeared into the reflection of Abigail with red lipstick.

"She's gone, mommy," Abigail said.

The vision faded and Abigail found herself with Raphael's hands on her shoulders.

"Abigail, it is your destiny to know what is on the other side of the mirror. That destiny will hound you all the days of your life if you do not follow it," he said.

"How do you know all this? How do you know what's going on inside my head?" she asked.

"All living things generate an energy field with a unique signature. Patterns within that field reveal characteristics specific to the organism. Your signature suggests not only who you are, but also who you may become."

"You have the mark," Michael explained. He then looked to Raphael and said, "Now tell her the rest."

Raphael swallowed before he spoke, "Your energy signature creates a unique vibration among the threads of life. The more you develop your abilities, the more other entities will detect your presence. Some of those entities possess malevolent intent."

Abigail laughed. "What? Are you saying the boogey-man will come after me?"

Raphael glanced at Michael, who nodded "yes," apparently to grant Raphael permission to continue.

"Certain forces are opposed to the evolution of Man, for their own selfish reasons. Others may simply seek to control your power," Raphael explained.

The somber tone in Raphael's voice said more than his actual words. Something deadly serious was out there. Abigail felt it in her guts. Goose bumps popped up on her skin and she rubbed her arms to warm the flesh.

"Now you're scaring me. Why don't you just tell me who's on the other side of the mirror? If it's not the boogey-man, then who is it?"

Urielle huffed. She glowered at Abigail with such a look of disdain that Abigail wondered if she might be one of the "malevolent entities" Raphael talked about. *What's her problem, anyway?*

"The world is larger than you know, Abigail," Raphael said, "and so is your life. The way is not easy but for the moment all you need do is put one foot ahead of the other."

Abigail turned to Urielle and asked, "How about you? Do you have anything to say?"

Urielle looked at Abigail with eyes that burned through her as though she didn't exist, and said, "I am the Fire of God."

Urielle's words hit Abigail like a slap in the face. She'd had just about enough of Urielle's rude demeanor, and it was time to push back.

"Well, that's not something you hear every day. S-s-so...," Abigail stammered, "Is it okay to call you 'Uri'?"

Urielle's mouth dropped open with surprise. She looked as though she had never been addressed with such flippancy. Rafael cringed as though struck in the head and Michael burst into laughter.

Urielle's hands dropped to her side and her entire countenance changed to a magnitude of fury the likes of which Abigail had never seen. Abigail realized she'd made a *severe* error in judgment. Urielle looked at her as though she had no more importance than a bug, and would leave an ugly spot on the ground where Abigail stood without even thinking about it. Urielle stepped towards Abigail in a purple rage. Michael moved between them and held up his hands to stop the crazed angel. Rafael stepped behind Michael. It looked as though Raphael meant to provide support, but Abigail noticed he hung back from the confrontation. Urielle frightened him, too!

Rafael turned to look at her and with desperation in his voice said, "Leave...*now!*"

Thus ended Abigail's question-and-answer session with the trinity of angels. She took a few steps backward down the path, then turned and ran. Rather, her guts pulled her away and her feet merely followed. Not even as the ape-girl on primitive Earth during the flood did she feel such terror! She ran with such panic that she could hardly control her limbs. She ran all the way back to the moon gate. Holding the side of the gate she stopped to regain her breath, and to calm her heart, lest it explode out of her chest.

Never Give Up

"It is not God who allows bad things to happen, it is you and me."

"There you are." Abigail turned to see Rayna, wearing grey workout pants and a sleeveless t-shirt that showed off her muscular arms.

"I have been looking for you," Rayna said, and then noting Abigail's breathless condition, "I see you're getting along with Urielle."

Abigail still hadn't caught her breath, so she simply nodded her head, "Yes."

"Come with me," Rayna said, "we have training for you."

Abigail didn't want "training" at this moment, whatever it might be, and besides, at what point had Rayna become a "trainer?"

"It will get you further away from Urielle," Rayna added.

"Okay, you have a deal," Abigail replied. "Just get me out of here."

They walked away from the gardens. Abigail regained her composure after a few minutes, and asked, "Is Urielle truly the 'Fire of God?'"

"Urielle...is the consolidated vengeance of every woman who has ever been raped by man," Rayna replied.

"Dear Lord," Abigail said, "that's horrible."

Thinking a moment she asked, "Then why is she so angry with me, another woman?"

"Her vengeance is a living thing that grows stronger every day, with each new atrocity, and she has become Wrath."

Abigail trembled from head to toe with the thought. She would sooner jump off a cliff than face Urielle in a fight!

"Then why doesn't God unleash her on the men who do those things?" she asked.

"Everything that happens is a thread in the Tapestry of Life. Only the Creator knows the purpose of each thread, and how it connects to all the other threads within the cloth. They explained this to you, yes?"

"They" hadn't explained it to Abigail in just that way, but she understood the idea.

"And besides," Rayna continued, "It is not God who allows bad things to happen, it is you and me."

Abigail stopped in her tracks. "What do you mean?"

"Think of it this way," Rayna answered. "Each year tens of thousands of people die in automobile accidents. Did those people die because God made unsafe vehicles?"

"No, they were probably going too fast, or got distracted."

"But in terms of vehicle safety, what about race car drivers? They get in horrendous collisions that destroy the vehicles around them. But more often than not, the driver is unharmed."

Abigail thought of the videos she'd seen of racecars rolling multiple times and disintegrating into hundreds of pieces, and yet, as Rayna said, the driver is usually unharmed.

"So, you're saying," Abigail responded, "that ordinary cars could be designed as well as racecars?"

"One is designed for safety, the other compromises safety for style and economy. It is a choice, a choice made by man. Again I ask, does God design unsafe vehicles?"

"No, we humans do that. As far as that goes, I suppose God doesn't drive drunk, either!"

"The world works the way it is supposed to work. It is up to people—me, you, and all of us together, to make it the best possible place, not only for ourselves, but for the Earth as a living organism."

Abigail had no idea that Rayna the warrior woman held such depth. Her respect for Rayna tripled in less than that many minutes. Rayna had one more point to make.

"The Earth was given to us by God," she said, "for the evolution of life on this planet. The Earth is not God's world, but ours."

They walked through an arched hallway that supported one of the long sides of the hacienda, and exited into a large rectangular patio with blank walls. The patio served as a storage area for items used in the garden. Huge pots were stacked high above Abigail's head, and thick columns stood more than a story tall. It looked like a great place to play hide-and-seek. Abigail's fear of Urielle had calmed considerably and she had more questions.

"I thought you said you were a guest. When did you become a trainer?" she asked. In other words, who died and put you in charge?

"Everyone comes here for a different reason, and possesses unique gifts. Training is something I do very well."

"Unique gifts?"

"You are like no one else in the world, and your life is a unique gift, a unique contribution to the whole."

"What is your unique gift?" she asked Rayna.

"I sharpen swords," Rayna said, and then looked at Abigail, letting her know that Abigail was the sword to whom she referred.

"What is the purpose of this training?" Abigail asked. *Maybe I don't want to be sharpened.*

Rayna paused to look closely at Abigail, as though she should already know the answer to the question.

"The spirits of men come to the Earth to experience the world as human beings. A few come to the Earth not only to experience human life, but also to master it. You are here and this is your path. Did they not tell you?"

She seemed to refer to Abigail's question-and-answer session with the angels in the garden. Apparently, Abigail should have listened more closely!

"Our chat was, uh, cut short," Abigail responded.

"That is unfortunate. But you feel a difference now, yes? Different than before you came here?"

"Yes, I feel different...more powerful. Except when I'm running for my life. So, am I a superhero now or what?"

Rayna laughed, and then gave Abigail a ruthless, calculated look. Abigail realized she'd made a mistake in jesting about her new power. *Yes, I'm a superhero, and my super power is putting my big foot in my mouth!*

"You are stronger, faster, and have more stamina than before, but not so much as that. You are not a 'superhero,' but you are in possession of something more valuable than any of those things. You now have the ability to see key joints."

"Key joints?" Abigail asked.

"A key joint," Rayna began, "is the most vulnerable point in any system. It's the thing upon which the strength of the entire system depends. You could think of it as the weakest link in a chain, but that is an oversimplification. For example, imagine yourself fighting the strongest, fastest man on Earth. How can you defeat him? What is his key joint? What is his weakest link?"

Abigail shrugged her shoulders and said, "I don't know."

"It is his brain!" Rayna said. "Destroy his brain and it doesn't matter if he is the toughest man who ever lived, without a functioning control center all that muscle is no more than dying meat."

Abigail understood her point. Rayna seemed to speak from experience, but Abigail had no idea how killing people could fit in with "mastering the human experience."

"So, you're in the brain destruction business?"

"You are too clever for your own good," Rayna answered, "I think you must learn the hard way." She took Abigail's shoulders and positioned her so that she looked down the long length of the patio.

"Your task is to get to the other end," she said. Then she swatted Abigail's butt and shouted, "Go! Go!"

Abigail took off at a mild trot. Almost immediately a man stepped out from behind a column and ran towards her, fists clenched. He wore a black t-shirt with a logo on the left chest, and grey athletic pants with white sneakers.

Abigail felt confident in her newfound strength. *If a little sparring practice is what you want, then bring it.* The man swung his fist in earnest. It wasn't an all-out blow using his full might, but nevertheless would have knocked her down had it landed. She slipped the punch and stepped aside, then struck his upper back with a hammer fist blow. She picked up her pace and trotted towards the far end of the patio.

Two more men, dressed like the first, appeared from behind stacks of pots. Further away another man stepped out from a column. All of the men ran towards her. She engaged the first two at almost the same time. Eyes, throat, groin, knees, those are the targets her self-defenses classes had taught her to strike. She feinted at the first man's eyes with her fingers and then delivered a low-powered kick to his knee. She turned to face the second man and the bottom of his foot struck her upper chest and knocked her to the ground. The man had executed a jumping sidekick without breaking stride. Worse than the physical blow was the realization that he intended to do genuine harm!

Abigail's kickboxing instructor flashed through her mind. "The essence of self-defense," she'd taught, "is the willingness to suffer injury and to do injury to another human being." But Abigail hadn't been ready for this. This was no friendly sparring match; this was Israeli military combat training, taught at the impact of fists and feet. She knew she had to get back into the fight but they were already upon her, kicking from all directions. She rolled back and forth on the ground, trying to block their blows and regain her feet. All four of the men kicked her, including the first man she'd fought. She covered her head and neck and curled into a defensive ball.

"*Stop!*" Rayna shouted. The beating stopped and the men stepped back a few paces. Their proximity menaced Abigail. She did not feel safe. She had no control over the situation, and anything could happen. She certainly did not feel like a superhero. She felt like a curled up little girl who'd just been beaten to the ground by four grown men. This can't be happening to me.

Rayna leaned over her. "*No! No! No!*" She screamed. "Never give up! Fight, you live! Give, you die! Always fight! *Always!*" Her spittle sprinkled Abigail's face, and in that moment Abigail felt more terrified of Rayna than all of the men combined. They might beat her to the ground, but Rayna would kill her!

Rayna grabbed Abigail's blouse; the pretty one with the red wasp Caroline gave her earlier that afternoon, and jerked her to her feet. Abigail felt bruises on her arms, legs, and ribs. Her elbows and knees were raw and bleeding. Her lip bled. Her right eye swelled underneath the scar. My god, did they re-open the wound? Her blouse was soiled. She was soiled. Tears welled in her eyes. How could this be happening?

Rayna stood in her face, with neither compassion nor mercy. "This is not a wrestling match where you tap the mat and give up," she said. "Go to the ground and you die! This is fighting for your life, for your very right to be here! *Do you understand?*"

Abigail thought back to her experience on primitive Earth, back to the flash flood and the lightning, back to the long line of women across the centuries who had endured unbearable hardship that she might be here. Fight for your life to survive. Live long enough to reproduce. Stare death and defeat in the face and curse the darkness. "Come and get me," we shout into the storm and stand defiant!

Something hardened inside her, like the rod of steel that the sword smith pounds with his hammer to create layer upon layer of sharpened metal, a deadly weapon. Anger rushed over her like a fire. They re-injured my face and my blouse is dirty. *Hell and fury shall now follow!*

"You are angry?" Rayna asked. "Good!"

Abigail glared at her with red rage. *How could you do this to me? How could you allow this to happen?*

"*Abigail!*" Rayna shouted. "Get out of your head and into the fight! Look for the key joints! Look for the key joints!"

Rayna pushed her in the direction of the far end of the patio. Her attackers had dispersed among the storage objects. Her body burned with fire. Her old friend anger came back. She thought of her father's indifference and lechery, her mother's loneliness, and Edgar's fist in her face. They didn't know what they'd unleashed. She straddled her anger like a wild stallion beyond control. She could only wrap her fingers in the creature's long mane and hold on!

This time she did not trot into the patio; she walked at her own calm pace. The first man came out of hiding at a full run, headed directly for her. She watched his feet and his swinging arms. A moment before they collided she sidestepped and swept his leg out from underneath him, just as he moved to place his full weight on the foot. He went down face first with a thud. Dust billowed from the impact. She thought to stomp the back of his neck, but instead delivered a safer blow to his shoulder.

The next two men came out of hiding and ran at her in unison. They would reach her almost simultaneously. She watched their legs, their torsos, and their fists. She ran toward them. Just as they arrived within striking distance she kneeled down and struck both fists into their groins with a wide u-shaped punch. She stood back up in an instant. They didn't. The men lay on the ground, doubled over in pain, grasping their crotches with both hands. She hadn't held back much on the punches. If they pee blood for the next few days, then screw them!

The fourth man came forward, but approached with more caution. He saw what happened to the others and closed the distance in ever decreasing arcs, looking for vulnerability.

What? You don't like it when little girls fight back? Does the big bad man like his girls on the ground, where they're easier to kick? A bestial rage welled up inside Abigail and she fought to maintain control. Her senses went wild. Time dilated. She closed her eyes and struggled to focus. She heard the soft rustle of the man's clothing as he moved, and the cautious placement of his feet on the stones of the patio. She smelled his fear.

She decided to beat him into the ground. She didn't care who he was, what he thought he was doing, if he had a wife and kids waiting for him, or still lived at home with his mother. She envisioned beating him to his knees, and then with the thick, dark fingernails of a beast, ripping out his throat.

"Stop!" Rayna shouted. "That is enough!"

Abigail opened her eyes. Everything in her vision bloomed with a red cast. The man backed away. Some dark core in her brain hungered for his demise. Maybe later. She faced Rayna and saw fear.

"Good, good," Rayna said, but her voice held a tremor.

Abigail's restraint faltered on the edge of a precipice from which she could not return. She had to get away before she lost all control. She hurried past Rayna without saying a word or a change of expression. The training session was over.

Boogey Man

"...get a grip."

Abigail's fury raged like an animal in a dark pit, prodded with sticks and taunted, and now it roamed unleashed, ravenous for vengeance.

She walked to the gardens and placed her forearms against a shaded wall to rest her head. The cool adobe felt good to her raw elbows. The open scrapes were probably picking up bacteria by the billions, but she didn't care, she'd kill them, too.

Abigail, get a grip! She hadn't been this angry in a long time. She hated the red rage that dominated everything. She knew she couldn't think straight. Worse, it stirred up the rejection she felt as a young girl when she realized her father cared little for her. She tried to be a loving daughter and got nothing. Her main crime, it seemed, was to be born with a vagina. That alone condemned her to eternal second-class status. Make good grades on her report card? That was less important than the football game on the television. Join the drill team? He never saw her perform. Earn a scholarship? Why couldn't she have earned two?

Nothing she ever did was quite good enough. He never said, "I love you." He never reached out with genuine affection. And then on her sixteenth birthday...

Her throat choked. She shook the tension out of her fingers and wiped tears from her cheeks. She stood up straight, inhaled deeply through her nose to expand her diaphragm, and then exhaled the full volume of air through her mouth. It helped release the anger, as long as she didn't allow her thoughts to start the cycle all over again.

She felt calm, and tired. The adrenalin had run its course and fatigue settled in. She went back to her room and lay down. At the moment it felt good to be alone.

She woke later that night and sensed Caroline standing over her. "Shhh...," Caroline said, "you're a mess. I'm going to clean you up."

Caroline washed Abigail's face with a warm, wet washcloth, and then cleaned her elbows and knees. She placed a cold, damp cloth over the right side of Abigail's face. It felt wonderful against the swollen eye, but Abigail expected to have a shiner in the morning.

Caroline removed Abigail's clothes with gentle hands. Abigail thought back to the first morning she woke at adobeDreams, naked in bed except for panties. It was Caroline who undressed her and she smiled at the thought.

Caroline lay down beside her, and pulled the bedcovers over them. Her warmth comforted Abigail's sore body. Caroline caressed the bruise on Abigail's chest, and gently massaged Abigail's shoulders and arms. Her hand moved down to glide across Abigail's upper thighs and slid between her legs. Her fingers played Abigail's mound in lazy, loving strokes that built to a slow, desperate crescendo. Abigail gasped, shuddered, and felt a healing release that no sedative could have accomplished. They slept.

In the night something stirred in the back of Abigail's brain. She smelled darkness. She struggled to bring the sensation to full conscious awareness, but could not. Caroline lay beside her, asleep, but someone or something else hung nearby, at the threshold of detection. She wanted to get up, but her limbs would not move. She listened for any sound, but heard only the faintest stir of air currents through the curtains.

An entity skulked on the patio outside the open doors. She could feel it! The presence moved into the room.

Fully alert, she kept her eyes closed and didn't move, lest "it" detect her conscious state. Even though she couldn't see the thing, she sensed that it was a dense ball of gravity, completely black, the size of a basketball. The thing traveled further into the room and approached the bed.

The ball lowered itself and depressed the mattress with its weight. She visualized it as a dense sphere that would sink to the Earth's core in an instant were it not under some kind of influence. The fact that the bed depressed only slightly with its weight demonstrated that someone or something exerted conscious control over the effect it had on the physical environment.

Wide-awake and terrified, she felt that she must do something. She drew up her legs, spun out of bed, and threw herself against the wall with arms outstretched. The dense ball sat on the bed, unmoving. Hair stood up all over her body and her heart drummed in her chest.

The ball levitated off the bed to the height of a large man's chest and began to rotate. Wisps of darkness curled up from its surface and created tendrils that fell back into the ball, and then rose again. The wisps grew larger and took on more solidity as the ball turned. The ball expanded and contracted in a slow rhythm. It pulsated like a nest of black snakes writhing to escape a dark pit. Warm liquid ran down Abigail's thighs. She'd peed herself.

The primal memories in her guts understood the identity of the thing even if her brain did not. Her limbs trembled and tears streamed down her face. The writhing snakes formed a beating heart, the heart of all darkness, *the heart of Lucifer*, the sworn enemy of Man!

The black snakes expanded, thickened and coalesced into the shape of a man. His hair hung loose and black below his shoulders. He wore a dark, long sleeve shirt, faded jeans, and a wide black belt with a large oval buckle. Shiny medallions embellished the ankles of his black boots. His face was lean with wide cheekbones, dark eyebrows, and a square, cleft chin. It was the face of the dark-haired man who frightened her in her ape-girl dreams on primitive Earth!

He stood tall, and stretched out his body and neck. His shoulders popped from the movement.

"Good evening, Abigail," he said, "It is so nice to finally meet you!

"Did your angelic friends tell you to expect me?" he asked, then answered his own question. "Oh, they did not, did they? Tsk-tsk! How can you appreciate the full scope of the game when you do not know all the players?"

Abigail didn't answer. She hung suspended against the wall with her feet off the floor and her arms outstretched in the shape of a cross.

Lucifer leaned over and inhaled her scent with his nose barely above her chest. She felt the air currents of his inhalation on her skin and wanted to vomit. She knew he could smell the residue of the sex pheromones from Caroline's earlier lovemaking.

"What a rare flower you are," he said. "And what is that perfume you wear? No, no, don't tell me."

He closed his eyes and inhaled deeply through his nose.

"Well, I don't think it's chicken," he said with a cruel smile.

He scanned her exposed body. He paused at her private parts, cocked his head, and blinked his eyes in slow motion, like a man raising and lowering a hot cup to his lips. His eyes drank her nudity and she felt violated, and ashamed.

The tip of his tongue traced the outline of his upper lip, and his eyes looked drunk with lechery. She knew he was going to rape her. He spoke:

"How ripe the fruit

"Plucked twixt thorns

"With sweet delight."

"Abby?" Caroline said. She sat up on the bed, and held the covers to her chest.

Without a turn of his head, Lucifer's eyes glanced back in the direction of Caroline's voice. He looked at Abigail and smiled. He wants me to know that he knows she's there. When he's done with me, Caroline will be next.

Lucifer kicked his left foot back with a slight thrust. The bed flew up and smashed into the opposite wall with a dreadful impact. Caroline's body hit the wall. The wall cracked and chips of adobe plaster fell from the ceiling as the bed recoiled and crashed to the floor.

"Oops," he said, with mock surprise, "girlfriend fall down and go boom!"

Abigail wanted to cry out for Caroline, but her voice would not work. She wanted to push herself away from the wall, but her limbs would not move. *Caroline!* The violence with which her body impacted the wall could easily have shattered her skull. Abigail gasped for breath, panic-stricken.

Lucifer drank every moment of her distress. Then he pointed to the cheekbone below his right eye, and swiped it with his fingertip, drawing a rough, crude line. "You had a boo-boo," he said, mocking the scar on her face.

He stood nose to nose with her and savored her fear. She looked away and stared out the balcony door as her body trembled against the wall. He chuckled and turned her head forward.

"The funny thing," he said, "is that you don't know what a dangerous young lady you are." She had no idea what he meant and gazed past him to the far wall with the wreck of the bed below it. He swiped her chest with his hand, and held it up for her to see. Blood covered his palm.

"You are leaking," he said.

What? A single rivulet of blood ran down his wrist. He turned his hand sideways and licked it off. His tongue was huge, like that of a bull. She looked down at herself. Red globules covered her skin like beads of sweat.

Hematohidrosis. She knew the word from her studies of the Crucifixion. Extreme terror caused small blood vessels to rupture around her sweat glands, and blood now oozed out of the pores like perspiration.

Lucifer looked at her dead on and began to unbuckle his belt. His pants bulged with an erection. *Think Abby, think!* What had Rayna said? "Look for the key joints!"

What constituted Lucifer's "key joint," his most vulnerable point? What did the success of the entire system known as "Lucifer" depend? She knew the answer as soon as she asked the questions. *Vanity. Stupid male vanity.* For the sake of vanity Lucifer refused to bow to Man, and God ejected him from heaven. At that moment she forgot that she wasn't religious and her soul cried out for salvation in the only way it knew how.

She looked Lucifer in the face and said, "In the name of the Father, and of the Son, and the Holy Spirit." It was something she remembered from one of the few times she went to church, or maybe it was from a horror movie. Either way, it didn't matter. In that moment she reached out to God with all her heart. She longed for God. She loved God, and she wanted God with her always.

She repeated "In the name of the Father, and the Son, and the Holy Spirit," like a lover crying out her beloved's name across a distance. She stared the heart of all darkness in the face and stood defiant in God's love.

Lucifer stumbled back, dumb struck. The tongue of his belt hung limp. His nose crinkled as though he smelled an abominable odor, and he looked on her with complete disgust. At that moment the door jam shattered and shards of wood exploded into the room. Urielle stood in the doorway, with Michael behind her. Raphael and Rayna were in the background.

Lucifer screamed at Urielle with primal rage. She fell upon him in a blur and struck a mighty open-palm blow that threw him into the wall. As he rebounded Michael skewered him through the guts with a heavy golden spear and pinned him against the wall. Abigail hadn't noticed the spear before; it seemed to appear from nowhere.

Lucifer roared with an anger that shook the room. Bits of adobe plaster fell from the ceiling. He struggled to free himself from the wall, but Michael held him fast with the spear. Lucifer glowered at Abigail with a hatred that said, "This isn't over. I will be back." His form reverted to black snakes writhing in a dark pit.

"Urielle! Now!" Michael shouted.

Urielle produced a sword in her hand, hesitated to gather strength, and slashed the apparition in half. Dark blood splattered the wall and Lucifer exploded into tentacles of swirling mist.

Abigail fell to the floor. She tried to stand but her arms collapsed when she tried to push herself up. Across the floor Caroline's limp hand protruded from underneath the wrecked bed.

"Caroline!" she screamed.

Aftermath

"Where one heart is true, others may follow."

Michael jerked his spear free of the wall and Urielle returned her sword to a scabbard within her cloak. It seemed she concealed a scabbard there, but for all appearances the sword simply materialized in her hand, and disappeared as quickly. Michael's spear also disappeared. *Neat trick.* Urielle spun and walked out of the room. She had done what she came to do, and the aftermath did not concern her.

Abigail pointed at the wrecked bed as Raphael and Rayna entered the room. The impact of Caroline's body left a pattern of cracks on the wall. The wall was solid adobe, not sheetrock, and Abigail cringed at the thought of how hard Caroline must have struck in order to leave that kind of impression. Every bone in her body might be broken!

Michael lifted the mattress and moved it aside. Caroline lay on the floor, nude, motionless, her hair matted with blood.

"Let me look at her!" Raphael shouted.

He kneeled beside Caroline and moved his hands above the length of her body. He paused at her head, then closed his eyes and settled into an apparent state of deep meditation.

"Her spine and organs are intact, but there is bleeding inside her skull," he said.

With Rayna's assistance he supported Caroline's neck and rolled her onto her back. Rayna covered her body with a sheet and stepped away. Raphael held Caroline's head between his hands with his fingertips supporting the occipital ridge at the back of her skull. At last he turned to Abigail and said, "She will live, but tomorrow will not be a good day."

Rayna squatted beside Abigail, grabbed her upper arm, and lifted her up.

"You look like road kill," she said, "We need to get you cleaned up."

Abigail didn't want to leave Caroline. "Don't we need to call an ambulance? Doesn't she need a doctor?" she asked.

"She is in our hands now, and will be well," Michael responded.

"You're not the only one with 'superpowers,'" Rayna said with a reassuring smile. "She will recover quickly."

Abigail's heart thumped with anxiety. The angels seemed confident in their diagnosis. She didn't like it, but if she couldn't trust angels, whom could she trust?

"Thank you," she said, to all of them.

Rayna walked Abigail to her own room. If they passed anyone Abigail could not say, but how strangely a dark-haired nude girl, covered with blood and wobbling on her feet, escorted by a tall, blond warrior princess must have appeared!

Rayna put Abigail in the shower and cleaned her up. She inspected her body for damage. Rayna's hands were not the loving hands of Caroline, but she knew what needed to be done and she did it. Once she determined that Abigail had not suffered a sexual assault, she remarked as much to herself as Abigail, "Thank God I heard the bed hit the wall."

She gave Abigail a pair of her panties and a t-shirt to wear. Both of them were too big, but all the more comfortable for it. She put Abigail in bed and lay down beside her, her arm over Abigail in a protective embrace.

"Sleep, Abigail. Tomorrow will be a new beginning," she said.

Abigail woke up alone in the bed. Rafael sat in a chair a short distance away.

"Good morning, Abigail," he said. "How do you feel?"

Caroline! What if he has bad news about Caroline? Her stomach went queasy, and she blurted, "Is Caroline okay?"

"She will be fine, but needs rest. In a day or two she will be fully recovered." Then with a twinkle in his eyes, he added, "We'll check in on her this morning, if you like."

If you like? Of course, she'd like! But he already knew that.

"We need to talk about last night."

Well, by all means, she thought. Let's talk about my attempted rape by the heart of all darkness the first thing when I wake up in the morning!

"I apologize for the abruptness," he said. "But this is urgent. You need to understand what is happening here."

"Lucifer isn't dead, is he?"

"No, but he is in retreat, at least for awhile." He paused, apparently trying to figure something out in his own mind. "His attack on this compound was unprecedented. Never has he dared enter these walls."

She noticed he said, "attack on this compound," and made it sound like a trespassing offense. Anger shot through her veins and she sat up, her fists clenched.

"That...that thing...didn't attack the hacienda. He attacked me," she sputtered.

"I am sorry, Abigail. This was not supposed to happen. We thought we had more time to prepare you for what is out there."

"You knew this was going to happen? The devil—the freaking devil—came after me, and you didn't think I needed to know that? Is there anything else you're not telling me?"

Raphael held up both palms to urge patience. He stood up and opened the doors to the balcony. Dust motes sparkled in the morning light. The fragrance of roses wafted into the room. Raphael inhaled deeply and surveyed the garden before he answered.

"The truth is nothing could have prepared you for the path you are now on. To understand what is happening, we must start at the beginning."

He looked at Abigail and asked, "Are you ready?" She nodded her head, "yes."

"Your legends are true. Lucifer was the most beautiful of all the angels. He exalted in God's light and became prideful. And then came the evolution of human beings. His jealousy of God's love for Man became a twisted thing that grew inside him. His heart surrendered to hatred and he refused to bow to the Lord's creation. For this he received a dreadful punishment."

"God threw him out?" Abigail asked.

"God cast him to Earth and bound him to the frailty of Man. His power is the power of Man's evil in this world. It is the pit of black snakes you saw, his heart of darkness."

Whoa. Lucifer's power is Man's evil? That was difficult to wrap her head around. Then again, men did do evil things. She supposed that energy—that destructive intent—had to go somewhere.

"So people do bad things, and Lucifer gets stronger?" she asked.

"Evil begets evil. Lucifer's hate feeds Man's evil, and Man's evil feed Lucifer's strength. It is a tide that ebbs and flows across the centuries."

"So why doesn't God do something? Why doesn't God just swoop down from the sky and kick Lucifer back to the pit?"

"It is not God who gives Lucifer his power, it is you. Human beings provide the force that keeps Lucifer alive. It is you who must change. It is you who must defeat Lucifer in your own hearts, and in your own intentions."

That made sense, but people did so many horrible things to one another. Was all that necessary?

"But why? Why must there be so much evil in the world?"

"Without suffering there is no will to change. That is the rule. Without suffering mankind cannot make the next evolutionary transition. That transition, Abigail, defines the survival of the human race."

Abigail struggled to put Raphael's words in a context she understood. Man and Lucifer were in some kind of sick co-dependent relationship, and without that relationship mankind couldn't evolve to a higher state. Was that it? The way to get out of a co-dependent relationship, she recalled from every pop psychology article she'd ever read, was to focus on your own self-interest.

"What has this got to do with me?" she asked. "Why did Lucifer attack *me*?"

"Human beings are on the cusp of a great evolutionary leap. Lucifer sought to degrade and destroy you because he wants that transition to fail."

Abigail remembered their discussion in the garden, before she offended Urielle and fled for her life.

"It's the tuning thing, isn't it? I have the potential, and he wants to stop it before everyone has it."

"Yes, that and more. Your spirit came to the Earth to master the human experience. Because your spirit is connected to all other spirits, your mastery advances the evolutionary transition of all mankind. Where one heart is true, others may follow."

He paused before continuing, "One bird may change the direction of an entire flock."

"Are you saying I'm that one bird?"

"You are one, among few, who have the potential to change the course of events," he replied.

"So there are others like me?"

He lifted his arms, palms up, to indicate the hacienda.

"You are here, and this is your path. Others follow similar paths."

"I'd like to see Caroline now," she said. *And as soon as I do, we're going to walk straight out of this mess.*

The Heart of Darkness

"Her only answer was the rain."

Caroline slept like a stone. One look at her and Abigail knew they wouldn't be going anywhere. As much as she wanted the two of them to get away, it wouldn't happen today.

She bent over and sniffed Caroline's hair. It smelled warm, fresh, and delicious, just like her. A purple bruise marred Caroline's forehead. Abigail kissed it with the softest of kisses. Michael stood at the foot of the bed with his palms raised toward Caroline, seemingly absorbed in meditation. He made eye contact with Abigail long enough to give a reassuring smile, then resumed his meditations.

"Abby?" Caroline stirred.

Abigail knelt beside the bed and rested her face on the edge. Caroline peered out, and then closed her eyes. Abigail loved her eyes.

"I had a bad dream," Caroline said.

"Yes, you did, but it's over now," Abigail replied, then leaned forward and kissed her closed eyelid. Caroline's hand wriggled out from underneath the covers and grasped Abigail's with a soft grip. Love, hurt, and anguish welled up in Abigail at that moment. She'd almost lost her! She had almost lost her! Then came the fire in her veins and she made a decision: *I will kill Lucifer. For all the Caroline's on this planet, I will kill him. And if I can't kill him, I will make him wish he were dead.* The last look she got from Lucifer told her they had future dealings together. "I will be back," his glare said. *And I will be ready*, she vowed.

Abigail leaned forward and kissed Caroline's lips, then whispered, "I love you."

"I love you, too," Caroline replied, and went back to sleep.

Rayna waited for Abigail outside the room. "How is she?" she asked.

"She's sleeping. I think she'll be fine."

Abigail needed to say something else to Rayna. "Thank you for taking care of me."

"You are welcome," Rayna replied with a slight bow of her head.

"It's more than last night," Abigail continued. "Thank you for what you did for me at the storage patio the other day, with the men and the training. That saved my life with Lucifer. If you hadn't pushed me to the extreme, I couldn't have survived what I went through."

"I had no idea the training would be useful so soon, but I'm glad it gave you what you needed." Rayna studied Abigail's face for a moment and added, "Your face is completely healed."

Abigail hadn't noticed, and didn't care. She had other things on her mind. She stood on her toes to kiss Rayna's cheek and then excused herself. She needed time to think.

Abigail walked to the Grotto of Hearts and found it empty. The mandala on the floor attracted her attention and she followed the path of one line. The line traced the outer curve of one radiating whirlpool, then branched off to join another. She stopped and looked at the intersections of the pools. If she followed any one line, the mandala became a labyrinth suitable for meditative purposes. The intricacy of the design amazed her, but she had no time for it. The only inspiration she sought was the means to kill an angel, *a dark angel*, to be exact.

Michael pinned Lucifer to the wall with a spear, and that only stoked Lucifer's rage. Urielle cleaved his dark heart with a sword, but that didn't kill him either. If magic weapons couldn't kill him, what could?

Through love of God she stopped Lucifer's advances before he assaulted her on the wall, but at this moment felt no love in her heart. She didn't want to stop Lucifer. *She wanted to destroy him.* Lucifer must die, and failing that, she wanted to mess him up so badly that he'd crawl back in his hole and never come out!

She walked the intersecting patterns of the mandala thinking about these things—how long she did not know. At last she stood at the center of the floor, looking up to the star at the top of the dome.

"How do I kill Lucifer?" she shouted.

Her equilibrium teetered. The floor rolled beneath her feet. The path she'd walked through the mandala vibrated with hypnotic energy. The oscillations mesmerized and sickened her all at the same time. Nausea washed over her in a hot wave and she closed her eyes to avoid throwing up.

Her disorientation subsided and she opened her eyes. She hung suspended above the seven-pointed star at the top of the dome, her head pointed to the grotto floor. *This is a neat trick.*

The spokes of the star glowed and formed a protective wall of light around the center of the star. The wall of light appeared more blue than white, a little different than what she'd experienced before. She looked down at the surface of the star and expected blue streaks of light to fill the micro fissures within the stone, become liquid, and travel across the surface. Nothing happened. Something was wrong.

She studied the surface of the stone and saw it blur. No, not blur, but *move* with a thin, dark mist. She didn't like where this was going.

The mist grew thick and rose in tendrils above the stone. She began to sink into the mist. She looked around in desperation but found nothing to halt her descent, and nowhere to go. She looked down at the floor of the grotto. Rayna stood there with her eyes reaching up. Abigail extended her arm as though Rayna might grasp it and pull her to safety, but neither of them could do anything to halt Abigail's descent.

She sank into the dark mist. It rose up her ankles, twisting and writhing like vaporous tentacles. The mist wrapped around her legs and pulled her down. Its touch felt like cold mud, oozing across her skin. The mist had her now, its grip tight, and she sank faster.

Abigail looked up one last time at Rayna, and remembered her words. "Fight, you live! Give, you die! Always fight! *Always!*"

She clenched her fists and looked down into the writhing mist. This situation was seriously beginning to piss her off, and then the mist had her.

Her eyes opened into darkness. She saw light filtering down from above as her pupils adjusted, but could not see her arms or legs. She sat in an earthen pit. She smelled damp earth, sweat, urine, and fear. Other women sat in the pit beside her. She heard popping noises in the distance. The women trembled in the darkness. They all hid from something but Abigail didn't know what.

She moved her legs to see if they worked. They did. Her anger with the black mist still burned, and she didn't feel like sitting on her butt in some dark pit. She moved toward the light and lifted the edge of a straw mat laid over the pit. A hand reached out to touch her shoulder and pull her back but she shrugged it off. She saw garbage everywhere. It looked like a garbage bomb exploded in the area, or perhaps the women hid in an actual garbage dump.

She listened and scanned the area, but detected no threats. She pushed up the straw mat and discovered it was heavier than she thought. A large piece of corrugated tin lay on top of the mat. She looked back into the pit and saw the faces of three black women. They wore dull dresses that were little more than unwashed rags. One of them held a baby girl in her arms. The baby was wrapped in strips from a black plastic garbage bag. *People in developed nations have no idea what poverty is.*

The women huddled together in terror. She looked at her arms and saw dark black skin. She touched her face and felt a wide nose with large nostrils. She realized she'd incarnated into the body of a black woman, somewhere in Africa. Africa! Freaking Africa, she railed. Just once, couldn't I go to France?

A heavy vehicle approached and crunched debris underneath its tires. It sounded like a truck. It creaked to a halt as the brakes screeched on naked metal. Men laughed. She lowered the mat and listened. A whole group of men shouted and laughed amongst themselves. The women in the pit gasped with short breaths and trembled against the dirt walls. This is what they feared.

There were sounds of a scuffle. The voices of at least three other men blubbered with tears and panic. Their words were unclear, but she understood the meaning. They begged for their lives!

More laughter followed and then angry shouts. The larger group of men exhorted someone to do something. Abigail's hearing extended. She heard the huffs of a crying child, a young boy, she thought. The exhortations continued. They prodded him to shoot one of the men. The boy cried out in pain. Someone in the group had struck his head, probably with the point of a rifle. The shouts of the men grew louder and became angrier.

BOOM-BOOM-BOOM! The discharge of a high-powered assault rifle thunder clapped and echoed through the air. The baby cried and the mother quickly put her hand over the child's mouth, and made shush sounds for the child to be quiet. The men shouted and laughed, their blood lust running high. The discharge of multiple assault rifles boomed across the sky. The shots echoed like thunder and the men burst into laughter and excited chatter. The baby began to wail and the mother silenced her once again.

The men continued to laugh and talk excitedly amongst themselves. Footsteps approached, kicking trash along the way. One of the men from the vehicle stood above them and unzipped his pants. He urinated on the corrugated tin covering the pit. If the baby made any sound now, they would be undone! The urine ran down a channel in the corrugation and seeped through the straw mat in amber droplets. The man shook himself off and walked away.

The men got back into the truck. They congratulated the young boy for his first kill. The truck started up and at last drove away, crunching more debris.

The women stayed silent in the pit. They held onto one another as involuntary tremors shook their limbs. Time passed. Abigail needed water. Her stomach also ached for food. She lifted up the corner of the mat to peer out and saw only garbage. She looked back at the other women and motioned her arm downward to urge quiet.

She began to crawl out of the pit and saw the mother with the baby. The mother's eyes were wide with shock and reminded Abigail of Caroline's ape-mother incarnation as she held onto her infant in the floodwaters on primitive Earth. The African mother's baby lay limp in her arms. At the cost of her child and her sanity, she had kept the baby silent and saved all of their lives. *My God, my God, what a choice to have to make!*

God wept and the devil danced in Africa. The devil? This was Lucifer's vision for mankind's destiny. This is what Lucifer wants for the entire planet. How can a creature that feeds on such evil be defeated?

Abigail had no answers. She crawled out from underneath the mat and lowered the tin with care, lest it make any noise. She wore dirty grey athletic pants, with a blue t-shirt that had an athletic logo across the chest, and old sneakers with ruptured side seams. She lay motionless on the ground and extended her senses in all directions, but detected no threats. She sprinkled the area around the pit with dirt and twigs to hide its location. Then she knelt behind a shattered wooden fence and surveyed the scene.

A large dead tree sat in the middle of a dusty intersection, the sun behind it. Three men lay on the ground with dark pools beneath their bodies. The twisted, bare branches of the tree gave it the appearance of some ancient deity, raised from the earth. The tree cast the shadow of its branches on the corpses, marking its tribute. This is what happens when people lack the means to defend themselves. This is why she was here. This is what she was meant to see. How can God allow these things to happen? Then she recalled Rayna's words, "It is not God who allows bad things to happen; it is you and me."

Warriors like Rayna did more for peace than anyone who sits on their butt and bemoans the state of the world, but doesn't lift a finger to help. If you want peace, if you want safety and security, then be prepared to fight for it! What a paradox!

She scanned the streets and listened, but detected nothing. She edged along an earthen wall pockmarked from machinegun bullets. The wall led to a corner of the intersection. There she looked and listened again, and once again saw the bodies under the tree. Okay, if this is what I was meant to see then let's get on with it!

She walked to the center of the intersection and put her back against the trunk to blend into the shadow. She looked at the bodies. All three of the men were nude down to their underwear, their shoes, pants, and shirts stripped away. Three bullet holes riddled the chest of the man that the young boy had been forced to shoot. The other two men had been shot through the head, their skulls burst open by high-velocity bullets. She wondered if the men were the husbands of the women in the pit. Perhaps they'd hid the women, and covered them up, before the gang of men in the truck arrived? Perhaps one of them was the husband of the mother with the dead baby?

She recognized one of the men who had been shot in the head. Though hardly anything remained of his face above the mouth, she knew him all the same. She remembered his smile and his laughter and the way he looked at her like nothing else existed. The man had been her husband in this life! She covered her mouth and fell to her knees. She wailed like Caroline wailed to mourn all the losses of her life.

She knew she shouldn't do this, but couldn't stop herself. She sat and howled for a long time before she regained control. She stood up with her back against the tree and surveyed the area.

Scruff marks on the ground revealed that the men had been shot with their shirts off, and then their shoes and pants removed post-mortem. Seven or eight shots rang out when the men were executed, but there were no shell casings on the ground. The gang had stopped to pick up the brass. In this place brass could be reloaded and had value, but human life did not.

She looked around and wondered if this was where she'd experienced life on primitive Earth. Millions of years can change the appearance of a place, she supposed, and then she thought more about the passage of time. Two million years of evolution separated modern man from her Australopithecus ape-girl, and this—*this atrocity*, is the best that humans can do?

Despair overwhelmed her. She felt ashamed to be human. Perhaps God should wipe us all out, or simply allow us to destroy ourselves? Or perhaps God had abandoned the Earth and simply allowed Lucifer to have his way, fueled by humanity's own evil? In another million years the Earth could be clean again, and teem with life that eats, and screws, and poops, but works no evil.

Abigail's stomach cramped from dehydration. The pit with the women escaped most of the day's heat but the accumulated body heat had been stifling. She needed hydration and she needed it now.

She crossed the intersection to a row of pockmarked buildings. Flies buzzed as she approached a blown-out window. She knew she didn't want to look inside, but felt compelled. With her back against the wall she slid to the edge of the frame. She peered around the corner and at first didn't see anything, but then looked again. The bodies of women and young girls lay on the floor, victims of rampaging troops.

Death had loosened the women's bowels and the stench of feces fouled the air. In this place sexual assault and murder is what Lucifer's dark heart meant for people that the world cared little about. It was too much. She turned away and wretched on the spot, throwing up what little food her stomach held. She stared down at the dirt and struggled to make sense of man's inhumanity to man.

Excited shouts forced her to look up. The truck with the gang of men was back. Men in the back of the truck pointed at her, laughed, and thrust their AK-47 assault rifles into the air. They wore a mix-match of military uniforms and civilian garb. The truck was a decrepit old diesel flatbed with wood slats for sides. They had returned to perform a second sweep of the area, looking for survivors who may have come out of hiding. No wonder the other women stayed in the pit and didn't crawl out with her!

Abigail knew she couldn't evade them on the open street. She hated those movie scenes where a victim runs down the middle of a road to escape a vehicle in pursuit. Whom were they kidding? Even in low gear a car travels faster than human beings can run.

She leapt through the window and stepped among the bodies. Her foot slipped in a pool of coagulated blood and she fell beside the body of a woman. The woman's eyes were clouded over and flies crawled across her lips.

Abigail regained her feet and shook the blood off best she could. It was thick as mud and smelled of burnt copper.

She entered another room and ran out an open back door that led to an alley lined with more decrepit buildings. She sprinted away from the main streets that passed the front and side of the building. The alley was strewn with trash, tires, and broken wagons with bare bicycle rims for wheels. The truck with the gang of men screeched to a stop. The men shouted and raced down the main streets looking for her. Some of them reached the head of the alley behind her, and pursued at a full run.

A supersonic bullet sizzled through the air over her head followed by the booming discharge of a rifle. She realized one of the men had taken a shot at her. I want a refund on this ticket, she thought, and then chastised herself. *Abby, this is no time for wisecracks! Run, woman, run!*

There were more shouts behind her. Members of the gang had come through the building, saw the chase down the alley, and shouted instructions to the men in the truck. She looked back and saw that the soldier at the head of the pursuit gained ground very fast, carrying an assault rifle with one arm. Just my luck, I get an Olympic-class sprinter playing for the opposing team! She heard the truck gear up and bounce in the rutted street, knocking debris out of the way with its bumper. She saw that the soldiers were flanking her on the main street. They would reach the opposite end of the alley ahead of her and cut her off!

A broken fence appeared on her right. She ran through the fence and immediately tripped on a wire woven through the fence to hold the slats together. The impact with the ground knocked the wind out of her. Her lungs burned and she didn't want to move. She forced herself to get up though pain gripped her chest like a giant fist. She fought to stay conscious. Her pants leg caught on a sharp piece of wire that protruded from the fence. She ripped the leg free and the wire slashed her ankle.

The soldier she'd seen in the lead of the pursuit leapt through the fence and came right at her. She swept his legs out from under him without thinking about it. He hit the ground hard, stunned by the impact. His assault rifle bounced away. Abigail picked up the weapon, pointed the barrel, and pulled the trigger. Nothing happened. She figured the safety must be on, but had never handled a gun before, and didn't know what the safety looked like. She grabbed a shiny handle on the right side of the receiver and pulled it. The handle opened a rectangular slot on the side of the gun and she saw the brass casing of a bullet. *It's loaded, but that's not the safety.*

She let go of the handle and the slot snapped closed. She looked at both sides of the weapon and in the one second she had to figure out the safety, could not do it. More men approached from the alley and she had no more time. Lifting the rifle up she threw it down sideways and hit the soldier in the head. The metal receiver impacted his skull with a dreadful thud and his body flopped from the impact. One down, how many more to go?

She turned and darted into the building ahead, burst the door inwards, and landed on all fours. She stepped through darkened rooms strewn with trash and then sprinted across the street into an abandoned storefront.

She dashed through the store and hit the back door at a full run, but the door didn't budge. Something blocked it from the other side. The impact knocked her flat on her butt and she sat dazed in a cloud of dust. Light infiltrated through the slats of a boarded window above a sink. She jumped on top of the countertop and kicked at the boards. The boards gave way one by one. She slipped through the window as men came through the front of the building. A shard of glass in the frame sliced the palm of her hand. She fell to the ground and gasped for breath.

She struggled to get up but had no wind. If she had just two minutes to recover, she could put some distance between these men and herself. But there was no time. The yard opened to another alley, but the walls along the opposite side were solid. She stumbled into the alley and looked down one length. There was less debris, but the sides were solid earthen walls or had fences without gaps. She looked down the opposite length of the alley. The truck came towards her, with three men in the cab, and two more in the back. More men had broken out the remaining boards of the window she'd just exited, and spilled out into the yard. One of the men sliced his hand on the same shard of glass and she smiled a little at that, but could run no further.

Eons ago this is how we humans ran prey to ground. We worked in teams and chased animals until they could run no further. Then we slaughtered them, while they stood panting for air and exhausted. Today she was just such an animal!

She walked across the alley to the solid wall and put her butt against it. She rested her hands on her knees and gasped for breath as her arms trembled with terror.

The truck pulled up and all the men got out. One of them had a young boy by the collar. He was surely the same child they'd coerced to execute the man at the intersection. They would probably force him to rape her, too, if he could sustain an erection. The soldiers removed the debris that blocked the back door of the building she'd run through, and more men came out the door. She didn't know how many of them there were, maybe twelve or more. This is so unfair, so cursedly unfair. No one deserves this!

She again remembered what Rayna told her. "Fight! Always fight!" Abigail resolved to fight to the death. A rifle butt to the head, crushing her skull, would be better than what lay ahead. "Look for the key joints!" Rayna had shouted at her. She saw the vulnerabilities of individual men as they approached. One on one, or even three on one, she could beat them. But even her super-powered self, rested and in good condition, with anger burning in her blood, couldn't prevail over this many men!

The men surrounded her in a semi-circle, and laughed. They had run her to ground, and now they relished the moment, just as Lucifer had relished her terror at adobeDreams.

A man standing in the middle of the group signaled for the soldiers on either side of him to grab her. She watched their arms, their legs, and their torsos as they advanced. She stumbled forward as though about to faint, and then punched the man on the right in the throat. He choked and fell down. She stuck her hand in the mouth of the man on the left, grabbed his lower jaw, and then pulled him forward and tripped him before his weight came down on the leg. He fell head first into the wall with a wicked thump. Two more down, only ten to go.

And then they were on her, beating her with their fists. She struck back with all her strength and speed.

She ripped at the flesh of their faces with her fingernails. The smell of their sweat and rapine lust filled the air. She concentrated on keeping her feet, but there were too many hands on her. Her legs were pulled out from underneath, while other men grabbed her arms and held her to the ground. She jerked and twisted but could not free her limbs. The ones who weren't holding her cursed and kicked at her torso, trying to stomp her ribs. One of the men shouted for the others to stop.

It was the man who first stood in the middle, who'd signaled the other two men to grab her. He was the leader, and she saw that her fingernails had found his face in the melee, and ripped it open. He was infuriated, eyes bloodshot with rage, spittle around the edges of his mouth. He gave her a wicked smile, letting her know that he was in control and that he would have her now. He looked her up and down and savored the moment.

Time dilated, and she saw past his face into his soul. An ethereal darkness shifted across his countenance and crawled, like a multitude of writhing maggots underneath the skin. He stood tormented and damned, and he had done it to himself. At some point in his journey on this planet he turned from life and embraced evil. His heart became a heart of darkness and it ate away the better aspects of his humanity. Momma would be so proud.

In that microsecond the side of his head exploded into a cloud of red mist, followed by the boom of a rifle at some distance. A distant voice in her laughed. *Well, that'll wipe the smirk off your face!*

A flurry of rifle shots followed, at much closer range. Other men fell within the crowd. Then women in black shirts were upon them, with bayonets and machetes. In their haste to assault Abigail the men had put down their weapons and assigned no guard. The women attacked them with relentless kicks and slashes. It was a slaughter!

A huge black woman with an Afro pulled back in a flared bun picked up a man by his throat and his privates, and then smashed him to the ground. She stomped his groin with a kick that doubtlessly ruptured everything in his lower pelvis. Another woman in an outlandish zebra-stripe pantsuit stood guard with an AK-47. The women could have shot the men with their weapons, but this was *personal*. They wanted to slaughter them in hand-to-hand combat.

All the men were down. Most were dead, but others moaned with primal cries that stood the hairs on Abigail's arms erect. The big woman whom she'd seen pick up the man by his privates walked through the fallen men with a machete and slashed their necks, one by one. There was no mercy. Abigail sat up and watched the slaughter.

A fit black woman with her hair restrained in a black bandana approached with an AK-47 slung over her shoulder. The woman had a hardness of character that was unmistakable. She was Rayna, no doubt about it. The woman said, "We are the Black Diamonds, and you girl, are with us."

Abigail had read about these women and knew where she was. During the reign of Charles Taylor in Liberia in the late 1990's, the Black Diamonds fought with the rebel forces to overthrow the government.

The Black Diamonds were women who had been victimized by Taylor's forces, and took up arms to defend themselves and take back their country. They were ferocious fighters and gave no quarter.

The young boy stood in front of the truck and trembled with shock. His pants were wet. I don't blame you, Abigail sympathized, I'd pee myself, too!

The big woman with the machete walked over to him and raised her arm to strike. The angle of her arm and the machete were identical to the way Urielle raised her sword to strike Lucifer's dark heart on the bedroom wall at adobeDreams.

"No!" Abigail shouted.

The big woman glared at Abigail with a look of disdain that instantly identified her as Urielle.

"Leave the child!" Rayna commanded.

The big woman lowered the machete and glowered at Abigail. She had no love for humanity, especially the males, and didn't appreciate the interruption. She pushed the boy with the bottom of her boot and he fell to the ground. He scrambled out of her immediate reach and then ran down the alley with his arms folded to his sides and his hands shaking like leaves in a storm. Abigail's heart broke at the sight of it. Where would he go? How would he survive? How many more were just like him?

Urielle gave Abigail one more dirty look and walked away. That look made it clear that Urielle tolerated the Black Diamonds because they were women, and because they were women who killed the men that assaulted and oppressed them. Left to her own designs Urielle would lay waste to this village until not one human of either gender remained alive!

It surprised Abigail that angels could play at this incarnation game, but it explained how Rayna traveled across time to find her. She'd had Urielle's help, and brought the angel along for back up.

Rayna explained that the Diamonds had been scouting the town for government forces when she and Urielle joined them. They'd followed the chase from a nearby rooftop, and closed in when they saw Abigail cornered. It took them a while to get into position so that they could out-flank the men and cover their positions. She'd been the one who headshot the leader before he could assault Abigail. She handed Abigail a canteen and allowed her to take two large gulps of the tepid water.

Only six members of the Diamonds joined this patrol, and because more government forces were in the area they needed to leave. Abigail persuaded them to look for the women who hid in the pit, but the pit was empty. They had probably fled into the countryside. Abigail had no doubt the mother still carried her dead baby in her arms.

The Diamonds led her away from the town and into the trees. They heard thunder in the distance. An hour later they reached the Black Diamonds camp, as light sprinkles fell. Abigail limped from the slash in her ankle. They'd given her a bandana to tie around her lacerated palm. Potatoes and beans were boiling in a pot when they arrived. How good warm food felt in her empty stomach!

The rain fell in earnest. While the others took shelter underneath camouflaged tarps strung among the trees, Abigail stood out in the rain. Yes, God, please let it rain, she pleaded. Please let it rain and wash away all the horrors I have witnessed this day!

She remembered standing in the hot sun as the Australopithecus ape-girl, while her troop of proto-humans slumbered in the shade. Now she stood in the rain while her troop took shelter under tarps. The rain fell in heavy sheets and she allowed it to soak her to the skin. She felt glad to be alive, preposterous as it seemed for everything she'd experienced that day. Even so, she wondered, *what is it with men and rape?*

She understood some of the classic rationales; things she learned in rape awareness class. Rape is about aggression, not sex. Men who rape have severe self-esteem issues, are social misfits, or are angry with a woman in their past. Entitlement plays a role, because God knows men rule the world, and we all know how well that's turned out! Both advertising and pornography objectify female sexuality as little more than a collection of body parts.

Some say men rape simply because they have the equipment to do so. Maybe it's too much testosterone and bad training. If young men grow up in a culture that idolizes stupidity and indiscriminate gratification, then why should anyone be so surprised when some carry it too far?

It really doesn't matter why men rape, so much as it had to stop. Do men not realize that attacks on women are assaults on the life force itself? Are they not shamed by their cowardice? Do these men not have mothers, and sisters, and daughters? *Have they no hearts?*

Her only answer was the rain.

The clouds began to part as the rainstorm passed and the full moon shone almost bright as day. The light sparkled on the wet grass and trees. A rainbow of flowering plants, their blossoms closed for the evening, led to a structure that glowed in the moonlight. At first she could see only the top of the structure, but as the clouds opened she recognized the moon gate at adobeDreams. She realized that she stood on a balcony above the gardens.

The last raindrops captured tears and pattered into a puddle around her feet. Her hair hung matted and soaked. She thanked God for the good rain and the good Earth, and wrapped her arms across her chest to ward off the chill air.

She walked inside and knew it wasn't her room. That wasn't the wall where Lucifer threatened to impale her. That wasn't the other wall where he'd thrown Caroline and the bed. The bed stood where it was supposed to be with someone sleeping in it. *Caroline.*

She felt unclean and didn't want to touch her. She went to the bathroom, shut the door, and took off her clothes. *Maybe I can have them burned.* She turned on the shower, adjusted the water, and stepped in. With tears and soap she washed the day down the drain, down through the building's plumbing system and out into the sewers where it belonged.

There was a knock at the door, and it cracked open. Caroline stuck her head in and said, "Abby?" Abigail opened the shower curtain and blew Caroline a kiss with one hand. Caroline stepped into the bathroom, dressed in a nightshirt and black panties with small red poppies on the left hip. The last time Abigail saw her she laid injured from Lucifer's attack. Now she appeared to have made almost a complete recovery. *My lover is healthy and alive.* Thank you, God! Thank you, God! Thank you, God!

Abigail hoped that Caroline would kiss her. Instead Caroline pulled her panties down her legs and pulled them off. Then she pulled her nightshirt over her head, with a slow, languorous movement, just to be tantalizing, Abigail assumed. It worked. *Thank you, God*, she thought, as her eyes drank the nuance of every move Caroline made.

Caroline stepped into the shower and gave Abigail a gentle kiss. Then she held Abigail's face with both hands, looked her in the eyes, and kissed her again with her tongue making slow love to Abigail's mouth.

Lovemaking is life affirmed. This time they didn't run out of hot water.

Indian Market

"How many blue cars did you see?"

The next morning Abigail and Caroline sipped tea on the balcony under a clear, blue sky. A cluster of pink day lilies blossomed in the garden below, their stigma curled up to the sun with pollen-filled anthers.

Abigail knew Caroline must be curious about her African adventure, but the entire thing had been a horror. With Caroline scarcely recovered from her injuries, how much more trauma could she tolerate? It was the kind of stuff best kept separate from loved ones, lest the stain pass between spirits.

No, she didn't want to revisit what happened in Africa. Not with Caroline.

"How long have you worked here?" Abigail asked.

"Almost three years. A friend in Taos hooked me up with Raphael."

"Let me guess. You met him on Burro Alley?"

"No, we had breakfast first."

"The corner café on Don Gaspar at Water Street?"

"That's the one. Their huevos rancheros are the best!"

"I guess he likes the place, because that's where we met. On the corner."

Raphael. Abigail's life had been a nightmare since the day she met him. He didn't have the integrity to tell her he was the guide she'd expected. Or maybe that was some sort of angelic test? And she passed? For what, all the horrors she'd experienced?

Only one thing went well, and she looked at her right now. She'd do it all over again, but only for Caroline.

"Raphael says you are special. Urielle hates you. Well, Urielle hates everyone."

Abigail envisioned Urielle's slaughter of the men in Africa. She shuddered and hoped Caroline didn't notice.

"Why does she hate me? Are angels even supposed to hate? Because they are angels, aren't they?"

"'Hate' is not really the right word. It's more like 'righteous anger,' that's what drives Urielle's behavior."

"Rayna told me Urielle is the consolidated vengeance of women who had been raped."

"I think it's bigger than that. Women represent the life force on Earth...," Caroline began to reply.

Abigail remembered standing in the rain and coming to the same conclusion as she pondered the atrocities of men. Caroline noticed that she went somewhere in her head, outside the conversation.

"Abby? Are you okay?"

"Yeah. Yeah. Just thinking about what you said, 'women represent the life force on Earth.'"

"That's how Urielle sees it. Men have raped the Earth just as they have raped women, and she's taking all that on herself."

Abigail wanted to have a conversation that avoided Africa, but it seemed everything they talked about led right back. She remembered the mass of wriggling darkness that crawled under the face of the gang leader in Liberia, just before he attempted to assault her. A hot mass rose in Abigail's throat, and she covered her mouth as she ran to the bathroom.

She leaned over the toilet and spewed black liquid as a violent spasm contracted her abdomen. Visions of the horrors she'd seen in Africa cascaded through her mind. All the sensations—the sights, the smells, and the fear, all of it—washed over her in a hot wave. She gasped for air, choked, and spewed again.

She flushed the toilet and then sat on the floor with her arms resting on the bowl. Caroline handed her a wet washcloth.

"Are you okay?" Caroline asked.

Abigail nodded her head "yes" and held the washcloth to her forehead. After a moment she stood up and washed herself at the sink.

"I think I just threw up Africa."

"That bad, huh?"

"Yeah, that bad. I don't ever want to go back there again."

"We'll take it off our vacation list."

Abigail beamed at Caroline. *We're going on vacation together!*

Caroline smiled back, and asked, "Where would you like to go? For vacation, I mean. Just for future reference."

"France. I want to go to France. I..."

Abigail paused while she processed a painful memory. She blew out a huff of air.

"I missed it the first time. It was our senior trip in high school. I worked two summers and part-time to get the money. Then two days before the flight, I came down with strep throat."

"That had to suck!"

"You said it! My classmates were in Paris, and I was home, flat on my back."

Caroline grasped both Abigail's hands and looked into her eyes.

"We'll go there, someday. I promise."

Abigail leaned forward to kiss, but Caroline held her palm over Abigail's mouth. "Brush your teeth," she said.

The women dressed in matching outfits with black shorts and black cup-sleeve blouses. They switched blouses so that Abigail wore the top with the red poppies, and Caroline the top with the red wasp. Who sewed these things, anyway? Both wore black sneakers with white bobby sox, the tops folded down.

Abigail put on her sunglasses as they walked down the hallway to the stairs.

"You never said why Urielle hates me."

"She's formed an opinion about mankind and she doesn't want to change it. Backing down or reversing course isn't part of her chemistry. It doesn't matter what Raphael says."

"What is it that Raphael says?"

Caroline hesitated before speaking, apparently to collect her thoughts. Abigail stopped to look at her.

"He says you're different. There's something new in your brain. Up here...," she said, rubbing her forehead with one finger, "...in the prefrontal cortex. I didn't understand it, exactly. It's something about frequencies. The brain is set to detect certain frequencies, and that defines our reality. Your brain can tune frequencies different from everyone else, or has the potential to do so. He says there are very few like you."

"Tuning. He called it tuning. Evolution made a leap, and I'm the lucky leap girl, or something like that."

Caroline leaned in so that her lips hovered only a few inches from Abigail's. She grasped the button flap over the crotch of Abigail's shorts, and ran her fingertips up and down the flap.

"I think you're lucky," she said. "In fact, I think you've 'gotten lucky' a number of times. I'm not spoiling you, now am I?"

Her voice sounded smooth as vanilla floating on air. Heat rushed to Abigail's face and she found it difficult to concentrate on anything but Caroline's eyes.

Caroline traced the outline of Abigail's lips with her tongue, smiled, then grasped Abigail's hand and continued down the hall. Abigail stumbled behind, pulled as much by the warmth in her pelvis as Caroline's grip. She watched the ripple of muscles in Caroline's thighs, and the flexion of her calves as they walked. She followed the sheen of Caroline's hair as it captured the light with each step. Abigail wanted to take Caroline inside herself and hold her there forever. *Oh, God. This has gotten so far out of hand!*

In the dining room Raphael and Rayna sat at a table across from one another. It surprised Abigail to see Raphael eating a huge plate of blueberry pancakes sopping with maple syrup. She never thought about angels needing food or actually eating anything. Rayna had a large omelet with black beans and spinach. All of it looked delicious, except for the pool of syrup on Raphael's plate.

"Good morning," Abigail said, then leaned over and kissed Rayna on the cheek. "Thank you for saving me, ...again!"

Caroline kissed Rayna's other cheek. "Thank you for saving her, too," she said.

"What happened to me? In the Grotto?" Abigail asked Raphael.

"It works like this. Imagine that you are driving down the street, and decide to count red cars. As the blocks go by, you first see one red car, and then another, and another."

He paused to chew a bite of pancakes, three layers deep and soaked with syrup.

"Now let me ask you a question," he continued. "How many blue cars did you see?"

Abigail laughed. "I suppose I didn't see any blue cars, because that's not what I was looking for."

"Exactly. That is how it works. You tend to find whatever it is you seek. If you look for problems, you find problems. If you look for opportunities, you find opportunities, and so on."

"If you look for bad things about people, you find bad things. If you look for good things, you find good things. That's what you're saying?" Abigail asked to confirm his point.

Raphael nodded his head "yes" and stuffed more pancakes into his mouth.

"So what does that have to do with getting chased by a gang of murderers and rapists in Liberia?" she asked.

"I think I can explain," Caroline volunteered, seeing that Raphael's mouth was still full.

Raphael held his hand up to stop her. He swallowed his food and looked at Abigail.

"You first approached the Grotto of Hearts with wonder and awe. And that is what the Grotto allowed you to experience. It tuned itself, so to speak, to your frequency."

Abigail could accept that.

"The second time you went with malicious intent," he said.

Abigail wanted to protest, but held back. Raphael hadn't finished his point.

"However justified your feelings, the fact is, you did go with malicious intent, and you did try to use the Grotto for those purposes. The Grotto responded in kind. It showed you the consequences of malicious intent, without conscience or control."

Abigail felt chastised, but couldn't argue with Raphael's explanation. Even so, his words didn't explain everything.

"What about Urielle?" she asked. "What about what she did. Did I ask her to massacre those men, too?"

"No," Rayna responded, "you didn't ask for the massacre. *I did*. I joined the Black Diamonds and I led them to save you. Remember? Those animals deserved everything they got."

Abigail could tell she was just getting started. Rayna's voice rose and her face flushed with anger.

"If we killed them ten times over, it wouldn't be enough. It wouldn't be enough to compensate for the atrocities they committed against women and little girls!"

Abigail hadn't intended to offend Rayna. What she wanted to hear was what Raphael had to say about Urielle's anger toward mankind, but the words came out wrong. Now she'd insulted the woman who saved her from a horrific death.

Rayna stood up, her fists clenched. She flexed her leg backwards against the chair and it crashed into the table behind her. Patrons at nearby tables jumped and then looked to see what was going on. Rayna stomped away.

"That went well," Abigail said with mock sincerity. *Oh, God, I did it again!*

"I think it's time we went for a walk, away from the hacienda. We can catch the last day of the Indian Market," Caroline suggested.

"The Indian Market! I forgot all about it," Abigail exclaimed.

"That is a good idea. But if I may suggest, return before nightfall," Raphael said.

Caroline stood up and kissed Raphael's cheek. "Okay, 'dad,' we'll be good girls!"

They retrieved Abigail's camera bag from the room and walked out the double doors of the main entrance. Hanging baskets overflowed with ivy and multi-colored petunias along a columned porch. A head-high adobe wall with a single pedestrian gate lay across a bricked patio with a fountain. In moments they stood on the streets of Santa Fe. Abigail turned around to see what the hacienda looked like from the outside.

A steer skull hung beside the gate with a bundle of ristras, dried chilies, hanging from each horn. No sign identified the location, nor did she see a street number. It looked little different from any other door in an adobe wall found elsewhere in Santa Fe. She pulled the camera from her bag and took several photographs of the skull and ristras.

"It's not the gate you came through," Caroline explained.

"No kidding," Abigail said, thinking of the narrow path behind the blue door.

"So what's with the whole pathway-behind-the-blue-door thing?" she asked.

"I'm not sure you're ready for the answer to that question," Caroline replied.

"After everything I've experienced, I should be ready for anything. Go ahead, hit me with it."

"The blue door, and the path, is a mystical conduit that leads to adobeDreams."

"But this is adobeDreams here, isn't it? Why not just walk in through the front door?" Abigail said, as she placed her hand against the adobe wall.

"You've seen the adobeDreams complex, at least part of it, and you must have wondered, how can anything that big stay hidden in Santa Fe?"

The question had occurred to Abigail when she saw the size of the gardens and the Grotto of Hearts.

Caroline patted the wall, and said, "This is a façade. The real adobeDreams... Well, it's in another place."

"'Another place?' Are you telling me there's more than one adobeDreams? Or it's in another dimension, or something?"

"Is that so hard to believe, with everything you've experienced?"

"I suppose not, but what about the dogs?"

"What do you mean? What dogs?"

"The dogs at the intersection, behind the blue door. If that's a mystical conduit, what were feral dogs doing in there? They were coming after me when Raphael scared them away."

The blood drained from Caroline's face and she looked frightened.

"Oh, Abigail, those weren't dogs!"

Abigail started to ask what she meant but Caroline held up a palm to signal, "Enough!"

"Let's talk about this another time. We're going to miss the festivities if we don't get going, and I think we're both due for a pleasant day."

Abigail grasped Caroline's hand and they walked to the Santa Fe Plaza and entered the Indian Market. Abigail couldn't believe that she had forgotten all about attending the fair, one of the main objectives of her Santa Fe visit. That seemed like two lifetimes ago, and the woman who'd made those plans? She was now only a distant memory.

They talked to the artists as they strolled through the tents, and admired their work. Caroline purchased a silver barrette with turquoise stones from one of the vendors. A set of black pots caught Abigail's eye and she thought to have them shipped home, but then had to ask herself, where would that be? What place do I have to call home? Medical bills claimed her mother's house years ago. Strangers lived there now. She had no idea where her father lived, and even if she did wouldn't have anything to do with him. She looked at Caroline and realized that her home was with her, for however long it lasted and wherever their path took them.

"So tell me about yourself," Caroline said, "Who

are you, anyway?"

Abigail laughed and asked, "What do you want to know?"

"Every sordid detail," Caroline replied, "the more sordid the better!"

Abigail thought for a moment, "Well, if you want sordid, you can't get much more sordid than my father." She swallowed and tried to continue, but couldn't. Then she began, "My father cheated on my mother. Actually, he cheated on her all the time. He's one of those men who are so self-absorbed they can't see the damage they do to the people around them. Or maybe they just don't care."

"You said, 'is one of those men,' so your father is still alive?" Caroline asked.

"Somewhere, I suppose. I haven't seen him since my senior year in college. That's when my mom died."

"I'm sorry," Caroline replied.

"He screwed around their entire marriage. She didn't divorce him until after I graduated from high school."

"Did you know," she asked, "about the infidelities?"

"Only a little. He was gone most of the time. He didn't pay much attention to me, anyway. I didn't have a dick, and I didn't play football."

"One of those, huh?"

"Yeah, one of those."

"How did your mom die?" Caroline asked, her voice soft with compassion.

"Cancer. Ovarian. Fourth stage. She was diagnosed in my junior year of college. It was downhill from there. I think she died from loneliness really. She lived alone in her marriage, and was alone again after they divorced. All her fight ebbed away."

Abigail stopped and wiped tears from her eyes with the back of her hand. She had more to say and wanted to continue, but the words were so difficult. Caroline squeezed Abigail's shoulder to offer support.

"Whew! This is tough," Abigail exclaimed. "In her last months all she had was bitterness towards my father, for all the years she wasted on him. She finally owned her anger, but it was too late. He didn't even come to see her while she was ill. Maybe she got a phone call, I don't know. I saw him at the funeral, and that was it...the last time I saw him.

"He came with a floozy," Abigail continued with a laugh. "Can you believe that? He came to my mother's funeral with some woman he lived with!"

"Did you say anything to him?" Caroline asked.

"No. He said, 'I'm sorry for your loss,' and I couldn't even look at him. The way he said it was like she hadn't meant anything to him." The memory shot warm anger through Abigail's veins.

"And then came Edgar," Abigail continued. "I suppose I got involved with him because it was what my family of origin trained me to do. If I hadn't seen what happened to my mother..." She choked on the words and couldn't continue.

"It's okay," Caroline said.

They kept walking and didn't say anything while Abigail sorted out her feelings. She didn't want this moment with Caroline to fade away because of a handful of difficult words. She had to get them out, no matter how much it hurt.

At long last she spoke, "My mother's example

saved me years of unhappiness with Edgar. He didn't cheat on me like my father cheated on my mother, but other than that he was a self-absorbed jerk who 'cheated' a hundred other ways. All he cared about was *his* buddies, *his* beer, *his* sports, *his* porn, and *his* toys."

"You know what they say," Caroline responded "'the only difference between men and boys is the size of their toys.'"

"Yes, the maturity level stays about the same. Only the size of their self-absorbed ego grows! Oh, if he wanted screwing or to shove his cock in my face he was always available for that, but otherwise he hardly displayed any awareness that I was alive."

Abigail could tell Caroline didn't like the part about Edgar putting his cock in her face and she immediately regretted saying it, but before she could say anything Caroline spoke.

"So what happened?" she asked.

"One day I looked in the mirror and realized how unhappy I was, and how little we had together. And then I made the correlation between my father's absenteeism in my parent's marriage, and Edgar's self-absorbed absenteeism in our relationship, and that did it for me."

"And then you ended it?"

"And then I *wanted* to end it. I wanted to end it for a long time. I tried to be more the person he needed me to be, hoping that'd make things better, but I lost myself in the process. I didn't like who I had to be, to be with him. It was the memory of my mother's dying bitterness that gave me the courage to leave at a time when I really needed it. I didn't want to look in the mirror thirty years later and see her face, not like that.

"She..." Abigail choked on the words, "...she deserved better than that. And I needed to be better than that, for her sake." Abigail wiped tears away with her fingers.

They stood and watched the Native American Clothing Contest, the highlight of the Market. The child models looked adorable in their costumes and Abigail took dozens of photos. They admired the bright colors and artistic patterns of the traditional designs, but the contemporary clothing truly caught their eyes. The women looked at each other and saw black-on-black. Yes, Abigail admitted, they were smokin' hot, but perhaps a little variety wouldn't hurt? They decided to get away from the Market for a few minutes and do some window-shopping. They walked down a side street and assessed the apparel in the windows. Some things they wouldn't be caught dead in, and others stirred their clothes envy.

"Abby! Abigail!" a voice shouted.

Abigail turned and saw Edgar. *That idiot.* He had come to Santa Fe looking for her; that could be the only explanation. He'd stalked her for months after the breakup, and no sooner than she thought she was finally free of him, he'd show back up again. How long he'd been watching them, she did not know. He looked scruffier than when she'd last seen him, and much less attractive. He walked up and tried to hug her, but she held her arms in front of her chest and pushed back.

"Abby!" He exclaimed with disappointment in

his voice. "Don't be that way! It's so good to see you!"

Maybe it's good for you, she thought, *but not so much for me!*

He tried to kiss and she saw it coming; she sidestepped.

"Stop," she told him.

"What's wrong with you?" he asked.

With you it's always the other person's fault, isn't it, she wanted to say, if they don't do what you want, then there must be something wrong with them!

"What do you want, Edgar?" she asked, but it really wasn't a question. It was more of a demand. Whatever you want, get it over with and then get away from me.

"I...I just want to talk to you," he said. Abigail saw his anger flare. Things weren't going the way he expected. Should she have jumped with joy to see him? *Not happening!*

"You don't want to talk to me, Edgar. You want me to be what you want me to be. That is not going to happen. Goodbye."

She turned to walk away and he grabbed her arm.

"Abby!" he shouted sharply.

At that moment Caroline noticed Edgar's grasp on Abigail's arm. Edgar caught her concerned expression and sensed that the women meant something to each other. He looked at Caroline and back at Abigail, and at least surmised that they were friends, if not something more.

His eyes went back to Caroline and he scanned her up and down, sexualizing her. His grip tightened on Abigail's arm. Abigail didn't like the way he looked at Caroline. Maybe he realized they were lovers, and thought less of them for it.

The memory of the breakup tumbled back in a rapid cascade of images. Edgar didn't take the, "It's over," conversation well. He held her face with both hands and tried to force his tongue between her lips. He liked to get a little rough like that at times; she supposed to demonstrate his manliness. He seemed to think that everything would be smoothed over if he could "just give her a good screwing." She refused to open her mouth and pushed him away, and said, "No." That's when he hit her.

She saw his fist coming and rolled with the punch so that his knuckles only struck a glancing blow. Another inch and he would have crushed her cheekbone or fractured her eye socket!

He hit me! He hit me! His fist tore a gash in her sense of security as much as her cheek. She never expected her partner to hit her. She never expected to become a victim of domestic violence. If anything, she'd felt protected by the presence of a large man in her life, and then that man became her attacker.

She erred in not having the cut stitched right away. She'd felt such shame that she didn't want to deal with it. She avoided friends and hid behind sunglasses to avoid questions she didn't want to answer. Oddly, she also acted to protect Edgar, lest anyone file a complaint with the police. The scar had become a permanent reminder of her foolishness, on all counts. Her psyche took even longer to heal, and her self-esteem didn't begin to recover until she completed her first self-defense class.

The images ignited an explosion in some deep

part of her brain and bestial rage surged throughout her body. Her forearms rippled with muscular contractions and hominid fangs protruded from her upper jaw. She growled and grabbed Edgar's testicles through his trousers and lifted him up onto his toes. He screamed and fought to release her grip.

She struggled to maintain control, lest she rip the flesh away from his body. Her eyes bore into his with animal bloodlust and he wailed with wide-eyed terror. She tasted blood in her mouth and wanted nothing more than to tear him to pieces with her bare hands.

"Abby! Abby!" Caroline screamed, her voice frantic. She grasped Abigail's shoulder with one trembling hand and squeezed.

The rush of Abigail's bestial rage collapsed with Caroline's touch. Caroline mattered. *Caroline mustn't see me like this!* Abigail relaxed her grip on Edgar's crotch. The hominid fangs retracted into her jaw, but she wasn't quite done with him yet.

She put her mouth next to his ear and asked, "What do ten thousand men with crushed balls have in common?" She flexed her grasp on his privates for emphasis, and then answered her own question, "They just won't listen!"

"Oh, God, please, ...Abby," he said in agony as he struggled to speak.

She released her grip and he sank to the sidewalk like a limp bag of potatoes. He gasped for breath and held his crotch.

"Abby! Abby! Let's go!" Caroline exclaimed while she tugged Abigail's arm. She seemed desperate to get away from the scene.

Abigail looked down at Edgar one last time and

said, "Touch me again and I'll kill you," then walked away with Caroline.

They hurried down the street, walking apart. Abigail rode the buzz of adrenalin in her veins. Caroline seemed anxious and her arms jumped with nervous spasms.

"Slow your breathing. It'll calm you down," Abigail suggested. It was a trick she learned in self-defense class.

They put a couple of blocks between themselves and the altercation before Caroline was able to speak. She looked at Abigail and said, "You're bleeding," and pointed to the corner of her mouth.

Abigail wiped her mouth at the same spot and looked at blood on her fingertips. She'd cut her lip with one of the hominid fangs. She wiped her hand on the side of her shorts.

"I'm sorry, that freaked me out," Caroline said. "What happened back there? The way you looked! I thought you were going to kill him."

"That was Edgar. He's the one who did this," Abigail said, as she pointed to the scar on her face. "I tell him to go away, but he keeps coming back."

"Can you get a restraining order?"

"Busting his balls was better. Maybe he'll get the idea this time."

Caroline chuckled. She seemed calmer. "Let's hope he doesn't reproduce," she joked.

"He may not be able to," Abigail replied, while she looked back over her shoulder.

Caroline laughed. "This could be your contribution to making the world a better place. You can walk around and crush men's balls."

"That works for me," Abigail replied.

They joined hands together and returned to the Indian Market for the remainder of the afternoon, then watched the sunset while sipping margaritas at a rooftop bar on top of a local hotel. The last rays of twilight cast a pink glow on clouds as they stood at the edge of the roof. Abigail grasped Caroline's hips with both hands and gazed into her eyes.

"My name," she said, "is Abigail Regan, and I am yours."

She kissed Caroline with a long, slow, deep kiss, their bodies locked together in a full embrace. Caroline kissed her back, giving Abigail everything.

Shadows

"I wouldn't want to be here with anyone else."

Their hearts rapid with anticipation, the women walked hand in hand along the streets of Santa Fe. They stopped to admire a hand-painted silk ruana in the display of a small boutique on Water Street, and talked about returning another day.

Abigail watched Caroline's reflection in the glass as much as she scrutinized the brightly colored poncho. *That makes you happy, baby? I'll buy you ten of them!* The altercation with Edgar shot her libido into overdrive, and she wanted nothing more than to press Caroline against the nearest wall, arms pinned up, and ravish her up and down with her mouth, right there on the sidewalk.

Whoa, put it in neutral. She tried to think of something, anything, to slow the rush of passion.

"What's your favorite color?" Abigail asked.

Caroline looked at her as though she'd chosen an odd question to ask at that moment. It was awkward, but Abigail had to do something to get her mind on a different track.

Caroline leaned in close, her breath hot on Abigail's cheek. She held her lips above the lobe of Abigail's ear, and exhaled. Abigail shuddered.

"My favorite color," Caroline whispered, "is a fine pink blush. With just a hint of brunette."

"You're killing me here, you know that, don't you?"

Caroline laughed, and then ran her tongue over her lips as she turned away. At that moment the headlights of a car illuminated a man walking two dogs on the opposite sidewalk and cast large shadows on the wall. The dogs had stocky shoulders with broad heads and thick snouts. The man struggled to keep the animals under control as they pulled him along by their leashes. As the car turned, the shadows of the dogs surged like giant wraiths on the wall.

"Did you see that?" Abigail asked.

"Yeah, I saw that. That didn't look normal, did it?"

Abigail looked up and down the street. A cold chill sent a shiver down her spine. "This doesn't feel right," she said.

Caroline covered her breasts with her arms, and scanned the street before she answered. She'd apparently felt a chill, too. For a fleeting microsecond, her eyes reminded Abigail of the little brown-eyed girl in the alley.

"Remember those dogs I told you that weren't dogs? We need to get out of here," she said.

Caroline grabbed Abigail's hand and led her away on a side street. Shadows seemed to threaten from every direction. They navigated on pure instinct. If a direction felt right, that's where they walked. If it felt wrong, they avoided it. They zigzagged through the streets and found themselves on West Palace Avenue near the north end of Burro Alley.

"Wait, wait," Abigail said as she held Caroline back. "This is ridiculous! We're running from shadows!"

"Abby, we need to keep moving before those shadows become real!"

Abigail wanted to feel annoyed, but Caroline's tone sounded serious. Beyond that, she decided even if Caroline were wrong, she'd follow. The only direction that seemed right was Burro Alley, where Raphael first led Abigail to adobeDreams. Was the blue door still there? Did it even exist?

They jogged to the north entrance of Burro Alley and stopped. The way looked clear to the statue of the burro at the opposite end. In the night the street looked like the set of a western movie where the hero confronts villains in a quick-draw contest to the death. Entering was a gamble. If in fact they were being pursued, there was only one way out, unless they found the blue door.

The women walked a short distance into the alley and then jumped at the sound of claws on pavement. A wall of deep shadows enveloped the entrance and blocked the light of street lamps and nearby stores. Multiple pairs of bright orbs glowed in the dark like moonlight in the eyes of predatory animals. The boundary of the wall expanded at the edges and cast images of long snouts and snapping teeth on the nearby walls. Low, angry snarls gathered in the dark.

"Now would probably be a good time to tell me about those dogs," Abigail said.

"They're *shadow wraiths*—devil hounds that pursue prey to ground," Caroline said.

Abigail shuddered. "Lucifer? Lucifer is here?"

Caroline looked around before responding. "No, not Lucifer. Just his hunters."

"What hunters?"

"The wraiths, and worse things."

Caroline pulled them further into the alley. The blue door wasn't where Abigail remembered it. It wasn't anywhere.

They moved toward the south end of the alley and then stopped as another dark wall covered the entrance. The statue of the burro could no longer be seen. The profiles of indistinct shapes rose up from the wall, fell back, and then rose again. Glowing eyes like blue-white opals paced in the shadows.

"What do we do now?" Abigail asked.

"We put our backs to the wall and wait. They're gathering strength to solidify, and then they'll attack."

"You fought these before?"

"They chased me, years ago, in dreams, then they lost interest. It's you they're after."

Oh my God. I've put her in jeopardy. *Again!*

"I'm sorry," Abigail said, her heart heavy with regret.

"No matter what happens, you're not responsible for what these things do. I wouldn't want to be here with anyone else," Caroline assured her.

They positioned themselves equidistant from the shadows at both ends of the alley, and put their backs against the west wall. Only a thin sliver of moon illuminated the walkway. The shadows surged towards them from both directions, black as tar, with snarls that flowed across the night.

"How do we fight them?" Abigail asked.

"We kick and punch, and tear them apart with our hands."

That didn't sound like a great strategy. Wouldn't the wraiths also be trying to tear *them* apart at the same time?

Caroline looked at Abigail and said, "Now would be a good time to get really, really angry!"

The shadows from both ends converged on the opposite side of the street, and rose to a thick, black mass. The stench of sulfur hung heavy in the air and hundreds of blue-white eyes burned with malevolent intent. The women were alone, trapped, and outnumbered. The whole thing was seriously beginning to piss Abigail off.

"I've had just about enough of this," she said.

She let go of rational control, let go of trying to think and figure things out. She dug deep down through the civilized layers of her brain and accessed the amygdala, the flee-or-fight center of the brain's limbic system, and allowed her anger to flow. Rage surged through her body. She felt primal. Her fingers bent into claw-like shapes with black fingernails, and her body's center of gravity sank. The hair on her forearms grew thick and long. Hunched over, she snarled in animalistic rage, her lips curled back to expose hominid fangs. Caroline underwent the same metamorphosis, somehow caught up in the power of Abigail's own transformation.

The shadows rose and fell, rose and fell, building momentum, and surged toward them in a tidal wave of blackness sprinkled with blue-white eyes. The long snouts of feral dogs snarled and snapped from the leading edge of the wave. The momentum of the mass seemed certain to crush them against the wall. Their civilized selves may have stood and waited for the impact, but their hominid selves knew better.

They raced into the surge with claws slashing. The shadow dogs recoiled and yelped as the women tore into them and sent shards of corporeal shadows flying in every direction. The wave rocked the women backwards but they held their feet and tore a swath out of the attacking mass. At last the wraiths retreated into the background. The corporeal chunks they'd slashed from the dogs de-solidified and drifted back into the larger mass.

The shadows fought amongst themselves and reached berserker pitch in their effort to regroup. More shadows poured in from the sides and the overall volume grew larger until the women faced a mass with hundreds of snapping jaws protruding from its bulk. When this wave attacked, they would surely be overwhelmed. The women exposed their fangs and brought their rage to a homicidal pitch.

The wave surged and broke toward them, full of jaws and snapping teeth. They rushed forward and tore into the mass with claws and fangs. The wave poured onto them and kept coming, pushing them back. Teeth tore into their legs, their arms, and their torsos. They ripped and slashed at the darkness but the surge held relentless. Their hearts pounded and they gasped for breath to keep fighting. Within seconds fatigue and the overwhelming mass of the wall would claim them.

Two bright flashes exploded into the darkness, one right after the other. A massive shock wave went out from the epicenter and wraiths splattered away in all directions. The women were lifted off their feet. They hit the wall and fell to the ground on all fours.

Michael. And Urielle.

The angels stood where the flashes hit the ground, their backs to the women. Michael held his golden spear in one hand and wore faded jeans with a black t-shirt and scuffed brown boots. Urielle held her sword at her side; wearing tan slacks, black polished boots, and a white blouse with ruffled sleeves. Even in Abigail's ape-girl form she could see that Urielle's black boots didn't match the rest of her outfit.

Michael turned to look at them and said, "Now, that's gonna leave a stain!" He surveyed their animal state, smirked, and then faced the wraiths.

Abigail's animal rage collapsed and she came back to her senses. Caroline's hominid fangs receded back into her jaw. They stood upright and reverted to their normal selves. In the background the wraiths lay in a disorganized mess, then one by one picked themselves up in an effort to regroup.

Michael pointed his spear toward the sky, and said, "Ladies, your magic pumpkin ride is over. It is time to go home!"

A blue door appeared in the air and swung open. Beyond the door a pathway extended up and out of reach of the gathering wraiths. With his free hand Michael gestured in the direction of the path and made a slight bow.

Abigail stepped through the door and pulled Caroline beside her. The wraiths snapped and howled below, but could do them no harm. Urielle sheathed her sword, and then held her arms at her side with the palms facing out. A look of pure wrath crossed her face as she brought her hands together with a loud clap. A shockwave of blue fire exploded out in all directions. The wave raced through the darkness and incinerated every wraith in the alley, leaving only swirls of smoke in its path.

Abigail's peripheral vision caught the movement of man-sized shapes at the far end of the street. They shuffled like black corpses and disappeared into the shadows. Were those the "worse things" Caroline talked about?

A glow appeared ahead on the path. They stepped into the light and faced the gates of adobeDreams, the same gates where Caroline initially welcomed Abigail. One door swung open to reveal Raphael.

"Welcome home, ladies," he said. "I grew concerned about your late return and sent Michael to look for you. I understand you have had quite an evening..."

The women stumbled forward, bruised, battered, and cut.

"...but we can talk about it in the morning," he added after seeing their state.

They retired to Caroline's room, showered and washed their wounds, then held each other and slept.

Paradox Rule

"...your evolution furthers the evolution of all
humanity."

Abigail dreamed. Two streamers of light
curved down a staircase between stone
walls. Acrid smoke burned her lungs. In each hand
she held an automatic pistol with slides locked
open on empty magazines. Something dreadful
came up the stairs, around the corner, out of sight.
She woke.

"Rayna. I need Rayna," she told herself.

Abigail and Caroline walked to the dining room to
meet Raphael for breakfast. Abigail didn't want to
spoil a pleasant start to a new day, but she had one
question on her mind.

"You said last night that there were worse
things than the wraiths. What would be worse?"

Caroline hesitated and then spoke, "*Scourge.*"
She turned away and avoided eye contact.

Abigail stopped and touched Caroline's
shoulder. "What's wrong?"

Caroline looked down. It was obvious she
didn't want to answer the question.

"Caroline?" Abigail prodded.

Caroline exhaled loudly. "Scourge are parasites
that feed on corrupt souls. The more they feed, the
more the victim hungers for corruption."

"So they feed on addiction, and make it worse," Abigail volunteered. "Is that what you're saying?"

Caroline nodded, "That's how it works. The longer they feed, the more the victim and the addiction become one and the same. That's why... that's why drug addicts end up looking like hell. The demon completely overtakes them."

Abigail sensed more to the story. "Have you encountered these Scourge?"

"Yes," she said. "I had an older brother. He struggled with drug addiction for most of his life."

Abigail's heart sank with embarrassment. What is wrong with me? I never asked if she had any siblings!

"He died?" she asked, and grasped Caroline's arm to add support.

"Yes," Caroline answered. "He lost everything he owned and wasted away to nothing. I always sensed darkness about him, beyond the addiction. Only after I came here did I realize what it was."

"I'm so sorry," Abigail said. She wanted to let the topic drop but needed more answers.

"If these creatures feed on addicts, then what danger are they to normal people?"

"The stronger they become, the more they manifest into our world." Caroline turned her forearm to display cuts from the previous night's encounter with the wraiths.

"So they can do real, physical harm?"

"Yes, but imagine being bitten not by dogs, but by rotted corpses."

"We're talking zombie time?"

"Yes, 'zombie time,' but Scourge ultimately want to eat your soul, not your flesh."

"Lovely," Abigail said in jest. "So how do you kill them?"

"I don't know, Abby, I don't know."

"I think I saw them... these Scourge, last night at the Alley."

Caroline's face went ashen. "Where, Abby? Where did you see them?"

"When we walked away on the path, I saw man-shaped things at the far end of the alley."

"Then they were truly after us. The Scourge waited only for the wraiths to beat us down."

The angels intervened before that could happen, but they'd been in more danger than Abigail realized. Wraiths? Scourge? Lucifer really wanted her dead. The more she understood what she'd gotten herself into, the worse it seemed.

In the dining room Raphael once again breakfasted on blueberry pancakes smothered in maple syrup. Across the table Rayna ate a vegetarian omelet with red bell peppers.

Abigail needed to make amends with Rayna. She sat next to her and said, "Good morning." Rayna smiled and responded in kind. That was a start. At least the warrior woman didn't stand up and leave.

Abigail looked at Raphael and said, "Tell me again what's happening here."

"Last night? In the simplest of terms you shape-shifted. In a moment of extreme crisis you accessed the oldest evolutionary levels of your brain and transformed into a primitive beast."

"How is that possible?" Abigail asked.

Raphael took another bite of his pancakes, a long string of syrup hanging to the plate. He chewed for a moment before he responded.

"It is possible because the situation pushed you beyond previous limits. You *tuned* to a different frequency. This is exactly your path. Your ability to tune expands the boundary of human potential. Because all spirits are connected, your evolution furthers the evolution of all humanity."

"So, you're trying to tell me that gay girls take over the Earth?" Abigail asked.

Raphael laughed before answering.

"A world that is safe for 'gay girls' is a world that is safer for everyone, but this has nothing to do with the sexual wiring of your brain. Your purpose on this planet is to explore the genetic potential of what it means to be human."

"And that's why the wraiths came after me?" she asked, then looked at Caroline and corrected herself, "I mean, us?"

"As you have already seen, your development conflicts with certain intentions within this domain."

"You mean Lucifer?"

"Yes, I mean Lucifer. If he distracts you from the path, then he blocks an evolutionary leap that mankind desperately needs in order to survive."

"So what am I supposed to do?" she asked.

"You already know what to do. Every generation has its challenges. You experienced life on primitive Earth. Was it any less difficult then, than now?"

"No, it wasn't," she said. "In fact, it was rather brutal. But it's always been something, hasn't it? If it's not starvation, disease, or predators, it's usually each other."

Abigail thought again about the long line of women across the centuries that struggled to survive so that the next generation might have a better life. Her existence in this place, at this time, was the result of an unbroken chain that spanned millions of years. On a much smaller scale, every twist and turn in her life also led to this juncture at adobeDreams. It was her time to seize the moment.

She turned to Rayna and said, "I need your help. Teach me to shoot."

Rayna looked to Raphael. Raphael nodded, "yes," then stood up and walked away. Caroline blew Abigail a kiss and followed him. She looked as though she had something to discuss with Raphael.

Rayna led the way to an underground room with a heavy metal door. Throwing a lock, she stepped inside and lifted a switch on the side of an electrical box. Three strings of lights flickered below the ceiling, and somewhere fans whirred to circulate air. Metal sheets at the far end of the room angled down into the floor.

"Two centuries ago, this was the powder room," Rayna said.

Powder room? The space looked as though it never contained plumbing or other amenities. Indeed, it seemed more suitable for livestock than a lavatory.

Rayna noticed Abigail's confusion and added, "Gunpowder, Abigail, gunpowder."

"Oh." Now the room's layout made more sense.

Rayna unlocked a tall rectangular cabinet bolted into the wall, and removed a black military-style rifle. She pulled a handle on the weapon, looked inside, and allowed the handle to slam forward.

"Today," she said, "you will learn operation of the AR-15 and AK-47 assault rifles. But more important than learning *how* to shoot, is understanding *why* to shoot."

She held up the rifle with both hands to allow Abigail a full view of the weapon.

"You had less of a fighting chance in your Liberian experience because you did not know how to release the safety on the rifle you seized from a soldier. Had we not intervened, the outcome would have been...horrific."

Abigail couldn't disagree, but she also had to wonder, how long could she have held off the troops before she ran out of ammunition? Against those odds it was a fight she could only lose, no matter how many guns she had.

Rayna bounced the rifle up and down in her hands. "There is a saying, 'If all you have is a hammer, every problem begins to look like a nail.' This is exactly the issue with weapons in your society. Conflict is a normal part of the human experience, and people need a variety of tools to resolve disputes. Can you talk? Can you reason? Can you negotiate? Can you compromise? Can you tolerate? Can you forgive? It seems in America you have too many cowboys, and not enough good sense."

She held up the rifle for emphasis, and added, "This is not a solution; it is a *last resort*, to be used only in defense of life or to escape serious injury. The consequences of using this tool are devastating and ugly. Understand?"

Abigail envisioned the bodies of the executed men under the tree in Liberia. The image of the destroyed face of her African avatar's husband was something she'd never forget. That's what these weapons did. Devastating and ugly? More than anyone should ever have to see!

Nausea coiled in her stomach. Was she on the right course? Or should she run the other way? Her dream came back to her. She stood on the empty stairway and inhaled gun smoke while holding two empty pistols in her hand. Something awful was coming and she had to be ready.

"Abigail?" Rayna asked.

"Yes, I understand. I understand very well."

"Your American president, Theodore Roosevelt, said, 'Speak softly and carry a big stick.' *He knew*. He knew that the reality of the world is that people, and nations, respect strength and exploit weakness. That for which you will not fight will be taken away from you. The boundaries you do not enforce will be invaded. This is human nature."

"That's very harsh. I don't know that I want to believe the world works that way," Abigail said.

"It does not matter what you want to believe. What you get as a person who is unable or unwilling to defend yourself is..." Rayna struggled to think of the right phrase, "...is 'screwed over.' What you get as a nation that is unable or unwilling to defend itself is the *Rape of Nanking*."

"I don't know that one," Abigail responded.

"History too often protects us from unpleasantness, lest the actual truth disturb tender sensibilities. In 1937 the Imperial Japanese Army captured the Chinese capital of Nanking. The invaders pillaged the city and raped women, young and old, by the tens of thousands. In six weeks they murdered half the city's population, some three hundred thousand civilians."

Such numbers were unfathomable, but Abigail didn't have to imagine the horror. She'd seen it in Africa. The dead women in the storefront shot through her mind. She tried to remember how many bodies lay in the heat, but the smell of coagulated blood and the steady buzz of flies overwhelmed her memory. She shuddered.

"I didn't know," she said.

"Abigail, are you okay?"

"Just remembering bad things. 'Screwed over' is what happens when you can't defend your interests. Nanking is what happens when you can't defend your country. If you want peace, then you must be prepared to fight to the death to defend it. That's quite the paradox, isn't it?"

"Appropriate boundaries are better for everyone. Ultimately *it's our world and it is we who allow these atrocities to happen,* not God."

Rayna had said that before. Abigail thought of Caroline, lying bloody and broken after Lucifer's attack. If she'd had the means to fight, she might have stopped Lucifer. Warm blood flushed her face and her heart hardened into a fist. She'd personally rip to pieces anyone who ever tried to harm Caroline again!

"Show me what to do," she said.

Learning to shoot wasn't what she thought. First came the safety rules: keep the weapon pointed in a safe direction at all times; never point the weapon at anything you do not intend to shoot; treat every weapon as though it is loaded; keep your finger off the trigger until you are ready to fire; check your backstop. Abigail recited the rules until she knew them by heart.

Rayna grasped the black rifle by the front handguard and narrow portion of the rear stock.

"The physical structure of the rifle," Rayna explained, "makes a far more effective weapon than your hands or feet."

She thrust the rifle directly forward, as though smashing the side of the receiver into an imaginary target. Then she whipped both ends back-and-forth in diagonal slashes, before thrusting the tip of the barrel forward in jabbing motions. She handed the rifle to Abigail and said, "Now you."

Abigail repeated the exercise until both arms seemed ready to fall off. When she thought she could take no more, Rayna retrieved a heavier, meaner looking rifle from the cabinet. She checked the chamber to ensure that it was unloaded, and then held it up for Abigail to see.

"This is the rifle you saw in Africa, a derivative of an AK-47," she said. She swapped rifles with Abigail and led her through the same drills with the heavier weapon. The drills had been difficult with the AR-15, but the weight of the AK-47 produced its own special misery.

Three men entered the room. Abigail recognized them from the training session in the patio and blushed with embarrassment. She'd left two of them on the ground in a heap. The third she might have killed if Rayna hadn't stopped the training. The men were a grim reminder of how much damage she could do when anger got the best of her.

"Fight!" Rayna shouted as the men surrounded Abigail with heavy sparring pads. They thrust the pads into her as she defended with the AK-47. At first they attacked one at a time, then two, then all at once. As she defended one direction a blow struck from another. Their attack was relentless. They pressed in from all sides until she had no room to maneuver. She struggled to keep her feet as the men pushed her at will across the floor.

She could hardly move the rifle an inch, let alone use it to defend herself. She wanted to ask for a chance, but remembered Rayna's "never give up" spittle from the patio training session. This was another no-quarters combat drill and she had to fight until she either won or could fight no more.

She struggled for breath as tears of frustration ran down her cheeks. The tears turned to anger and the anger turned to rage as the power of the beast surged within her. She sank her hips and thrust her legs upward with everything she had and pushed the men away. She slammed her body and the rifle into the pads and sent the men stumbling back. The rage built until she wanted nothing more than to throw down the rifle and tear them to pieces with her bare hands. At any moment she would transform to full beast mode and do just that.

"Stop!" Rayna shouted. The men backed off.

Abigail stood looking down, the rifle at her feet, her body hunched over, and her fingers curled into claws. A deep growl rose from her chest as she bared her teeth at the men. They kept the pads in guard position and exchanged uncertain glances as they edged further away.

A shock of cool water struck her face. She shook the water off and looked to the source. Rayna held a large water bottle in one hand, the top sliced off with a lock-blade knife she held in the other. She'd doused Abigail with the entire contents.

"Abigail! Look at me!" Rayna shouted. "Who am I? Who am I, Abigail?"

Abigail struggled to speak. Fog filled her head and her mouth struggled to form English sounds.

"Ray-na. You are Ray-na," she said at last.

"What day of the week is it?" Rayna asked.

Abigail couldn't remember. "I don't know," she said.

"I don't know, either," Rayna responded with a shrug of her shoulders.

They both laughed. Rayna nodded at the men and they left the room.

"Raphael told me to keep an eye on you," Rayna said. "When you get angry, you really lose it."

"I know. I think it's worse now, after the wraiths," Abigail confided. The thought made her uneasy. What if the bestial part of her psyche took control? She could kill someone and not even know it!

With protective glasses and earmuffs in place, Abigail pushed the safety of the AK-47 into the "off" position. After a few minutes training with Rayna, she couldn't believe how she'd missed it in Liberia. It seemed obvious now. She pulled the butt of the weapon into her shoulder, aimed, and squeezed the trigger. The recoil and concussion startled her.

"This isn't like on TV!" she exclaimed.

"No it is not. TV bullets bounce off cars with pretty little sparks," Rayna answered.

She held up a bullet as long as her index finger. "A bullet such as this will cut through the sheet metal of an automobile like it was paper. What you see on TV is..." she paused trying to think of the correct word, "...is manure that comes out of rear end of bull."

Abigail understood. She struggled to hit the target at the opposite end of the training room. Her shots hit the paper, but danced all around the bullseye.

"Abigail, remember the key joints," Rayna advised. "When the rifle becomes an extension of your body, together you become the weapon. Strike the key joints. Strike the key joints together!"

In that moment Abigail understood that her mind and body were as much a part of the weapon as anything else. Together they formed one unit. *How very zen!*

She allowed her intent to become one with the target, then squeezed the trigger. The shot punched a hole through the outer edge of the center ring. Much better. Rayna smiled approval.

The day wore on, much longer than Abigail wanted. She'd learned how to shoot, but her shoulder ached from firing hundreds of rounds of ammunition. She hoped to never see a firearm again.

Taos

"I didn't know you could do all this."

Abigail stumbled out of the shower, dried off, and opened the door to the bedroom. Caroline sat on the edge of the bed with her legs in the lotus position. She wore a black t-shirt and from what Abigail could see, nothing else.

"How was training?" Caroline asked.

Abigail rolled her eyes. "Brutal, as usual," she said.

Caroline laughed. "I had the 'pleasure' once, in Israel, when we recruited her."

"You recruited Rayna?"

"Well, we extended an invitation to visit, and she decided to stay."

"I see, so you and Rayna have known each other for awhile?"

Caroline grabbed Abigail's hand, and pulled her on top as she lay back on the bed. Abigail waited for the answer to her question.

"I talked to Raphael," Caroline said. "We're going on a little field trip, to visit a friend."

"Oh, yeah? And just where do you think you're taking me?"

Caroline pulled Abigail down beside her, then rolled on top, straddling Abigail's legs. She smiled with a twinkle in her eyes.

"We're going to be on the road for awhile, so we'll have to get up early, okay?"

"You're not going to tell me where we're going, are you?" Abigail asked.

Caroline leaned forward and put her face directly above Abigail's.

"I'd tell you," she said, "but then I'd have to lick you up... and down... and in... and out... until you were nothing more than a quivering mass of girl-jelly."

Her tongue traced the outline of Abigail's lips, and then probed her mouth. She straightened her arms and stared at Abigail with lecherous intent.

"Oh, sweetie, that's a lovely idea," Abigail said as she turned her head away, "but I'm so tired! I need to sleep, especially if we're going to get up early."

Caroline bent down and caught the bottom of Abigail's exposed ear lobe with her mouth. She sucked for a moment, and then whispered, "Up, and down, *and in, and out,*" with her breath hot against Abigail's ear.

Girl-jelly? Was that some kind of lubricant? Abigail allowed her arms to flop back over her head.

"Oh, god..." she said in surrender.

Caroline jostled Abigail awake two hours before sunrise.

"What?" Abigail asked.

"You need to get dressed! They'll be here soon."

"They who?" Abigail asked. The last time Caroline prepared her for "they," she ended up running for her life from the Fire of God.

"The girls," she said, "the girls!"

Abigail surveyed her with one open eye. Caroline's enthusiasm would not be denied. Capitulation was Abigail's only choice.

"Okay," Abigail said. "As long as they're not angels."

"Wear these," Caroline said, pointing at a pile of denims on the seat of a chair, "and bring a change of clothes."

Abigail went to the bathroom and returned to see Caroline packing a small overnight bag. Caroline placed two pairs of long rubber gloves in the bag. Abigail picked up a pair of jeans from the chair only to discover that they were overalls, pants with a bib front held up with suspenders. Hmmm... long rubber gloves and overalls, what does this mean?

"Are we going to a farm? We're not going to stick our arms up any cow butts, are we?"

Caroline laughed. "No, no, it's not that. But thanks for the visual!"

The women dressed and waited on the front porch of adobeDreams. Caroline dropped her bag and skipped around the fountain while she sang, "I have a surprise! I have a surprise!" Her face looked like that of a little child, all innocence and delight. Abigail glowed with the love she felt for Caroline in that moment. At the same time her rational self wanted to ask, "What are you, eight years old?"

A vehicle approached in the distance and Caroline raced to pick up her bag and take Abigail's hand. They walked outside the gate and waited. A red pickup came up the street. The truck was an old Dodge, circa 1950's, with a large chrome-plated ram ornament that projected from the top of the hood. Its headlights illuminated faint wisps of dust that dissipated in the air as the truck came to a halt. Even in the dark Abigail could see that the truck had received loving restoration, but at the same time it didn't look like a show vehicle. This truck was a workhorse that received daily use. Blond and red Labradors looked out over the rail of the bed in the back.

A woman in a plaid long-sleeve shirt, faded jeans, and cowboy boots stepped out of the truck. She looked to be in her mid-40's, with red hair going to gray, freckles across her nose and cheeks, and permanent wrinkles around her mouth and eyes. A pair of sunglasses sat on top of her head. She looked a little bit cowgirl, a little bit hippy, and as lean and tough a woman as Abigail had ever seen. Truck, dogs, woman—it was a delightful slice of Americana!

"Abby, this is Sam," Caroline said. "Sam, meet Abby."

Sam shook Abigail's hand. Her palm felt calloused with a firm grip, but not so firm as those idiot men who turn a handshake into a hand-crushing contest. Why do they do that, anyway? Are they just stupid?

"Good morning, Sam," Abigail said, "It's good to meet you."

Sam smiled and nodded, then looked back and forth between Caroline and Abigail, and smiled again.

"You can put your stuff in the back," Sam said, "and say hello to Susannah and Tristan."

"This is Susannah," Caroline said, stroking the head of the Labrador with the red-fox coat. "And this is Tristan," she continued, petting the Lab with the blond coat. "Tristan's a girl," she added. The dogs seemed to know Caroline and were excited to see her. Then Abigail understood. These were "the girls" Caroline expected to arrive.

Caroline stored their bags among cardboard boxes in the back of the truck where the dogs were leashed. The truck had three rear windows, one on each corner, and a longer one in the middle. All of the windows were small and could be better described as portals. They walked around the pickup's hood to get into the truck.

"Is Sam short for Samantha?" Abigail asked from the passenger side.

"It's just Sam," the older woman replied.

Caroline sat between them so that Abigail got the window seat, the so-called "shotgun" position dating back to stagecoach days. The overall appearance of the cab could only be described as "funky." A center divider separated the windshield into two separate panes. The steering column thrust up out of the floorboard with the steering wheel permanently tilted at a backwards slant. The wheel had three spokes, unevenly placed so that if the middle spoke pointed up, the two bottom spokes stood further apart. Through the steering wheel Abigail saw a vertically oriented radio faceplate with big push-button controls on the dash next to the driver side door. A tall stick shift angled up from the floorboard on a long shaft, with a round knob for the grip. The speedometer was to the right of the steering wheel, followed by engine indicator dials and a chrome-grilled speaker. The ignition keys plugged in below one of the indicators, not next to the steering column. It was charming!

Sam opened the hood of the truck and pulled something out from underneath. She juggled a small package wrapped in aluminum foil in her hands as she brought it to the cab, and then tossed it to Caroline to hold in her lap.

"I love your truck," Abigail said.

"Thank you," Sam replied. "It was my grandfather's, then my dad's, and now mine."

Sam started the truck and they pulled away. Caroline unwrapped the mystery package, revealing three oblong objects wrapped in aluminum foil. "Breakfast burritos," she said, handing one to Abigail. The burrito felt warm, but not too hot to handle. Abigail unwrapped one end and took a bite. It had scrambled eggs, fried potatoes, and chopped chilies. Delicious!

"So how do you two know one another?" Abigail asked, in between bites.

Sam laughed. Caroline held Abigail's hand and replied, "Sam helped me out when I was going through a tough time with my family. She gave me a place to stay while I finished school."

Abigail wondered if they'd been lovers, but didn't want to think about it. Besides, Caroline told her that she had a girlfriend in college. Before the thought totally eased, Sam spoke up.

"What she means is that I taught her the ways of lesbian womanhood," she said.

"She taught me that it was okay to be who I am," Caroline explained.

"So where are we going?" Abigail asked, ready to change the subject.

"Taos," Caroline replied, "we're going to Taos. Sam is building a house there and we're going to help her."

Sam drove the high road to Taos, up highway 503, then north on highway 520 through Chimayo, and on to highway 76 through Truchas and Las Trampas. Abigail wanted to stop along the way, but Caroline explained they were in a race to start work before the day became too hot. Abigail made a decision to come back and explore the route in more detail at a later time.

They passed through Taos as the sun rose above the horizon and then headed northwest. Turning off the highway, they drove down a narrow country road for a few miles before Caroline said, "That's it!" She pointed to a group of single story adobe structures in the chaparral. Sam stopped the truck in front of a metal gate with a cattle crossing, and Caroline scooted out over Abigail to unlock the padlock. Abigail noted that Caroline already had a key. A one-room adobe cottage with an exterior staircase stood behind the main house, together with a small storage building and an outdoor shower with an elevated water tank.

Once inside the gate Sam pulled the truck to a sudden stop and got out. "Coyote," she said, and then pulled a .30-.30 lever action carbine from a scabbard that hung below the front seat. Abigail knew something hung below the seat but never suspected a rifle! "They kill my cats," Sam added, then cocked the rifle's hammer back to the ready position.

Abigail looked in the direction Sam aimed the rifle and saw the pointy ears of a coyote a football field length's away.

"Hold your ears," Caroline said.

Abigail covered her ears but jumped nevertheless at the boom of the discharging rifle. The shot echoed and burned across the sky like thunder. A plume of dust rose beside the coyote in the distance. Either Sam missed, or she meant only to warn the animal, not kill. The coyote jumped straight up in the air on all fours and then landed in full sprint off into the bushes. The dogs in the back didn't make a sound. The sunglasses remained in place on top of Sam's head.

"And don't come back," Sam commanded. She worked the lever to eject the spent cartridge and place a new bullet into the firing chamber, and then carefully lowered the hammer into the down position. Holding the rifle so that the barrel pointed straight up, she squatted down and retrieved the spent shell casing. She shook the dust off while juggling the hot casing in her hand, and then placed it in her pocket. Abigail thought of the absence of shell casings on the ground in the Liberian town where the three men were executed, then pushed the memory away. Sam re-holstered the carbine, then went to the back and released the dogs.

"Let me show you around the place," Caroline said. "We'll be staying in the guest house. That's the first house Sam built on the property. She's been working on the main house for a couple of years. We're here to help finish the wall for the addition."

"Do you notice anything missing, from the skyline perhaps?" Caroline asked. Abigail looked around but didn't see anything that could be identified as "missing." She saw sky, that's all.

"It's the power lines," Caroline said. "That's what's missing. Sam is off-grid." They walked behind the house where an array of photovoltaic modules stood mounted on a pedestal. She nodded toward the small storage shed Abigail noted earlier. "Back up batteries for nighttime use are in the shed. Maintenance is sometimes a pain, but if you want power when the sun's not shining..." She shrugged her shoulders and allowed the thought to drop.

"A heat exchanger pumps fluid through a slinky loop in the ground for heating and cooling."

"I don't know what that means."

"If you get far enough under the ground, the temperature stays the same. In the winter you use it to pump heat into the house, and in the summer you pump the heat out."

Caroline pointed to the top of the main house. "A solar thermal panel provides hot water. Rainwater and snowmelt is collected in underground cisterns. During the day water is pumped into the water tank. That way she has water pressure during the night without using any battery power. It also means she isn't entirely dependent on well water."

"Wow, this is impressive," Abigail said. "I didn't know you could do all this."

"Sam grew up on a ranch, so she did most of the work herself. Otherwise it can be really expensive to setup, but hey, there's no utility bills.

"Graywater from the shower and kitchen is recycled for the vegetable garden," she said, pointing to a small greenhouse attached to the back of the main building. "We also use it to make adobe bricks."

"Adobe bricks?" Abigail asked. "Are we making adobe bricks from toilet water?"

"It's not toilet water," Caroline corrected. "That's called black water, and that goes straight to the septic tank."

"So you could live out here indefinitely, and not go to town?"

"Well," Caroline responded, "at some point you're going to get tired of eating carrots and tomatoes!"

"Are you ready to get started, ladies?" Sam called from the new addition to the house. They walked over and saw a galvanized washtub and short shovels in a wheelbarrow. Sam handed each of them a sun hat. "What we're doing is adding another layer to the existing wall. The thicker the wall the more thermal mass it has."

"What does that mean?" Abigail asked.

"It means it gets hot during the day, and then releases that heat at night when it cools off. That keeps the temperature comfortable most of the year, with only a little help from the ground loop."

Sam pushed the wheelbarrow around the side of the house, and explained how adobe bricks are made, "Here's how it works. The soil here has just the right clay content to make good adobe bricks. We shovel dirt in the washtub, add water and straw, and then mix it up. Next, we pour it into wooden frames to form the bricks. The frames come off the bricks, and then we allow them to dry in the sun."

Abigail realized the explanation was for her benefit. Caroline already knew how to make the bricks. She also noted Sam's use of the word, "we," when in fact it appeared that only she and Caroline would be doing the work!

"How soon will we be able to use the bricks?" Abigail asked.

"The bricks have to dry for two weeks before they can be used. They also have to be turned over every few days to ensure even drying."

"So the bricks we make today will be used at a later time?"

"Yes. The bricks we make today will be used to finish the last bit of the wall, a few weeks from now."

"Welcome to the real New Mexico," Caroline said, handing Abigail a well-worn pair of work gloves, dried stiff by the sun. Caroline threw several shovel loads of dirt from a nearby pile into the tub, and then added a small coffee can full of cement from a nearby bag. Sam poured water into the mix from a hose running from the house.

The use of cement surprised Abigail. "Hey, isn't that cheating?" she asked.

"Compared to what," Sam responded, "plywood glued together with formaldehyde, or Chinese sheetrock that releases sulfuric acid?"

"Good point," Abigail said, and then made a mental note. Don't tease the Taos country folk about their building methods!

Moving the conversation along, Caroline said, "Now we add straw." She grabbed several handfuls from a nearby bale and stirred it into the mix with a shovel. Lastly, when the mix was just the right consistency, they poured it into a wooden frame, tamped it down with the flat side of the shovel blade, and then eased the frame off the brick.

"Ta-da!" Caroline sang. "Our first brick!"

The women found a rhythm for making the bricks and used up the pile of dirt. Sam brought cool water from the house and they stood sweating in the morning sun.

"What do you think?" she asked.

"I could do this," Abigail answered. "Dirt, water, straw, equals house."

"Yes," Sam said. "A house you built with your own hands. A house that connects you to the Earth as no other house can."

"That's why I feel so grounded here!" Abigail blurted with a sudden moment of insight. "It's the connection of the adobe to the ground!

"Another convert," Caroline said to Sam as she laughed.

Next they harvested dried bricks cured by the sun, and then added them to the wall of the addition using the same adobe mix they'd used to make new bricks. Caroline dug the long dishwashing gloves out of her overnight bag to make the task a little less messy, but they quickly stripped those off and worked with bare hands. In short order they both had goo smeared up to their elbows, and it reminded Abigail of playing with mud as a child.

"This is so much more fun than sticking our arms up a cow's butt," she said. They both laughed.

The women made a good team but the bricks were heavy and the sun was relentless. They both welcomed the moment when Sam stuck her head out the back door of the house and shouted, "It's getting too hot out there, girls, come in and cool off!"

They washed their hands and arms over the tub, then saved the wastewater to make more bricks.

Inside the house Sam blended ingredients in a bowl. "I'm making watermelon salsa," she said. "There's beer in the frig."

Caroline twisted the top off of a beer and handed it to Abigail. Abigail normally didn't drink beer because it reminded her too much of Edgar, but accepted the bottle to be polite. Two cats wandered into the kitchen, a calico and a tabby. Pointing to the Tabby, Caroline said, "That's Isabel," and then indicating the calico, "and that's Alfred."

"What happened to Isabel Two?" Caroline asked Sam.

"Coyotes got her," Sam answered.

"No! That's awful," Caroline responded. "Next time you get a bead on a coyote, blow its freaking brains out, will you?"

"Already done," Sam replied, "but they just keep coming."

They watched Sam make the salsa. Sam drained two cans of black beans and added them to chopped onions, watermelon, cilantro, and diced jalapeno peppers already in the bowl. She squeezed fresh limes over the mix, and blended it together with a wood spoon. Caroline took two of the remaining lime slices and stuffed them down the necks of the beer bottles. Sam dished the salsa out into black bowls and served them on the table with blue and red tortilla chips.

"Dig in, ladies," she said.

The salsa tasted delicious and the ice-cold beer was the perfect complement to their hot work and spicy meal.

"Did you hear about the two cowgirls who had an affair?" Sam asked.

"No," Abigail said, expecting a true love story, "What happened?"

"They rode off into the sunset together, lickety split!"

It took a moment for the meaning of the "lickety split" expression to sink into Abigail's consciousness, but then she burst with laughter. Her mouth hung open. She couldn't believe Sam said that! She'd just heard her first lesbian joke, as told by a lesbian!

"You're awful," Abigail said to Sam.

Sam giggled and took another sip of her beer. "That's seasoning, honey," she said, "just seasoning."

They sat and drank beers as Sam told more stories and risqué jokes. The watermelon salsa steadily disappeared until none remained. Sam didn't own a television, but had a sizeable library with many reference volumes for medicinal herbs. Caroline and Abigail sat on Sam's couch and flipped through books until they both fell asleep, the aftermath of full bellies and beer. Sam passed through and eased the last book from Caroline's lap.

Late that afternoon they all rocked on the front porch in chairs and sipped herbal tea while the sun went down. The dogs lay nearby, while the cats slept on windowsills and made funny snoring sounds. The stars popped into view a few at a time until the night sky filled with them.

Caroline slipped away to take a shower and then returned in shorts and a t-shirt. "The shower was wonderful," she said, "it feels so good to be clean!"

Abigail took that as a hint and carried the overnight bag with her change of clothes to the outdoor shower. Battery-powered Oriental lanterns, recharged by solar cells during the day, illuminated the path. The walls of the shower were little more than head high, affording a clear view of the landscape of the sky. The water felt wonderful after the hot day in the sun.

Abigail opened the shower door to retrieve her clothes. The towel hung where Caroline left it, but her overnight bag was gone. Only her sandals remained. Caroline had run off with her clothes. Cute, perhaps, but not funny!

Abigail dried off and wrapped the towel around her waist, then put on her sandals. She'd give Caroline a good scolding as soon as she found her. She walked past the corner of the shower and stopped in mid step. A stream of luminarias, candles in paper sacks, illuminated the path to the guesthouse and led up the stairs to the roof. How beautiful they looked with the adobe buildings and New Mexico sky overhead!

Abigail looked around. There were no lights for miles. The main house had gone dark. Sam must have retired for the evening. One of the dogs barked from inside and then settled down.

She threw the towel on top of the shower wall and stepped out onto the path. What freedom to feel the night air on her skin! She reached up to the night sky, stretched her entire body and laughed. Here she could be herself, without pretense, without concealment, and without clothes. She skipped along the path to the guesthouse.

At the bottom of the stairway she looked up. The luminarias, it seemed, led up the steps and into the stars. "Wow," she said, as she savored the moment.

She watched the flame of the candle in each luminaria as she walked up the stairs to the roof. Each candle created a small environment of light inside the bag; outside only a yellow glow warmed the night. She imagined the luminarias as a string of warm hearts, each sharing the glow of its love with the world.

The luminarias reached the top of the roof and then formed a circle. Caroline lay under a blanket in the center of the circle, her arms behind her head, looking up to the night sky.

"You've been a very busy woman," Abigail said.

"Come join me," Caroline replied. "The stars are beautiful!" She lifted up the blanket for Abigail to enter.

Abigail couldn't remember the last time she'd seen so many stars. Caroline identified several of the constellations. She pointed out the Northern Cross, and told Abigail the story of Cygnus, the Swan constellation, of which it is a part. The constellation formed, she said, after Orpheus died at the battle of Troy. The gods transformed him into a swan and cast him into the night sky with his harp, Lyra.

Less mythically, she explained that the constellation also contained Cygnus X-1, a black hole that emits strong X-ray signals across space. She explained that a black hole is a cosmic singularity, the masses of many suns collapsed to a single point, with a gravitational field so strong that light cannot escape.

Abigail had trouble keeping up with all of it. The sound of Caroline's voice and her enthusiasm enthralled Abigail more than anything she said. The night cooled quickly and they pulled additional blankets over themselves.

A shooting star streaked across the sky and quickly disappeared. "Now that's just too corny," Abigail said.

"What do you mean?" Caroline asked.

"I mean, here we are, in each other's arms, having a romantic evening, and a shooting star streaks across the sky. It's such a cliché!"

Caroline turned her face to Abigail and said, "Maybe it's not a cliché; maybe it's an *agreement*."

"Maybe it is," Abigail answered, and then kissed her. Caroline kissed her back, and pulled her close. Their tongues made slow love to each other's mouths, and their hands teased and caressed each other's bodies. It was the slowest, gentlest, sweetest lovemaking Abigail ever experienced. Long minutes passed as they lost themselves in one another. Their orgasms, when they came, were not passionate explosions, but rolling waves released upon a grateful shore.

Looking down from a vantage point somewhere above the scene, Abigail watched the two women make love on the roof. The luminarias on the stairs swept to the roof like the spiral arm of a galaxy, and surrounded the lovers with a constellation of stars.

Underneath the blankets, the heat of the women's sexual energy circulated through their bodies. The energy changed colors as it moved, from warm red in the depths of their loins to orange, yellow, green, and hues of blue and violet as it rose up their torsos. The vibrancy flowed from one color to the next so that as the intensity of one color grew, it passed the vibrancy to the next, coursing in a slow wave as it traveled.

The energy of the women ebbed and flowed in a perfect harmonious circuit, *Yin* and *Yang* in motion, action and reaction united and indivisible. The vibrancy of the swirling energy intensified and built to a crescendo so that all the colors were amplified, and then in slow, pulsing waves the energy released, washing over them. The women surrendered to the waves and quavered in their passing. The vision mesmerized Abigail, and for a time she forgot that she was one of the two women making love on the roof!

I'm dreaming. I must be dreaming. She looked at her body and saw a hairless, white form with an internal glow. Her breasts were little more than smooth mounds, but retained a feminine quality, as did her torso and limbs.

Still me. But am I my spirit self, or some future version, looking back on this moment? Perhaps both. Then the revelation occurred to her, this was my state before birth, and this is the state to which I will return when I pass from this life.

Drowsiness beckoned her to slumber. The Earth itself seemed to pull her down, back into her flesh, bundled together with Caroline in body, mind, and spirit. They slept in each other's arms, huddled close to stay warm in the chill night. As the adobe walls grounded the building to the Earth, so too were they grounded in one another.

Rio Grande Gorge

"The addiction was bigger than all of us."

Caroline shook Abigail's shoulder. "Wake up, Abby! Wake up!"

Abigail peeked out from underneath a warm blanket. "Wh-what?" she asked.

"Let's go for a run!"

Abigail pulled the blanket shut. This must be some kind of mistake. It was dark and cold out there.

Caroline shook her again. "Come on, Abby. Wake up!"

She stuck her head out and looked around. The sky was still black and full of stars.

"Are you kidding? It's still night!"

"Come on," Caroline said. "It'll be fun!"

Abigail turned over and shut her eyes.

"Abby! Abby! Come on! Wake up! This is why we came," Caroline persisted.

Abigail sat up and glared at Caroline.

"Caroline, darling, the sun is not up. This is what sane people call 'nighttime.' Can't this wait?"

"No, Abby, it'll be neat! We'll run through the desert and watch the sun come up over the mountains!"

Abigail hadn't thought about where they'd do the alleged "running." The desert...at night, was she kidding?

"The snakes will get us," she said.

"No, they won't," Caroline answered. "It's too cold for them to be out right now!"

That sounded like another perfectly good objection to Abigail. "If it's too cold for the wildlife, then what are we doing out there?"

"Come on, this is special," Caroline prodded. "It's why we came!"

Why we came? Abigail leaned close to Caroline so that she could see her face in the dark. Caroline's eyes sparkled with excitement, and her lips... as usual her lips were most convincing. *Oh crap.*

"Alright, alright" she replied, but offered nothing more lest it be confused for any level of enthusiasm.

They went into the guesthouse and put on shorts, light jackets, caps, and sneakers. Caroline placed a small daypack across her shoulders and tightened the straps. When they stepped outside the night air raised goose bumps on their exposed legs. Abigail rubbed the flesh with her palms.

"We'll start slow so our muscles warm up," Caroline said, and then took off at a mild jog through the chaparral.

"This is freaking crazy," Abigail said under her breath. "If you wanted exercise we could have stayed under the blankets!"

Abigail followed Caroline's dancing ponytail and scanned the ground for obstacles, like half-frozen rattlesnakes. They jogged for a good fifteen minutes before Abigail's body warmed up. Caroline increased the pace and they sprinted through the desert under a canopy of twinkling stars.

They ran through several patches of low-lying fog while the sky brightened and the stars faded. Onward they ran as the fog grew thick and obscured the landscape around them. Caroline had an obvious destination in mind and knew how to get there despite the fog. Abigail followed close behind to avoid losing her.

A few minutes before sunrise they broke out of the fog onto a rocky escarpment. The wide gash of a deep canyon cut through the desert running north. With the sun behind them, red alpenglow illuminated the opposite wall of the canyon and the desert in the distance.

"Wow," Abigail said. "Tell me we didn't run all the way to the Grand Canyon! We're not in Arizona are we?"

Caroline laughed and said, "No," as they walked to the edge of the canyon. "This is the Rio Grande Gorge. Not quite as impressive as the Grand Canyon, but not bad!"

"Not bad at all," Abigail echoed.

They stood on the edge of the canyon and listened to the river below.

"How deep is it?" Abigail asked.

"Eight hundred feet at the deepest, but not so deep here. This is probably six hundred feet," Caroline said as she unbuckled her pack.

"Thank you," Abigail said, no longer willing to feel cross. "This is a beautiful way to start the morning!"

Caroline offered a small container of water and Abigail drank thirstily. Caroline grabbed Abigail's other hand and pulled her to a flat area near the edge.

"Watch," she said. She stood with her feet spread apart, and inhaled while stretching her arms out sideways at shoulder level. Then she exhaled while pulling her arms back into her chest and touched her palms in a prayer position. She repeated the movement several times.

With her arms outstretched, she pointed her feet to the left and looked down her outstretched arm, then sank down on her left leg. Her opposite leg stayed straight. Abigail recognized the position as a yoga exercise.

"This is the warrior pose," Caroline said.

"It's beautiful," Abigail responded. *And you look beautiful doing it.*

"Come join me," Caroline said, then led Abigail through several variations of the pose.

"I didn't realize you practiced yoga," Abigail said. *Or I'd have been attending class a lot more often.*

"It comes and goes," Caroline answered. "I get out of the habit for awhile, and then I get back into it."

Mist drifted out of the chaparral and moved closer to the women. Something about it did not feel normal.

"What's with the fog?" Abigail asked.

Caroline stopped her practice and stood up. They faced the mist with their backs to the canyon. The morning sun created a diffuse glow across the top of the fog that made it difficult to see any distance into it.

The shape of a man appeared and drifted toward them. Caroline stepped back and Abigail clenched her fists. They were trapped between the apparition and the edge of the canyon with nowhere to go. The shape became more distinct and Caroline rocked on her feet. A young Hispanic man in his mid-twenties stepped to the inside edge of the fog. He wore a dark grey t-shirt over faded jeans and sneakers.

"Patricio!" Caroline exclaimed. She covered her mouth and trembled.

Abigail didn't know who "Patricio" could be, but Caroline obviously did not expect to see him here.

"Hello, Caro," the young man said, using a nickname Abigail hadn't heard before. He pronounced it, "K-row."

"What is this?" Caroline asked. She shook her head, "no," as though to say, "this cannot be."

"You're dead," she said, and took another step back.

Abigail looked back-and-forth between the two. There did seem to be a resemblance. Was this the brother Caroline lost to drug addiction?

"I am sorry to startle you," he answered. "You are correct. I am dead to this world, but I live on in the next."

Tears rolled off Caroline's checks and her body shook with tremors. She looked like she might collapse on the spot. Abigail grasped her upper arm to lend support.

"Wh-what do you want?" Caroline asked.

"I came to apologize," he answered. "I came to apologize for everything. I lived my life like a fool, never thinking about how much damage I did to the people around me."

"Patricio..." Caroline tried to respond. She cupped her mouth with one hand and burst into tears.

"I put mom through hell," he said. "I took advantage of you every time you tried to help me. All I wanted was money, or something I could sell. That is all it ever was. It was wrong, and I am sorry."

Caroline wiped tears from her cheeks. "Why wouldn't you let us help you?"

"I stole your class ring," he volunteered. "I stole it and I pawned it for ten dollars so I could buy drugs."

"My class ring?" she asked, incredulous. "I thought I lost it. You stole my ring...for drugs?"

"Yes, sis, I did," he responded. "Every time I came to the house in those last months I took something. I took something from the house, from the garage, or the tool shed.

"You think that there should have been something you could do, but there was not. I want you to hear that very clearly. There was nothing you could do. There was nothing anyone could do. The addiction was bigger than all of us."

"But the darkness..." Caroline responded. "I sensed it, and should have done something!"

"Caro! How could you know? Besides, the demons are just an excuse for what we already have in our hearts. I went down a wrong path and I got what I had coming to me. It's that simple."

"I'm so sorry," Caroline said. "I'm so sorry your life turned out the way it did. You were my best friend in the family. I loved you...so much!"

"I know, sis. I know. I let you down. I should have been there for you, to help with papa."

"He...he beat me!" she responded.

"Forgive him, Caro. His life experience did not prepare him to understand your sexuality. He doesn't understand that it isn't a choice. He doesn't understand that it is as much a part of you as the color of your eyes."

Caroline covered her mouth and huffed while more tears streamed down her cheeks.

"I miss you so much," she said.

"Caro," he responded. "You need to listen carefully. I also came to warn you. There are difficult days ahead, but you will get through them. No matter what happens, never give up!"

His words made Abigail uncomfortable. She and Caroline already passed through some difficult days, how much more difficult could it get?

Caroline nodded her head, "yes," and took a step toward him.

"I have to go now," he said. "I love you."

"I love you, too," she answered. Then he stepped back into the fog and disappeared.

Caroline collapsed into Abigail's arms. This was the loss Caroline mourned in the shower at adobeDreams, before they made love for the first time. Abigail held her until the tears stopped and then cradled her face and kissed her. Caroline looked in Abigail's eyes and kissed her back, and then they rested their foreheads together.

"That was intense," Abigail said. "If I hadn't seen it with my own eyes..."

"I don't know what happened. Sam says this is a special place, especially at the moment of dawn, when the world changes from night to day, but I never expected anything like that."

Caroline pulled back and studied Abigail's face. "I've been here many times and felt a spiritual connection to the Earth, but nothing like this has ever happened. I think it's you, or maybe us. Somehow the two of us together made this happen," she said.

"I had a dream last night, about being out of my body, but it wasn't anything like this," Abigail responded.

"We'll ask Sam when we get back to the house," Caroline offered.

Abigail's peripheral vision detected movement in the fog. "There is someone else in there," she said, as she moved Caroline aside.

Another figure approached the inside edge of the fog and stopped. The second apparition was smaller, female, with long dark hair. Abigail strained to see. There was a faint resemblance to her mother, as she appeared in earlier years when Abigail was a child. Her heart rose to her throat.

"Momma?" Abigail asked.

"Abigail, come to me," the figure said, as it reached out.

"Momma, is that you?"

"Yes, child, come to me!" the figure answered.

Abigail stepped toward the apparition and then halted. Something didn't add up. Her mother never called her "child," and the figure didn't appear as distinct as the vision of Patricio, as though it didn't really want to be seen.

"Abby, that's not your mother," Caroline said. Something about the situation apparently didn't seem right to her, either.

"Come to me, child! Right now!" the figure insisted.

Abigail felt compelled to embrace the apparition's outstretched arm. She took another step forward, almost within reach of the fog.

"Abby!" Caroline screamed. She grabbed the back of Abigail's collar and pulled her back. She spun Abigail around and slapped her.

"That's not your mother! Do you understand?" she yelled.

Abigail felt herself pop out of a trance. Somehow the figure in the fog had pulled her forward against her will. Caroline moved to slap Abigail a second time and Abigail caught her hand before it made contact. Abigail's anger surged from out of nowhere. *Slap me again and I'll break that arm.* The intensity shocked Abigail and she pulled the rage back into herself.

"I'm okay now," Abigail reassured Caroline. Then she re-directed her rage toward the figure in the fog and shouted, "You are not my mother! I don't know who you are, or what you want, but you are not my mother!"

The figure shifted and grew taller. An older Hispanic man, with a gray beard and long stringy hair stood in place of the figure. He frowned at Abigail with disgust, and then stepped back into the fog. His form disappeared in a swirl of black tendrils that dissipated in the air.

"What the heck was that?" Abigail asked.

"I don't know," Caroline answered. "I'm certain my brother was here. I don't know about the other apparition. We should go back to the house and ask Sam."

"You keep saying 'ask Sam,' what does she know about this?"

"More than you might expect. She's known Raphael for years."

Abigail remembered something Caroline said a few days earlier and put the pieces together. "She's the 'friend in Taos' who introduced you to Raphael?"

"Yes, after I graduated from college, she hooked me up with Raphael, and that's how I started working at adobeDreams."

Sam, Sam, Sam! All roads seemed to lead to Sam. No, that was just her jealous imagination working. She should be grateful that Caroline had someone who helped her along the way. Abigail didn't want to think about it any further.

"Is it safe to go back through the fog?" she asked.

Caroline surveyed the desert before answering. "It looks like it's burning off."

Abigail helped Caroline strap on her daypack and they ran back into the chaparral with Caroline leading the way.

Castro

"...don't hold anything back."

Caroline knocked on the back door to Sam's kitchen and the women stepped inside. Sam was grilling pancakes on the stove and had a thick stack piled on a plate.

"Good morning! You girls certainly made an early start to the day," Sam said in greeting.

"An early start wasn't the half of it!" Caroline exclaimed.

Sam reacted to the tone of Caroline's voice, and asked, "What happened?"

"I saw Patricio!" Caroline blurted, as her eyes once again welled with tears.

"Oh, honey," Sam replied. "Tell me what happened."

Abigail stepped in to take over pancake production so that the two of them could talk. Caroline told Sam about seeing Patricio in the fog, what he said, and his warning of "difficult days." The two of them embraced several times while Caroline shuddered with tears.

Abigail felt jealous even though she did not want to be. She still did not know the full story of Caroline's involvement with Sam, and in any case she should be the one giving Caroline comfort. Isabel, the tabby cat, sauntered into the kitchen and rubbed against Abigail's leg, hoping for treats.

At last Caroline said, "Abby has a story, too," and the two looked her way. Abigail explained the apparition she saw and how it tried to induce her to walk into the fog.

"And when the illusion fell away, he had shoulder-length, stringy hair?" Sam asked.

"Yes," Abigail said, and nodded her head in confirmation.

"I think that was Castro," Sam said.

"The Cuban President?" Abigail asked.

"Fidel or Raul?" Caroline chimed in.

Sam laughed at both of them. "No, I'm thinking of Emilio, Emilio Castro. He's a local *brujo*, or I should say, a *brujo* want-to-be."

"A *brujo*?" Abigail asked.

"A male witch. A sorcerer," Caroline explained.

"What would he want with me?"

"Your power," Sam answered. "That can be the only reason. He wants your power, but first he needed to snare you, and bring you under his control. Then he could figure out how to use your power. Or, at least, that's what he thinks he's doing."

"What do you mean?"

"Emilio is one of those men who take themselves a little too seriously. He fancies himself a master of the dark arts, but he's only a dabbler; a 'wannabe.' I'm surprised he could pull off the illusion you describe. I wouldn't think him capable..." Sam said, and then trailed off in thought.

"What is it?" Caroline asked.

Sam looked at Abigail before answering, "He has something of yours; preferably something with

DNA. Maybe it's a lock of hair, or a fingernail, or an article of personal clothing."

"He has my dirty underwear? That's gross!"

"Not necessarily your underwear, but something. You should look through your things and see if anything is missing."

Abigail started for the guesthouse, but a sudden thought occurred to her. "How did he know my name?" she asked. "He called me 'Abigail.' How could he know my name?"

"No one knew you were coming," Sam responded, and then her face tightened as some realization rolled through her mind. She uttered an expletive and slammed the flat of her hand on the kitchen table. Abigail and Caroline jumped.

"Someone had to tell him you were here. Someone at adobeDreams, or..."

"Or what?" Abigail asked.

"Something worse."

Abigail's heart dropped. "You mean Lucifer, don't you?"

"We chased Lucifer out of Taos a long time ago. If he's involved, then it's only through exerting his influence on weaker minds. He's reaching out, and messing with you."

"We... I should leave. I didn't mean to bring this trouble to your house," Abigail said.

"Trouble comes, troubles goes. It's not the first time, and won't be the last. Besides, I'm afraid this is something you girls carry with you."

"I told her about your abilities," Caroline explained.

"You're the tuner," Sam said to Abigail, then looked at Caroline, "and she's the dial. When you're together, strange things can happen."

"That's why I saw Patricio?" Caroline asked.

"I think it was a manifestation of the great subconscious, the group mind that we all share."

"So it wasn't real?"

"Sentience is not lost at the point of death, but continues in another form. Years ago you brought Patricio here to visit, remember? And you showed him that overlook above the Gorge. I think your subconscious memory of that, and Abigail's ability to access different frequencies, allowed Patricio to materialize in the mist."

"And Castro, was he there?" Abigail asked.

"He had to be somewhere nearby. I can't imagine he has the power to create that kind of illusion from any distance. That means he's been snooping around, and that pisses me off."

Ugh. Some weird old man in the chaparral spied on them? Not a pleasant thought.

"I'll check my things," Abigail said, as she walked out the door.

"My hairbrush is missing," Abigail reported when she returned from the guesthouse. "What do we do now?"

"Where was it when you last saw it?" Sam asked.

"In my overnight bag, in the guesthouse," Abigail answered. She didn't explain that Caroline put the bag in the guesthouse after sneaking it away from the shower. Abigail only found the bag when she began looking for the hairbrush. A glance at Caroline confirmed that she understood the omission.

Sam uttered an expletive. "That means he went into the guesthouse to get it! Not only did he spy on us, he came into my home!"

She exhaled loudly and appeared quite flustered.

"You want I should crush his balls?" Abigail asked.

"She's really good at that," Caroline added.

Sam laughed. "No, but we do need to break the spell. He's using the brush to establish a link between the two of you. We need to break that link. Then we need to do something to discourage further meddling... but at this moment, I don't know what."

"Why don't I simply go knock on his door and ask for my brush?" Abigail asked.

Sam laughed again. "Yes, that's probably as good as anything. The main thing is that we don't want to offend him in a way that will invite retribution."

She studied Abigail for a moment and explained, "We want cessation, not escalation." Had Caroline told Sam about some of Abigail's more violent exploits?

"Meanwhile," Sam added, changing the subject, "these pancakes are getting cold! Dig in, ladies!"

After breakfast Sam gave Caroline her pickup keys and sent her to harvest plant fiber from a grove along the Rio Grande Gorge. The Labradors—Susannah and Tristan—accompanied her. Sam explained they needed a natural fiber to break Castro's spell. Sam and Abigail cleaned up the kitchen and then sat in rocking chairs and drank hot tea on the front porch while they waited for Caroline's return.

"Caroline mentioned that you know Raphael?" Abigail asked.

"Yes. It seems like we met lifetimes ago, but I was your age, or thereabouts, and explored every alternative spiritual practice I could find. And then one day I heard about adobeDreams."

"That's when you met Raphael?"

"I lived there for a couple of years, but then one day decided to rejoin the real world." She laughed as though "real world" was a joke.

"What made you decide to do that?"

Sam paused before answering.

"I had a vision; a vision that I had a child. That didn't seem likely to happen at adobeDreams, so I left, and then..." She looked down and sighed, then focused on her hands. "And then I met the wrong man. Oh yes, he was handsome, and dangerous, and irresistible."

"What happened?" Abigail asked, not knowing whether she should.

Sam looked directly at Abigail and asked, "Do you love her?"

"Yes, I do. My heart practically melts every time I look at her."

"May I offer you some advice, then, from an older woman who's had some experience?"

"Certainly. I'd love to hear what you have to say."

"What you feel may not last, and you have to know that. Nature wants you to *screw*. It wants you to make babies, regardless of whether that's anatomically possible. At some point that lust for procreation will subside.

"But I tell you this, there's hardly anything better in life than what you feel right now. So what I want to say to you is, don't hold anything back. Dive in deep, because you never know if you'll ever have anything like this again."

Sam's face twitched with emotion. She'd loved and lost, and knew what she talked about. Something seemed left unsaid.

"You said, 'hardly anything better.' In your experience, is there something better?"

Sam hesitated, and then spoke. "Yes. There is one thing better. You can't know how much it is possible to love someone until you have children."

Abigail waited for her to continue.

"However much you think you love your significant other, the love you feel for your child surpasses even that. Nothing else compares." She hung her head and fell silent.

Abigail didn't know if she should continue the conversation, but this woman had opened her heart, and she could only honor that by hearing her story no matter where it might lead.

"Do you have children?" she asked.

Sam took a deep breath and exhaled before continuing. "I had a son," she began. "He and Patricio went to the same high school. That's how I know Caroline. He signed up after the attack on the World Trade Center. He was only nineteen, and I let him go."

She leaned down and scraped dirt off the toe of her shoe. She lifted her head up and looked at the far horizon. "He signed up to defend his country. Instead he died defending an oil tanker in Iraq. He was twenty-one when he died, and wanted to be a teacher."

"I'm so sorry," Abigail said, and squeezed Sam's hand.

Sam patted Abigail's hand, and then wiped tears from the edges of her eyes. "Evil comes in many forms, so often wrapped in a lie."

Sam stood up and brushed off her jeans, then looked up to the sky with her hands in her pockets.

"It is what it is," she said. "It's one of those things that no one can ever make right."

Abigail didn't know what else to say. Her son had only been a few years younger than she when he died. A lot of mothers' sons—and daughters—had only been a few years younger when they died in service to their country.

Sam noticed her discomfort and said, "It's okay. You can't know until you've gone through it, and I hope you never know."

Abigail got up from her chair and hugged Sam, and they held each other for a few moments.

A line of dust on the road announced Caroline's return. She parked the truck in the driveway and let the dogs out of the back, then walked to the porch with a cloth bag in her hand. "Got it!" she said, while the Labs slurped water from bowls beside the front door.

Sam looked in the bag and then handed it to Abigail. "Here's what you need to do to break Castro's spell. Take the fibers in your hand and roll them back-and-forth until you have a cord at least a foot long. You want to end up with something that can be tied into several knots."

Abigail didn't put much stock in all this talk of spells, but she couldn't deny the unusual influence Castro exerted when he tried to lure her into the fog. That spooked her enough to go through the motions. Even so, she had to ask, "Is this real magic?"

"What we're doing is a physical representation of what needs to occur on a psychic level. The 'magic' is in your intent, but it's helpful to involve as many senses as possible in order to anchor the experience."

After a few false starts Abigail produced a thick strand of twine about a foot long. It wouldn't win any awards for beauty, but it'd hold together well enough to tie a few knots.

"Okay," Sam said, "that will work. Now tie three knots in the middle of the twine as tight as you can get them. If you can tie the knots on top of each other that'd be best, but otherwise just get them as close together as you can."

Caroline brought a white candle and a small box of matches from inside the house. Abigail's knots weren't any prettier than her twine but Sam assured her that she'd done well, "You put your sweat into it, and made it yours, and that's all that matters.

"Now light the candle and hold the twine from both ends. Think about breaking the connection that binds you. Think about the strands of your life swinging free from the knots that bind them."

Abigail lit the candle and focused on flying free from Castro.

"Now hold the knots over the candle until the flame burns through them," Sam said.

The knots caught fire and burned through in seconds. The strands of twine swung free, trailing streamers of black smoke.

"Now blow out the candle," she said, "and take the twine out into the desert and bury it someplace where it cannot be found. There is a shovel in the wheelbarrow behind the house that you can use."

Abigail walked out into the chaparral a good distance from the house and made sure no one could see her. She dug a pit as deep as the blade of the shovel and laid the strands of twine in it, then covered it up and smoothed the surface so that it looked the same as the surrounding terrain.

Late that afternoon the three of them pulled up in front of Castro's house on the west side of Taos. They kept the windows up until red dust from the unpaved road rolled over the pickup and settled down. Abigail went to the house and knocked three times. The door partially opened and the man she'd seen in the fog peered from behind it.

"Mister Castro," she said. "I'm not here to cause trouble, but you have something that belongs to me."

He shut the door in her face and locked it from the inside. She knocked again three times. He did not answer. She waited exactly thirty seconds and then knocked again. "Mister Castro?" she called, "Hello, Mister Castro?"

He still didn't answer so she pounded the door with her fist. She could break through with one kick, but on the way over Sam had coached her to "take the high road." That's what she intended to do.

"Please, Mister Castro?" she pleaded.

The door flung open and Castro stood defiant in the frame, feet apart on stiff legs, his arms crossed over his chest and face flush with anger.

"Thank you, Mister Castro," Abigail said. "I'm so sorry to disturb you. All I want is my hairbrush and I promise I will not bother you again." She tried to make herself look as friendly and unthreatening as possible.

His face changed from anger to disgust, as though he smelled something bad, and the objectionable odor came from Abigail. He scanned her up and down and then stopped at her breasts. A smug smile twisted his lips. *And then she knew.*

She knew he'd seen her breasts before, and she figured it out. He'd been in the chaparral near Sam's house when she walked nude from the shower to the top of the guesthouse. Then he'd snuck into the guesthouse and taken the hairbrush from her bag while she and Caroline made love on the roof! Blood surged to her face and everything in her vision turned red.

What was that Rayna told her? "People respect strength and exploit weakness." Castro looked at Abigail and laughed, and then moved to slam the door in her face. She kicked the bottom plate before it closed and sent it crashing back into his face and pushed her way inside.

Castro held his nose with one hand and clenched his other hand into a fist. His face went purple with rage and he looked as though he meant to strike her. *Just like Edgar.* Abigail's rage exploded in a shock wave that burst out in all directions. She bared her teeth and growled as hominid fangs extended from her jaw. Her fingers twisted into claw-like shapes. Castro's eyes went wide and he backed away.

Thoughts raced through Abigail's mind as she struggled to maintain the last vestiges of control. This pervert hid in the weeds and spied on them. He snuck into the guesthouse and took something that didn't belong to him. He tried to work magic and use it against her. This ridiculous little man with his illusions of grandeur tried to steal her power!

"You want my power... Mister Castro? Do you really want my power?" she asked as she backed him down his own hallway.

"I WANT... MY MOTHER RIPPING... HAIRBRUSH!" she said, so angry that she could hardly form coherent words. How good it would feel to tear him to pieces right now. She battled to maintain control, but in that moment must have looked as much a wild animal as a human being.

He cowered with his hands out to her and bowed his head. "I'm sorry, mistress! I'm sorry," he said, "I'll get it! I'll get it for you right now!" He backed further into the house, not taking his eyes off the spot where she stood. He ducked into a side room for a moment and came out with Abigail's hairbrush. His hands trembled as he extended the brush, but wouldn't look into Abigail's eyes.

Abigail wanted to screw with his head for a while, but lacked the self-control. The energy required to contain the beast threatened to explode her body. The seconds passed while the bloodlust burned and she battled to maintain control.

"I'm sorry, mistress," he said. "I'm so very sorry!"

She slid the hairbrush with excruciating slowness from his shaking grasp.

"Look at me," she said. He kept his eyes on the floor and trembled. The crotch of his pants darkened with pee. He would poop himself any second.

"*Look at me*," she said.

He finally looked up but refused to hold her eyes.

Abigail tapped the wall with her hand and said, "This is your head." She snapped the hairbrush in half and buried the handle at head level into the sheetrock, creating a melon-sized crater. "And that's your head the next time I see you!"

Castro fell to his knees and begged for his life. "Please, mistress! I'm so very sorry! I will never bother you again!"

She dropped the other half of the brush on the floor, and walked out of the house without looking back.

She released several deep exhalations on her way back to the truck and got herself under control. She felt drunk with fatigue from the effort it took to suppress the beast, but a nagging realization plagued her head. *Someday I am going to kill someone.*

"Did you get it?" Caroline asked after Abigail sat down beside her.

"I let him keep it," Abigail lied.

Sam drove the women back to Santa Fe, and dropped them off at the front gate of adobeDreams. She said farewell while the truck ran in neutral with the emergency brake engaged. She hugged Abigail and kissed her cheek, and then stroked Caroline's hair as they held each other. She whispered something in Caroline's ear and then kissed her full on the lips. After all Abigail's doubts about the nature of their history, she hadn't been ready to see that!

Caroline turned Abigail's way and stared with defiance in her eyes. This woman had been a key player in her life. It was up to Abigail to deal with it.

Abigail took Caroline's hand and walked towards the gate.

"Y'all get along now," Sam said in an exaggerated Southern drawl, "lickety split!" With that she laughed, got in the truck, and drove away. The old pickup faded down the street with the dogs leashed in the back and turned the corner.

"I love her, too," Abigail said.

Altered States

"What if everyone just did that?"

That night Abigail walked in the gardens of adobeDreams. White roses glowed in the moonlight and a chill raised goose bumps on her arms. A young girl giggled somewhere nearby.

A small dark figure approached and stepped into the light. It was the little brown-eyed girl she'd seen in the intersection of the path near Burro Alley. Had she come with another warning? Abigail immediately scanned the bushes. The little girl laughed and grabbed Abigail's hand to pull her along.

"What's your name?" Abigail asked.

The little girl didn't answer, but led Abigail further into the garden. As they passed through patches of moonlight, Abigail caught glimpses of the red flowers embroidered at the end of the girl's black shawl. They looked like poppies. At last they came to the moon gate with the second story of adobeDreams in the background.

The little girl faced the gate, tapped her forehead and then pointed through the aperture. She rotated her palms in large circles, looked up to Abigail, and repeated the motions.

"Are we pretending to wash the gate?" Abigail asked, and mimicked the same movements.

The view of the garden through the gate became less distinct, as though seen through a fine mist.

Moonlight struck the edge of the inner circle and it took on a diffuse glow that intensified. The little girl continued to "wash" the gate with her palms.

"We're on to something here, aren't we?" Abigail asked, and then put more effort into her own circular movements.

Light burst across the aperture of the gate and solidified into a silvery screen. Ripples echoed from the center and then settled into a bright mirror-like surface.

The little girl laughed and poked the surface with her finger. A glob of reflective material stuck to the tip and she held it up for Abigail to see, and then flicked it back into the mirror. She smiled broadly then grabbed Abigail's hand and pulled her toward the aperture.

Abigail could easily have broken the child's grip, but allowed herself to be drug forward. A cold wave washed over her as she stepped through the reflective surface. A momentary flash of light obscured her vision and she woke up. Caroline lay beside her. The curtains swayed drowsily in a negligible breeze. Moonlight cast rectangular shadows on the floor.

"Welcome back to adobeDreams," she whispered to no in particular.

Abigail decided to take photos of Caroline in the garden. With the exception of the visit to the Indian Market, her camera gear had sat dormant since her arrival at adobeDreams. What had she been thinking? How could she *not* take photos in this place?

Caroline stood beside the bed wearing a midriff exposing chocolate top with spaghetti straps and red high-cut panties. She pulled a pair of straight-leg jeans up her legs, bounced on the balls of her feet a few times to settle her butt, and then zipped and fastened the pants. How could Abigail not take photos? She supposed she got distracted!

A few minutes later Abigail grabbed the canvas bag with her gear and they descended the stone steps into the gardens. The size of the adobeDreams complex continued to amaze her. She hadn't thought of it before, but the layout could be seen as a fortified enclosure. From that perspective the area occupied by the gardens could be utilized to grow food within the walls of the fort, without exposure to the outside.

She stopped Caroline near the bottom of the stone steps. Morning shade extended over the staircase but the quality of the light was exquisite. The bright blue sky provided even illumination while the walls of the hacienda reflected a warm glow. Caroline placed one hand on the stone banister and the other on her opposite hip, and then cocked her head with a smile. Perfection! Abigail framed the shot and held the shutter for three frames.

Abigail grinned. Great lighting, a beautiful model, and an engaging pose, for what more could a photographer ask? Then she also realized, as a male photographer might say, *I'm tapping that ass*. She blushed at the thought, and then chastised herself. *Abby, you are too bad!*

"I think I died and just went to heaven," she said under her breath.

"What did you say?" Caroline asked.

"I said you're beautiful!"

Caroline smiled and blew a kiss. Abigail hadn't removed her eye from the camera's viewfinder and caught the entire sequence with a flurry of frames. Abigail pressed the camera's playback button and they watched the entire sequence amidst giggles and laughter. Caroline kissed her cheek.

They stopped for more photos as they walked deeper into the gardens. Caroline posed and teased for the camera. The look she gave Abigail said, "I want you. I want you right now!" Or perhaps that was simply Abigail's imagination. She wasn't sure if the message crossed over into the images she captured, but her pelvis stirred with the warmth of it.

"Have you modeled before?" Abigail asked.

"Only for you, baby, only for you," Caroline replied, then batted her eyelashes.

"You are a big, fat fibber!" Abigail answered. Caroline's skill at posing was no casual feat. She'd had experience, but how and when?

"Tell me truly, you've done modeling before, haven't you?"

Caroline laughed. "Yes," she said, "I did some shoots for local print, but that was the extent of it."

"Why didn't you stick with it? You have a natural talent for looking good in front of a camera." Or maybe, Abigail thought, I'm just so madly in love with you that if you stood there picking your teeth I'd still find it adorable!

"No, no," Caroline answered, "I was quite awkward at first, but I was fortunate to have good coaches. The wife of the first photographer I worked with had been a model and she showed me how to use my eyes for the camera. Her husband was a patient man and taught me how to find the light in every shot. They really built my confidence."

"So they helped you become a better model, and in return they had a better model to work with?"

"Yes! I hadn't thought of it that way, but I suppose it was a 'win-win' for everyone."

"Everybody comes away a better person," Abigail mused. "Yes, I suppose that's how things should work."

Abigail realized Caroline hadn't answered her question, so she prompted her again, "So what made you stop?"

"There are some good people out there, and then there are some creeps," she answered. "One of my last assignments involved working with a creep. He...looked at me...like I was meat, and wanted to do nudes. Well, not nudes, really, but 'spread your legs' kinds of stuff. *As if!* I wouldn't have modeled parkas for that guy! Anyway, it took the gloss off the business for me. Beyond that, I made up my mind to be more than eye candy."

A jolt of anger shot across Abigail's face. "You want me to crush his balls for you?" she asked.

Caroline laughed, "I'll let you know if we come across him!"

As they approached the moon gate Caroline skipped ahead a few steps and struck a pose. She braced her back against the inner curve of the gate, and posed with one hand behind her head. She smiled, puckered her lips, and pouted for the camera. Abigail captured it all with multiple bursts of exposures. She zoomed in for a head and shoulders portrait and clicked the shutter, then adjusted the zoom for a different composition and stopped. For a moment the camera's auto focus zeroed in on one of the strange symbols engraved into the gate. Abigail's breath caught in her throat as she realized that she knew what the inscription said.

Abigail lowered the camera and approached the gate. Caroline noticed the change in her demeanor and looked at Abigail with a question on her face. Abigail touched the symbol, and then followed the inscription with her fingertips, reading out loud, "Take what you need but do not harm other spirits."

She took a step away from the gate, looked at Caroline, and exclaimed, "I can read this stuff!"

"When did you learn to read Tibetan Sanskrit?" Caroline asked.

"I don't know that I did. Is that what this is?"

Abigail examined the inscriptions. Other than the passage she'd read, the remaining characters remained elusive, and yet somehow ever more familiar. It seemed if she possessed a fraction more insight, she could read them all. Then something dawned on her.

"These are the same symbols that appear on Raphael's purple shirt, aren't they?"

"You've heard of Tibetan prayer flags?" Caroline asked.

"Sure, they send prayers to heaven as the wind blows through them."

"Not exactly. The prayers are for everyone, and the wind carries their message all around the Earth. Raphael's shirt is a chorus of such prayers. He says that way he carries good will with him wherever he goes."

"Wow. That's kind of awesome, isn't it?" Abigail asked.

"You have done well, 'grasshopper,'" a familiar voice said from behind. Raphael walked toward them wearing a white v-necked t-shirt with grey athletic pants and sneakers. Did he just make a kung fu joke? He folded his hands over his midsection and took a very Chinese-like bow.

"Come," he said, "I am about to practice."

"How is it that I can read the gate?" Abigail asked.

"It is a matter of where you are on the path," he said. "When you are ready the characters will reveal themselves."

Abigail and Caroline both raised their eyebrows, doubtful.

"Does that mean I'm not ready?" Caroline asked, with a slight pout.

"It means that everything makes sense in its own good time," Raphael replied.

They walked for some distance into the garden, to the clearing where Abigail met Raphael, Michael, and Urielle. Raphael stood still for a moment, then lowered his center of gravity and shifted his weight from side to side. Then he began practicing tai chi, one movement flowing indivisibly to the next, seemingly without beginning or end.

He paused to speak. "What you call time is a change of state in the ever present now. Each change of state is a transition. Changes of state are constant and interact with other changes of state. When two interconnect, it creates an agreement, a confluence of events by which they may flow together."

Abigail recalled that according to Raphael her arrival at adobeDreams had created just such an agreement.

"From this point of view there is no 'this' or 'that,' only the flow of transitions in the ever-present now. Billions upon billions of changes of state occur every microsecond. All changes of state added together at any moment may be said to create a tapestry, and that tapestry is the universe. Your life is a thread within that tapestry, and together with the threads of all other life on Earth you create a weave that makes this a living planet."

Some part of Abigail's brain understood what he said, even though she could hardly keep up with the words. One movement of the form flowed to the next without stopping. Each movement expressed a purpose, but had no beginning and end. Was that how the universe worked? Was that what he was trying to say?

His voice took an apologetic tone, "Language is clumsy when describing this phenomenon, and creates divisions where none exist. The consciousness of man is a dim glass through which this may be glimpsed."

Abigail had known quite a few dim men, so she understood what he meant. Then she thought of her troop of proto-humans and the direct way in which they experienced life and their connection to the universe, and it all made a little more sense.

Raphael resumed the form. The energy of the chi shifted and flowed through his body with all the beauty of the aurora borealis. Abigail saw the form as she'd never seen it before.

Then came the blue lines. They flowed up through the earth, across the ground, and up through Raphael's legs, up through his torso and out through his limbs to create swirling whirlpools in the air. The energy hummed with an electric buzz that touched her skin and raised the hair on her arms.

She looked at Caroline, whose eyes were wide with amazement. Abigail lowered her camera gear to the ground and stepped beside Raphael, then mirrored his movements. Caroline joined them. The three moved through the form, living the energy, and flowed together in perfect harmony. The energy passed through Abigail and reached deep into the Earth. She and the Earth had become one living organism, manifesting the tapestry of life with Raphael, Caroline, and all other living things.

At last they stood silent as the energy washed through them with a gentle rush.

"Whoa," Abigail said, as she stumbled forward a step. "That was amazing."

"That is reality according to God," Raphael answered. "Everything is connected, and everything works in harmony from one moment to the next. Everything happens exactly as it is supposed to happen, according to the laws of physics, and literally nothing—*not one thing*—can go wrong."

"It was beautiful," Caroline said. "I would stay in that state forever, if I could."

"It is always a part of you, whether you perceive it or not," Raphael explained, "but human consciousness serves other purposes. The path of Man is to learn what life has to teach, and to create a better world with others of your kind."

"Thank you, Raphael," is all Abigail could say. She didn't want to hear another philosophy lesson. The experience had been sufficient unto itself and didn't require further explanation.

She threw her gear over one shoulder and joined hands with Caroline as they walked back to the hacienda. Neither said anything, nor did they feel any need. The moment completed them without words. When they reached the moon gate, Abigail once more read the inscription she deciphered: "Take what you need but do not harm other spirits."

"What if everyone just did that?" she asked. "What kind of world would we have then?"

Catharsis

"...markets have the power to change the world."

Rayna intercepted the women as they walked into adobeDreams.

"Abigail, would you check in with Michael, please? He's waiting for you in the Grotto of Hearts."

While Caroline returned to their room, Abigail walked to the grotto and found it empty. Empty except for a single rustic chair sitting in the middle of the floor beneath the huge dome.

"Hello?" she called out, as she looked up into the vaults to see if any of the triangular portals were open. No one replied and the portals were closed. Dust motes sparkled in rays of light that shone down from the gashes of the seven-pointed star at the top of the chamber. The beams cast diffuse spotlights around the chair. It seemed obvious that she should sit down.

"Okay, I'll play," she decided, and sat down with her forearms on the rests. She sat for a while, fidgeted, and then extended her hearing to determine if anyone approached. The minutes passed.

"I'm here!" she shouted, and then exhaled loudly. Great, another game, let's see who gives up first.

She sat in the chair with her eyes closed and followed her breath. She inhaled through her nose and exhaled through her mouth, with only a slight expansion of her diaphragm. She simply allowed herself to experience the air flowing in, and the air flowing out. If her mind wandered she re-focused on her breath.

The minutes passed and she felt a concentric wave rush outwards across the floor from where she sat. When she opened her eyes it looked much like the ripple produced when a stone is thrown into a calm body of water. The waves expanded across the floor of the grotto, then struck the walls and bounced back. The returning wave appeared stronger and faster than the outgoing wave. That didn't make sense because its energy should have diminished as it crossed the floor and struck the wall.

She jerked her feet up as the returning ripple accelerated into the epicenter beneath her chair. A shock wave exploded out in all directions, traversed the floor in seconds, then hit the sides of the dome and rocketed back toward her. The walls of the grotto, she saw, acted as an amplification chamber.

She stood up, relaxed her knees and sank her weight into her hips, tai chi style, in anticipation of the approaching ripple. The wave hit and rocked her on her feet. She anchored herself to the ground and held on. The energy surged and sloshed against her.

Michael and Urielle suddenly stood beside her. "Abigail, surrender to the waves," Michael said as he placed his hand on her shoulder.

She let herself go. Her body opened to the waves and the energy poured through. Her body hummed as layer after layer of power collapsed into her being. She looked to either side and saw Michael and Urielle standing with her. Luminous, oval membranes completely surrounded their bodies, and she saw their hearts, their beating spirit hearts, pulsate within their chests.

The vision collapsed and she fell onto her hands and knees, the floor of the grotto underneath. "Whoa," she said. "What was that?"

"You have experienced a *quickening* like none I have ever seen," Michael said. "Your spirit is opening itself to new levels of awareness."

"Lucky me," she responded while she tried to stand on shaky legs. Michael put his hand under her arm and helped her up. Her eyes struggled to focus as ghost-like images of people and places appeared in every direction, like multiple movies projected onto the same screen.

"Something is wrong," she said. "I can't see straight." She closed her eyes to shut off the images and clear her head.

Michael laid his hand on her shoulder. She peeked out between partially open lids. Overlapping visions still affected her vision, but appeared less severe.

"What you are seeing," Michael explained, "are projections of what is and what might be. These are pieces of a puzzle; a puzzle that reveals more of who you are and the challenges you may face.

"You must stop trying to see with your eyes and simply allow the visions to reveal themselves to your spirit. Find the red wasp, Abigail. Find the red wasp."

"How do I do that?" she asked, but no sooner than the words left her mouth one of the visions took precedence over the others. She saw herself on the pathway off Burro Alley before she arrived at adobeDreams. Collapsed onto her knees and hands, she'd focused on the red wasp that landed in front of her.

The wasp groomed its forelegs with a selfless lack of concern for the giant human above it. Nature does what it does, without doubt, without hesitation, and without deliberation, Abigail recalled from the first time she observed the wasp. She envisioned Caroline's red poppies, and Rayna's red dragonfly. Each woman witnessed a similar expression of nature, but what truly connected their experiences was the color of the totems. The red represented the blood that women shed in preparation for bringing new life into the world. The rhythm of the blood connected women to the natural rhythm of the world, and to one another, in a way that no man could ever experience.

The red wasp flew away and she tracked it for a moment with her eyes. She looked down and saw that she still sat on her knees but her hands were submerged in black goo. The goo expanded and sloshed up her wrists and legs, like the waves that rippled across the grotto. She jerked herself away from the mess and stood up on her knees. Black goo covered her hands and wrists, and slid down her forearms. *Oil. Crude oil.*

The angels once more stood beside her and Michael helped her up. They stood in the surf on a rocky shore and oil covered everything as far as could be seen. The surf came in and sloshed black goo up their legs.

"We should walk," Michael said.

The three of them trudged through the oily surf with dark gray skies overhead. Abigail's feet slipped on the rocks underneath the floating slick. Michael grasped her upper arm so that she would not fall.

Dead fish floated in the goo and blackened seabirds flopped their wings helplessly on the rocks. The oil glued the feathers of the seabirds together in a tacky mass, too heavy to gain their feet, let alone walk or fly. Dead fish and dying birds littered the blackened sea as far as she could see.

"Dear God! Why am I here? What is this?" Abigail demanded.

"God had nothing to do with this," Urielle snapped. "*You* did this."

Abigail started to protest, but rationalized that Urielle meant human beings created this disaster, not her personally. They continued through the surf and came across the bloated bodies of sea otters bobbing in a cove, their long whiskers jutting from the oil.

"The oil," Michael explained, "negates the water repellant characteristics of the animals' fur. They lose their thermal insulation and freeze to death."

Abigail wept for the tragedy of it all. She wept for the Earth. She wept for what humans have done to it. She wanted to wipe the tears from her face but her arms were nasty with the goo. She shook her hands trying to get it off, and wiped them on her pants, but the oil permeated every wrinkle and line of her hands and fingers. She could not get free of it.

"I had no idea," she said. "I had no idea this is what happens. Is this Prince William Sound?"

"It is only one of more to come," Michael replied. "Four thousand otters will die in this spill, and five hundred thousand seabirds. Twenty years from now the oil will persist under the sand and rocks. Every careless act leaves a trail of destruction."

She wrapped one arm around her waist, and covered her mouth with the opposite hand, even though the oil smeared her face. She had to hold onto herself or she'd have thrown up.

The trio continued walking, and rounded a bend in the shoreline where a large blackened lump lay washed up on the rocks. Abigail recognized the shape of an orca as they neared the bloated mass. Even killer whales succumbed to the oil!

"Man did this," Urielle said, as her eyes burned into Abigail. The tone of her voice made it clear that she held Abigail as responsible for this tragedy as any other human being.

Abigail flinched under that glare like an abused child reacting to the threat of a raised palm. She wanted to run, but held her ground.

"And Man must stop it," Michael added. "It is your world and your choice. Will it become a paradise, or a garbage heap?"

She welcomed Michael's voice, but Urielle's accusatory declaration frightened her to the core. The full scope of the angel's disdain for humanity included the destruction that mankind had wrought on the life forms and ecology of the planet. Her wrath manifested the vengeance of the life force itself.

Abigail stood on the rocks and stared at the carcass of the orca. She trembled with fear for what mankind had done to the Earth and the creatures that share this planet with us. Tears streamed down oily smudges on her face. Her peripheral vision collapsed until only the body of the orca remained in sight.

Bright light blinded her. As her eyes adjusted to the glare the dark shape of the orca morphed into the rectangular shape of a large, dark boardroom table. Outside the windows the skyline of a large city appeared in the distance.

A dozen or more men in business attire sat around the table. The men were in the midst of a meeting, and Abigail assumed they were all vice presidents of a large corporation. She sat against the wall at one end of the table with Michael and Urielle beside her. The occupants of the room were oblivious to their presence.

An older gentleman stood at the far end of the table. Abigail understood that he was the CEO, the Chief Executive Officer, of the organization. Strong frown lines etched his face, suggesting that he seldom smiled. His skin tone appeared as though he'd taken a shower in a spray-on tanning booth. Through the façade of the false tan his skin looked yellow and jaundiced. Darkness seemed to hang over him and she felt an immediate revulsion.

"What's the status on the bay?" he asked a blond man at the table.

"The grad students are still poking around and digging pits. They're getting hits on thirty percent of them," the blond man answered.

"What are we doing to discourage them?" the CEO asked.

"Why do we care?" A younger executive piped up. "The American public has a two-day attention span. It doesn't matter what they find, the public will have forgotten about it in less than forty-eight hours."

"I'll decide what we care about," the CEO snapped back. Then he returned his attention to the blond man.

"We're approaching the court Monday and requesting subpoenas," the blond man responded. "We want their research data and their personal income tax records."

"Can we do that? Ask for tax records?" the CEO asked.

"We can ask. If we get them it may give us more leverage. If we don't, we're still letting them know that it's *personal*."

"Keep tightening the screws. Let's send them back to the university with their tails between their legs."

"Why don't we offer them a grant to go study owl poop or something?" the young executive asked.

The CEO thought about it for a moment, and then said, "Check into it." Then he looked back to the blond man and asked, "Do we have anyone on the board?"

"We do," the blond man answered with a smile, "The regents like their football program, and so do we."

The CEO nodded his head affirmatively. The young executive smiled with glee. Not only had he scored an approval from the CEO, he now had access to the resources of another player at the table.

"They can't hear us, can they?" Abigail whispered to Michael.

"No, they are oblivious to anything but their own self-interest."

The men all looked much the same. They wore starched long-sleeved white shirts with gold or silver cuff links, and silk ties with pins. Each man had a diamond-encrusted school ring on one finger, and Abigail wondered if they'd all attended the same schools. Their appearance could be described as clean, crisp, and sterile, but "sterile" was the operative word.

"They don't have any *connection*," Abigail observed. "They don't have any connection to nature."

"That's part of the problem," Michael replied. "These men work in isolation from the natural world. Their daily lives are cocooned in artificial environments where any contact with the outside world feels like an inconvenience. They move from air-conditioned homes to air-conditioned automobiles to air-conditioned offices. The real world, when they experience it, is too hot, too cold, or too wet. They have no respect for life on this planet because they are completely disconnected from it."

"There's a darkness about them," Abigail said.

"Keep looking and tell me what you see," Michael responded.

Abigail noticed a dark quality about the CEO the moment she saw him, but as the meeting progressed she saw that the same essence hovered around all of the attendees. The longer she watched the more it began to take form. Individual shapes coalesced around the men and became ghouls with dark, rotted, man-shaped bodies.

"Oh, my god," she said, as she covered her mouth with one hand.

The ghouls rocked back-and-forth behind the men, and moved their arms in and out. At first Abigail didn't understand what they were doing, but then she saw.

"They're feeding! Oh, god, they're feeding!"

The ghouls reached into the hearts of their victims and scooped out handfuls of wriggling black corruption, then stuffed it into their mouths. These creatures were the "worse things" Caroline warned her about!

"Are those Scourge?" she asked Michael for confirmation.

"Yes, the demons are Scourge, but the men you see, and others like them, are the worst of their kind, the *Whores of Greed.*"

"What makes them 'the worst'?"

"They are the worst because they serve neither man, nor god, nor nation. They serve only greed, and greed without limit."

"If they're..." she hesitated because she didn't want to say the word, "whores," to an angel, and then continued. "If they're as you say, then why call them that when they're not female?"

"Only men can betray the life force with the impunity that these creatures desire," he answered.

Abigail thought about it. All around the globe men did dreadful things with little concern for the web of life on the planet.

"That makes sense," she said.

Abigail shut the ghouls out of her mind and turned to Michael. He seemed to accept the boardroom scene at base value; a moment in time that somehow played a necessary role in the future evolution of man. The Scourge would have their way, and the Whores of Greed would receive no more or less than they deserved.

Then she looked at Urielle. Urielle's face betrayed hardly any emotion at all, but her eyes glared with disgust. These men were destructive of life on the planet and she in turn wanted to destroy them. Abigail wondered how long the angel could contain her vengeance before it exploded out of control. She wouldn't want to be in the vicinity when that happened!

She could bear Urielle's glare no further, and turned back to the men at the table. She studied the way they carried themselves and looked for their key joints. What made them vulnerable? How could they be defeated?

She decided it was the same for all of them. Their power and their arrogance also represented their greatest weakness. They believed in their own superiority. They thought they were infallible. They thought they were beyond flesh and blood. They thought they were bigger than life.

Take away that false sense of power, and they are nothing.

That power could be denied with one simple word, "No." "No" to their products. "No" to their marketing campaigns. "No" to their candidates. "No" to their lobbyists. "No" to regulatory agencies staffed with industry insiders. "No" to all their machinations and lies in whatever form they may take.

"We need a revolution," she said, as much to herself as anyone.

"A revolution in the way people think, and use their purchasing power," Michael said. "When consumers change what they value, they change markets, and markets have the power to change the world. It is as simple, and as complex, as that."

How long might such a transformation take? Abigail had no idea. She supposed it depended on the amount of direct pain involved. As Raphael explained, without suffering there is no will to change.

"Is this why I'm here? Is this what I was meant to see?" she asked.

"Man's avarice is destroying life on this planet," Michael responded. "You've seen the consequences, you've seen the cause, and you've seen how it may be defeated. The question is: What will you change in your own heart to make the world a better place?

"It's not a matter of what you think other people should do, it is what you can do, right now, today, to make a difference. Can you smile and say 'hello' to a stranger? Can you wait five seconds for someone to move out of the way before rushing past in a parking lot? Can you make more healthful choices for yourself and the planet? Can you look in the mirror and see what you need to change?

"What of your own heart, Abigail? What dark influence affects your own judgment?"

She didn't know what he was talking about and he was beginning to sound too much like Raphael.

"Get me out of here," she said. "I don't want to see any more."

The vision collapsed and she found herself sitting in the chair under the dome of the Grotto of Hearts. The angels were gone. Another chair faced hers, and in that chair sat her father.

"You have got to be kidding. This is not going to end well," she said under her breath.

He had more gray hair than when she saw him at her mother's funeral, and his wrinkles were deeper. Red splotches covered the end of his nose and the cheeks under his eyes. She forgot that he was a "drinking man." He'd done the bulk of his drinking away from home so it wasn't something she witnessed but on a few occasions. The effects of his alcohol consumption now wrote themselves across his face.

He looked confused. "Abby? Abigail?" he asked. "Is that you?"

What? You don't recognize your own daughter? You may remember me from your wife's funeral!

"Yes, it's me," she said, "your daughter." She added that last part just in case he forgot who she was.

"What... What am I doing here?" he asked.

"I guess we're supposed to talk," she offered. "How's tricks?"

"Well," he answered, "I suppose things are okay."

How about me, she thought. Don't you want to know how I'm doing? He sat there, looking around, and didn't even face her direction.

"It's always about you, isn't it?" she asked. "Do you ever think about anyone else?"

"I don't know what you mean," he answered.

"I mean you were a lousy father, and a lousy husband! That's what I mean! You broke mother's heart!"

"I... I don't know what to say," he answered.

Since he appeared too stupid to figure it out on his own, Abigail decided to explain it to him. "You broke mother's heart. You abandoned us. You..." She tried to continue but tears swelled in her eyes.

She wiped the tears away with her sleeve and continued, "You never said you loved me! Never! What's wrong with you?"

Oh, boy, here it comes, she thought as the emotions welled up.

"What was wrong with me, dad? What was wrong with me that you didn't love me? Did you want a son? Was that it? Did you want a son so that he could play football and be a big hero for you? Wouldn't that have made you look good, your son, the football hero? Is that it? It's all about you feeling good about yourself, isn't it? And a daughter just couldn't do that!"

"I... I..." he struggled for words.

"I watched my mother die in agony and you never even came to see her! You left her alone for all those years while you went out and chased your whores! She stayed home..." She stopped as a realization hit, something she'd never thought about.

"She stayed home with me."

Once she said it, the thoughts rolled over her and it made sense. Her mother stayed home with Abigail. Her mother stayed with her father to provide the best possible home that she could, for her. Her mother gave up her life to be with her. Abigail never before understood the sacrifice that her mother made on her behalf. Her mother never complained or said anything; she simply did what she had to do for her child. Abigail felt horrible guilt in that moment, and covered her mouth in anguish.

She wiped the tears out of her eyes and looked at her father. He looked confused, but had no empathy. Her heartbreak was of no concern to him. Her tears only presented a problem in that he wanted them to go away. He simply wanted to extricate himself from this conversation so that he didn't have to deal with it.

Him, him, him! It's always about him! What an incredible, self-absorbed narcissist!

"You are a worthless piece of crap," she said, matter-of-factly. "Mother hated your guts in the last months of her life, and that's all she had for you. Hatred! And you know what? *I hate you, too!*" Her eyes bored into his with all the rage she could muster. He needed to know that she wasn't joking, not about any of it.

He jerked back with surprise. As much as he treated other people with a lack of respect and empathy, he couldn't understand how anyone could be offended by his actions.

"Abby! Abigail," he said, reproaching her, "I did the best that I could!"

"No, you did what you wanted to do. You always did what you wanted to do! Did you ever think about the consequences to the people around you? To your wife? To your daughter? *To me?*"

She looked in his face and saw that he had no capacity to understand what she asked. His self-absorption overruled any awareness of how others might think or feel, or any appreciation of the consequences that his actions had upon them. Compassion? Love? Empathy? People can't give you what they don't have, and he had none to give.

"I... I had to follow my heart, Abigail," he responded.

That was the wrong response. "Heart? Heart? You didn't follow your heart. You followed your dick!" she shouted. "Here, let me show you!"

She raised both forearms with the palms of her hands upward. "This is your heart," she said, pumping her left arm in the air while holding an imaginary heart in her hand. She extended her arm and "threw" the heart away. "Oops! There goes your heart," she exclaimed.

"And this is your dick," she said, pumping her right arm in the air while holding imaginary genitalia in her hand.

She looked him square in the face, her eyes burning into his. "And this," she continued, "...is ...your dick ...in my fist." She squeezed her hand in a grip so strong that all her knuckles popped.

His eyes went wide with fear, and he trembled at her fury. Then she remembered. She remembered her sixteenth birthday. He missed the party, as usual, and came home late after her mother had already gone to bed. Limp balloons hung from the dining room chairs while she watched a late night television show in the living room.

He retrieved a beer from the kitchen, and then stood in the middle of the floor with his eyes fixed on her. She sat up straight on the couch and pulled the edges of her sweater together with her arms folded over her chest.

"Your birthday today, huh?" he asked. "Sweet sixteen?"

She shook her head "yes," and avoided eye contact.

"Happy birthday," he said, and held out his arms.

The bottom seemed to drop out of her stomach and her pulse raced. Her father seldom ever touched her, or expressed affection of any kind. Now, on her sixteenth birthday, she gets a hug? She didn't want to stand up, but feared that he might raise his voice and wake her mother.

She walked over and put her forehead on his chest, but kept her arms in front to create a barrier. He wrapped her in his arms, squeezed, and then rubbed her back. Beer stink clung to his clothes and smelled like a toilet with pee all over the lid. *Oh, god, just hug me and get it over with.*

His hands moved down to the top of her glutes, and she tried to push away, but he held her tight. His breath smelled like cigarettes and piss. He kissed her lips and she jerked her head back. He grabbed her face with both hands and tried to kiss her again with his tongue in her mouth.

"St... st... stop!" she shouted, and squirmed out of his grip. She stomped off to her room, locked the door, and barricaded it with everything she could grab. She spit and tried to wipe the taste of him off her mouth. What kind of disgusting, filthy pervert kisses his own daughter like that?

There was a soft tap at the door. "Abigail?" he said in a low voice. The doorknob rattled but wouldn't turn with the lock engaged. The doorframe groaned as he pushed against the door from the other side. Frantic, her eyes searched the room for anything she could use to keep him out. She didn't want to scream, she didn't want to wake her mother, but what could she do? She grabbed one object, and then another, but nothing seemed substantial.

The pressure against the door eased and she heard him walk away. She stood in the middle of her room and trembled like a frightened dog, with a teddy bear in one arm and a tennis shoe in the other.

In the grotto everything in Abigail's vision turned red. She stood up, grabbed the armrests of the chair and swung it in a large arc over her head. In one long step she crossed the distance to her father and with all her momentum and all her "superhero" strength smashed the chair down on top of his head.

Both chairs exploded into broken slats and splinters. Her father was gone. Some part of her understood that the vision had been another manifestation of adobeDreams magic, and some part didn't care. If she knew it had truly been her father, in the flesh, would she have lashed out just the same? She didn't know.

She surveyed the mess on the floor. "All the king's horses and all the king's men," she rhymed, "won't put those chairs together again." The destruction of the chairs and the rhyme were a good allegory for her relationship with her father. No one would be putting that back together, either.

For the first time in her life she finally *owned* her anger. She'd always wanted to confront her father for what he did to her mother and to the family, and for that dreadful kiss. She'd wanted him to suffer for all the damage he'd done. Looking back, she realized that she played that anger out, at some level, with every significant relationship she'd ever had.

The chairs lay on the floor in shattered pieces like a bus had hit them. If she'd struck her father with that much force pieces of his head would also be on the floor. She shuddered as she imagined what the scene would look like, with an old man's body on the floor and blood all over the place. Sure, he was a lying, cheating, self-absorbed, dysfunctional piece of crap, but did that warrant murder? Maybe hitting people over the head with chairs wasn't such a good idea.

For so many years she'd held that anger under her skin and allowed it to fester. Isn't that what women are "supposed" to do? Sit and smile and swallow their anger? Keep the peace and pretend that everything is okay. Try not to think. Try not to feel. Live vicariously through soap operas and romance novels. Drown it with a tub of ice cream. Stuff it deep inside until it manifests as cancer, heart disease, or an autoimmune disorder. Whatever you do, don't scream. Don't react to the violence and inequity of the world that *men* have created.

If you can't express your anger, then how can you defend yourself? How can you enforce boundaries? How can the world ever become a better place? It was like Rayna said, people respect strength and exploit weakness. If you are unable or unwilling to defend yourself, then all you get is screwed over. But Abigail's reaction had gone too far. She'd held her anger inside until it reached critical mass and exploded.

She picked up a chunk of wood and examined the splintered end. Maybe she could learn to assert herself in more constructive ways. Maybe she could put pieces together instead of breaking them apart. Maybe she could defend herself and enforce boundaries without getting angry. Yes, maybe she'd actually try all that someday...but not today. She let the piece of wood fall to the floor.

She didn't know if the angels were watching, but she held her empty hands up to the air and said, "Okay, I admit it! I have issues!" She shrugged her shoulders and walked out of the chamber. Passing through the hallways she saw that it was dark outside. She'd been in the grotto for hours.

Rogue

"You need to let go of this..."

Abigail was eager to share her experiences with Caroline, but there was one more thing she had to do. She had to know what lay on the other side of the mirror. In the dream the little brown-eyed girl had shown her the way, now it was up to her to make it work. She went to the garden and stood in front of the moon gate.

"I want to know what's on the other side of the mirror," she said. Talking to the moon gate seemed silly, but the little girl had tapped her forehead and then pointed through the gate, and Abigail took that to mean focused intent.

Abigail copied the same polishing motions the little girl had made. Nothing happened. She exhaled and dropped her arms. The open space within the circle of the moon gate stayed empty. Where was a little brown-eyed girl when you needed one? Someday she'd also like to know who the child was, but for now she had other things on her mind. She controlled her breathing and put herself into a calm state, then without force or effort, restated her intention.

"I want to know what's on the other side of the mirror."

A diffuse glow rose from the inner edge of the gate. Abigail circled her palms in the air and willed the mirror to appear. Her heart pumped faster and her eyes widened. Something was about to happen.

A wave of energy burst from the aperture and condensed into a silvery surface. She saw herself in the reflection with lights from the second story of adobeDreams in the background. She reached to touch the mirror and hesitated, then ran her fingertips across the surface. It felt cold and smooth to the touch, but when she lifted her hand reflective matter stuck to her skin like taffy. She examined the goo and saw miniature reflections of herself.

Should she step through the reflection? Would she be able to breathe? What if she got lost? Who would find her? What if she can't get back? Where is a robot probe when you really need one? Abigail's head spun with all the things that could go wrong. "Paralysis through analysis," isn't that what the management boys say?

Screw it. She stepped through the mirror with one giant step. A cold shock burst over her like an ocean wave and then she stood in front of the bright façade of a theater. Throngs of people milled about and she heard conversations in French. What the heck? The movement of the crowd overwhelmed her equilibrium and she stumbled to keep her feet.

A group of women headed for the entrance of the theater. The lead woman stood a head taller than the others and had a severe Egyptian-style haircut. The other women were dressed in Goth attire with whiteface and black lipstick. All of the women wore black. The tall woman gave Abigail a puzzled look that said she had not expected to see her here. Then she laughed and looked away. A second later Abigail saw why.

A girl with dark hair below her shoulders trailed the tall woman. At first Abigail saw only the top of the girl's head but then the crowd parted and Abigail saw her face. The girl wore heavy whiteface with thick mascara streaking from both eyes. A crimson slash below her right eye marked the same location as the scar on Abigail's face.

The girl turned towards Abigail and her blue eyes looked into Abigail's blue eyes. The girl's jaw dropped with recognition. She continued to stare as the group passed, then faced forward to enter the theater.

Abigail jumped as a voice beside her said, "Good evening, Abigail." It was Raphael, wearing a sports jacket with padded elbows. Somehow he looked different from the Raphael she knew, as though he'd jumped forward months or years into the future.

"This is not your time. Go back," he said.

The vision collapsed and Abigail fell to her knees. There didn't seem to be enough air and she gasped for breath. She searched for an anchor and realized that she sat inside the circle of the moon gate at adobeDreams. For a few brief seconds she saw what was on the other side of the mirror, but Raphael had sent her back. Why? What wasn't she ready to see? And why were people speaking French?

She pushed herself up in a fatigued stupor and wobbled back to Caroline's room. Rayna stood at the door and looked grim.

"Abigail," she said, "there is a problem. Caroline has been injured."

Abigail's heart sank. "What happened?" she asked, as her throat trembled. "Is she okay? Where is she?"

"Raphael is administering to her," Rayna replied.

Abigail rushed into the room. Raphael sat beside the bed, talking to Caroline in a low voice. Her head lay propped on a pillow with an ice pack across the side of her face, the purple edges of a black eye showing from underneath.

"Caroline," Abigail exclaimed as she hurried to the bed.

A black cut split Caroline's lower lip and bruises darkened her cheeks. When she opened her mouth Abigail saw a missing tooth.

"My god, what happened?" she asked.

"She went shopping this evening," Raphael replied, "and three men attacked her when she walked out of a store. She carried shopping bags, and when she turned a corner a man punched her in the face. She didn't have a chance to react."

"Why, why?" Abigail shrieked, "Who would do this?"

"Edgar," Caroline said, "Edgar did it. He hit me, with his fists." She put her hand over her face and shook with body-wracking sobs.

"Easy," Raphael said. "Easy! You need to lay still." He looked to Abigail and explained, "She has two cracked ribs and a bruised spleen, but no other internal injuries. She will recover, but needs to lie still for a few days. I administered a sedative to help her sleep."

Rayna entered the room and spoke, "It could have been worse. Passersby saw the altercation and yelled at the men, then began dialing the police on their cell phones. Caroline was able to walk away from the area before the authorities arrived."

Edgar. I should have torn his balls off when I had the chance!

Men...men and their fists. "Might makes right," isn't that the way it works, boys? Give you a dick and more muscle mass and suddenly you are the rulers of the Earth! And that's worked out so well for everyone, hasn't it? What if we all just started saying, "No?" "No" to your way of doing things! "No" to your smug sense of entitlement! "No" to you being in charge! "No" to football, pornography, cigars, video games, and all the other stupid things you do! And "no" to holding down the home forts while you go off and screw other women!

The last thought took the air out of her, as more memories of her father came rushing back. How self-absorbed he was, just as his doppelganger had been in the grotto! Everything they'd done as a family was either about him...or without him! She thought of her mother wasting away with cancer, just as she'd wasted away the years of her life, waiting for Abigail's father to become a better man.

I have issues, and I am about to do some damage!

Abigail set her jaw to destruction and turned to leave the room. Raphael stood in the way, his palms up to urge calm. She moved to step around him and he blocked her exit. She stood and glared with murder in her eyes. His eyes remained firm, but compassionate.

"Abigail," he said. "I know what you are feeling. Your anger is very strong. You need to let go of this and allow the authorities to handle the situation."

Oh boy, now he's trying to reason with me. Like that will work!

Raphael continued, "You cannot go after these men!"

He was doing fine until he told her what she couldn't do. That's what they all did, wasn't it? They try to control us. They try to define our reality and tell us what we can and cannot do. She looked at Raphael and lost all restraint. She didn't care whether he was an angel with a heart, an angel with a dick, or a heartless, dickless angel. It didn't matter. At that moment he represented the male of the species and stood in her freaking way, trying to tell her what to do!

"No," she said, and she liked the sound of the word as it came out her mouth. "No," she said with more force. "Whether I am right or I am wrong you cannot tell me what to do!"

She tried to step around and he moved with her. She pressed forward and he blocked her with his palms, but otherwise made no attempt to restrain her.

Tai chi, is it? He grounded himself with the Earth, just as he'd done in the garden. They moved together. He matched every move she made with a counter move. They flowed together like two partners gliding across a ballroom floor. She danced her way out of the room and down the hall. He couldn't stop her, not peacefully, anyway. If he tried to restrain her by force, then they'd see what angels are really made of!

Rayna stood out of the way the entire time. Her non-participation let Abigail know that she understood Abigail's feelings and would do nothing to intervene.

"Abigail," Raphael said at last, as he lowered his hands, "I cannot stop you, but I beg you to consider what you do! Think about the consequences before you act. Think, Abigail, think!"

She stepped around him and walked outside the gate of adobeDreams. Where were Edgar and the other men? The hour was late and only the bars would be open. She extended her senses and walked in the direction that felt right, without thinking about it. If she had to check every bar in town, she'd find them.

She found herself at a restaurant with a rooftop cantina, a few blocks off Sandoval. They were here; she knew it. She stood in the dark and waited. When she saw them, what would she do? Her rage told her to rip them to pieces, but she knew she shouldn't do that. She'd confront them, but then what? Ask them to surrender to the authorities? As though that would work! Maybe she'd beat some sense into them and drag them one by one to the police station?

Three men exited the bar. It was Edgar and two of his friends, Ray and Todd, or "Toddy" as he liked to be called. They all wore ridiculous Hawaiian shirts over knee-length shorts and sandals. They were liquored up and laughing as men who have had too much to drink do. She supposed they were celebrating, celebrating their victory over a girl that weighed hardly half as much as any one of them! Cowards!

She knew Ray and Toddy from visits to the apartment when Edgar hosted card-playing night. They were creeps. If she walked into the room their eyes tracked her breasts. When she walked out they watched her buttocks. She hated those nights and tried to avoid interaction with them as much as possible.

Sometimes Ray cornered her in the kitchen. He'd make small talk and the kind of asinine remarks that men make to impress women, but that actually have the opposite effect. He'd try to steer the conversation so that he could work in some sexual innuendos along the way. He usually said something stupid about "headlights" or "cherries." *Idiot!* The more he drank, the more crude his remarks.

Of course, he didn't really want to know her as a person. What a joke! He kept testing the limits because he wanted to screw her. That's all it ever was. Did he even possess the neural capacity to recognize her as another human being?

She looked up at the glow from the rooftop cantina, where they'd no doubt just had drinks. Too bad she didn't catch them sooner, she thought, as she envisioned their bodies falling off the roof. They came all this way, they came all this way to find us and hurt us, and probably thought it would be funny! Nothing more than a drunken lark! They'd be telling stories and laughing about it for years!

They stumbled further out onto the street and saw her.

"How's your little girlfriend?" Edgar asked with a smirk. The others laughed.

God, she wanted to destroy them! She stepped towards Edgar and his obnoxious smirk. Abigail met his mother once, when she came to visit. Her name was Ellen. It was easy to see how Edgar the boy became Edgar the man. His mother spoiled and coddled him, and allowed him to escape any consequences for his misdeeds. If he got a speeding ticket, she paid it. If he wanted something and couldn't afford it, she bought it. Mother's little precious! What an ill mannered, immature, self-absorbed little narcissist you raised!

Ray and Todd stood together with Edgar and exchanged lecherous smiles. They looked her up and down, stripping her with their eyes. She smelled their drunken lust and the animalistic surge of domination in their veins. She was meat. She was tits and ass and nothing more.

She hardly knew these guys, really, but she looked at them and wondered. *What the hell is the matter with you?* What were you going to do? Drag Caroline into an alley and beat her into the dirt? Was that your fantasy? Is that what this whole thing is about? Making you feel powerful? How did you think you were going to get away with it?

Then she realized they were never really after Caroline. They'd come for her, and simply saw Caroline first. Edgar knew she meant something to Abigail so they hurt her, and may have done worse if things had gotten more out of hand.

Abigail surged with bestial rage and everything in her vision threatened to turn red. If she lost control...!

A wind blustered across the street. Small particles of grit peppered the bottom of her legs. Black swirls of dust snaked around her feet before they dissipated in the wind. *Lucifer.* This is what Lucifer wants, for people to give in to their basest instincts and to destroy one another. She thought of the shattered chair in the grotto. It didn't change anything. All her anger over all the years didn't change anything. Beating up Edgar and his friends wouldn't undo the damage done to Caroline, either.

"You're not going to get away with this," she said. "I'm going to see you in jail for what you did to..." her voice cracked, "...to Caroline."

"Awww... did your little girlfriend have an accident? Maybe she tripped and fell down?" Edgar said.

"Yeah, three or four times," Ray added. They all snickered.

She felt her control slipping. She had to walk away, right then, while she still could. "This isn't over," she said, and backed off from the confrontation. She put a safe distance between herself and the men, then turned and walked down the street.

Agonizing pain shot through her body as all of her muscles contracted. Her body stiffened and she fell backwards to the street. The back of her head hit the pavement. The pain stopped and she gasped for breath. The stars shone in the sky overhead and seemed somehow peaceful. She blinked her eyes and tried to figure out what happened.

Footsteps approached and then Edgar and his friends looked down on her. Ray held something in his hand. Something with wires.

"How was that?" Edgar asked. He nodded at Ray and her muscles again twisted into knots. She thought she screamed but wasn't sure if anything came out of her mouth. The pain stopped and then came back, then went away again.

"St-stop," she said, and gasped for breath. Dear god, what was happening to her? It was Ray. He had some kind of electric stun gun, like the ones police use, and had shot her with it. She knew he could keep giving her jolts.

People shouted from the second floor of the cantina. They'd apparently heard some kind of altercation on the street and looked down to see what was going on.

"That's enough," Edgar said. "Let's get out of here."

"Why don't we all go someplace *more private*?" Ray asked.

The other men looked at him, and understood his intent. Abigail knew what he meant, too.

"That's not going to happen," Edgar said. "This has gone far enough. We did what we came to do. Now it's time to leave."

He looked down at Abigail and said, "You've learned your lesson, haven't you?" And then he called her the "b" word.

Edgar was a spoiled brat, and he'd made bad decisions that warranted criminal prosecution, but at least he wasn't a rapist. Perhaps there was still hope for him after all.

"Eddie's right. I'm drunk, *but not that drunk,*" Todd said. Perhaps Toddy could be salvaged, too.

"Maybe I'll see you again," Ray said as he leaned over. Then he gave her another jolt with the stun gun. Her body stiffened and her muscles twisted in pure torment.

"That's enough!" Edgar shouted as he shook Ray's shoulder.

"Just one more," Ray said.

"Ray, that's enough!" Todd shouted in protest.

Abigail heard every word but couldn't respond. She wanted to beg Ray to stop but couldn't put the words together. Whatever happened she didn't want to endure another shock. Her mind reverted to pure animal instinct. She couldn't reason with them and she couldn't run away. All she could do was fight.

Ray hit the trigger of the stun gun and the beast exploded out of Abigail at the same moment. She flew off the pavement with a roar of hominid fangs and slashed his neck with black fingernails like claws. Her swipe ripped a hand-sized chunk from his throat and he fell to the pavement with air and blood gurgling from the wound. Edgar and Todd jumped back in horror, and ran. Todd sprinted down the street and looked back over his shoulder just as a car roared past on Sandoval. The vehicle hit him dead on and threw his body thirty feet into a curb where he landed headfirst.

Edgar ran up the street in total panic. In three strides Abigail's beast form caught up and leapt upon his back. She rode him to the ground, rolled, and then came back at him just as he regained his knees. She bared her fangs in a loud snarl and tore into the side of his neck. He had just enough time to scream before her teeth tore a horrific gash from his flesh. She spit out the meat and surveyed the street, hunched over and ready for more adversaries. People screamed and shouted from the rooftop bar. She turned and ran.

She ran through the streets, unthinking, possessed by pure instinct. She ran for miles in the shadows. As she began to regain her senses she found herself inside the walls of adobeDreams, leaning over the fountain. Blood covered her hands, mouth, and throat. Gore plastered her blouse to her chest. *Oh, my god, what have I done?*

She tried to wash herself in the fountain, but couldn't get the blood off. It soaked into her skin and seeped into her soul. The stain would never come out. *This can't be happening!*

She stumbled inside the hacienda and wanted nothing more than to stand in a hot shower until the sun came up. Raphael sat inside the lobby, like a parent waiting for a child to come home from a date. He sat in a thick-cushioned chair with large armrests, and beckoned her over.

"Abigail," he said, "we must talk. You had the right to defend yourself when Edgar accosted you at the Indian Market, but the violence of your response only served to invite retribution.

"Tonight you crossed another line. You do not realize the power of your own intent. You went looking for revenge, and though you turned away, your original purpose was so strong that your mind found a way to achieve vengeance. You chose this path and the consequences will be yours, but this is not the way of adobeDreams. You must pack your things and leave, immediately."

Abigail couldn't disagree with anything he said. She shouldn't have gone to town. She shouldn't have walked out the door with vengeance in her heart. She looked at Raphael with her soul in torment. His face held a sadness that could not be measured with words. She wished she were dead.

"I'll say goodbye to Caroline, and pack my bag," she said.

Assault on adobeDreams

"Fight like amazons."

Abigail entered Caroline's room and paused as she waited for her eyes to adjust. Rayna sat in a chair watching over Caroline, asleep in the bed.

Rayna came to her and saw the dark stain on Abigail's blouse.

"You look awful," she whispered.

"Things went bad."

"You killed them, yes?"

Abigail nodded her head affirmatively.

"Good," Rayna said, and then said something in Hebrew that must have meant, "Damn their souls to hell!"

Abigail shook her head "no." How could she explain the revulsion she felt for what she'd done? Those idiots deserved *prosecution*, not *execution*.

"Raphael asked me to leave," she said. "Can you give us a few minutes?"

Abigail took her travel bag into the bathroom and looked in the mirror. Traces of blood stained her lips and the spaces between her teeth. She pulled off her blouse and thought to wash it out, but decided she never wanted to wear it again. She crushed it into a tight ball and stuffed it into her bag. She'd throw it away elsewhere so that Caroline wouldn't find it in the trash.

She stood there in a black bra, looking into the mirror. The reflection wasn't the same, nor would it ever be. She retrieved a small pair of scissors from her bag, grasped a few locks of hair between her fingers, and started cutting. The bottom of the sink filled with hair.

If some other Abby, in some other universe, looked into this same mirror, she apologized for the mess she'd made of their hair. It lay short and choppy on her head and looked like a pile of layered crap, but she didn't care. The new Abby looked back, and the old Abby fell into the trash.

She went to the bed and kissed Caroline's head, then stroked her hair. "I had another bad dream," Caroline said, her voice thick with sedation.

"Yes, you did, sweetie, but it's over now," Abigail replied. She told herself that Caroline couldn't converse any further, but perhaps she simply didn't want to face the pain of saying goodbye.

She put on a fresh blouse and walked out with more questions than answers. When will I see her again? How will I find her? What will she think of me once she knows what I've done?

Rayna waited for her in the hall. With a flash of insight Abigail saw Rayna's short-cropped hair and had a better understanding of what she may have experienced in her own life.

"Thank you for looking after her," Abigail said, then hugged Rayna and kissed her cheeks. Rayna responded in kind, and Abigail saw that the warrior woman's eyes were damp with tears.

Abigail took two steps away from Rayna and the ground swayed with a rumble that rolled through the building.

"What was that?" Rayna asked.

"Stay here," Abigail said. "I'll check it out!"

The rumble came from a definite direction, the Grotto of Hearts. Abigail ran toward it and met Raphael at the top of the staircase.

"What's going on?" she asked.

"There is no time to talk," he replied, and then raced down the stairs.

She followed behind but could not catch up. When she reached the bottom he stood a few steps out onto the floor of the dome and looked up. The grotto shook with a rumble of thunder as dust and small bits of stone fell from the ceiling and walls.

Raphael turned and said, "Michael fights Lucifer and Urielle in the vaults of heaven."

His reply didn't make sense. Why would Urielle fight Michael?

"Urielle has no love for Lucifer," Raphael answered in response to her unvoiced question, "but her disdain for mankind is even greater. With Michael suppressed, Urielle will be free to annihilate the human race. Then she will turn all her attention to the destruction of Lucifer."

"Why does she want to destroy mankind?" Abigail asked. "Why doesn't she just go after Lucifer, and leave us alone?"

"Lucifer obtains his power from the darkness of mankind. With mankind out of the way he will be vulnerable enough for Urielle to destroy."

Abigail thought back to Urielle's reaction to the oil spill and the machinations of the executives in the boardroom. Man's unconscionable destruction of life had pushed the angel over the edge; she'd simply held her vengeance until she could bear no more. In defiance of heaven she would now sanitize the Earth of the human race.

At that moment a stone the size of a small automobile fell from the ceiling. Abigail watched it as though it were in slow motion, and realized that she perceived the "key joint" of the falling rock. If needed she could run circles around the spot where the stone would impact the ground and not be injured. The stone hit the floor with an impact that sent an expanding shockwave out in all directions. The shockwave knocked her on her backside. *Okay, Miss Smarty Pants, if you can dodge the stone why not the shockwave?* Raphael still stood, anchored to the ground in a tai chi stance.

"I must aid Michael," he said. Then he jumped into the air and disappeared into one of the triangular openings in the ceiling. For a split second as he leapt, the thrust of luminous wings appeared behind his body.

The dome shook with thunder as more dust and stone fell from above. She regained her feet but nausea rose in her stomach. The thought of the angelic confrontation reminded her of how she felt as a young girl when she walked in on a loud argument between her parents. It was awful then; it was worse now.

Stones exploded from the top of the ceiling and a male figure with long dark hair flew out, struck the walls and then landed on all fours in front of her. Abigail knew who it was before he looked up. *Lucifer.* He coughed, laughed, and then spit out black blood.

"Abigail," he said, stroking his face where the scar crossed hers. "How nice to see you again!"

Always poking fun at my scar. That is just rude!

Lucifer inhaled to absorb her scent. He undoubtedly detected traces of blood on her skin.

"Smells like chicken," he said.

In the background Raphael fell from the ceiling and hit the ground, standing up. Just before impact he extended wide luminous wings and slowed his descent like a bird. Then the wings were gone. Dark shapes fell from cracks in the ceiling, smacked the floor and joined together in larger puddles. The shapes pulsated from within the mass and tried to rise. *Shadow wraiths!*

Lucifer stood up. Black blood ran from his mouth and nose. His clothing was soiled and tattered. The dome continued to rumble with the sound of battle. Michael and Urielle must be fighting in the upper vaults.

Lucifer smiled, and said, "This shall be an interesting day. You will await my pleasure, will you not?"

She liked him better when he didn't talk.

Dark figures fell from more holes in the ceiling. They landed broken on the floor, then gathered themselves and stood up. *Scourge. Ghouls.* The "worse things" Caroline warned Abigail about. This could only mean one thing. The shadow wraiths and Scourge joined forces with Urielle and Lucifer to attack Michael and adobeDreams.

A huge explosion at the top of the dome destroyed half of the seven-pointed star and sent it falling to the floor together with more automobile-sized stones. Two figures fell in the midst of the debris. Urielle and Michael struggled with their hands locked on one another's throats. They hit the floor sideways and created a fearsome impact. Dust and dirt flew out from the epicenter like the tendrils of a fireworks explosion. The shockwave sent all the stones that'd previously fallen up into the air before they fell back to the floor. A cloud of dust obscured the point of impact and Abigail couldn't see anything. Lucifer rocked on his legs but smiled, relishing the moment. Abigail kept her feet but stumbled back to the entrance of the stairs, reaching out to one wall for support.

"How is our dear Caroline doing?" Lucifer asked with a wicked smile.

She tried to think of a smart aleck reply when Lucifer's body rose in the air and then shot to the opposite side of the dome. His body struck the far wall and fell to the floor. Raphael stood facing her. He'd grabbed Lucifer by the hair and the back of his trousers, lifted him overhead, and tossed him across the dome.

"Way to go Raphael," she cheered.

"Abigail, we must contain them here. Get Rayna! Now!" he shouted.

He didn't have to tell her twice. She raced toward the top of the stairs and nearly ran into Rayna as she rounded a corner. They both jumped back, fists clenched.

"What is happening?" Rayna asked.

"Michael and Raphael are fighting Urielle and Lucifer," Abigail replied.

"Urielle?" Rayna asked with surprise.

"Yes, Urielle," Abigail confirmed, "but it gets worse. Demons are invading the Grotto. We must stop them before they gain access to the floors!"

Rayna reached both hands behind her back and produced two automatic pistols, and handed them to Abigail. *That's my girl, always prepared to kick butt and take names!*

Rayna showed her the safety and said, "Flip this up. Point and squeeze the trigger! I'll be back with more!" With that she turned and raced back up the stairs, then stopped and looked back at Abigail.

"Fifteen rounds," she shouted, "fifteen rounds!"

Abigail understood that she meant each pistol could fire fifteen times. Then Rayna ran up the stairs, out of sight. She hadn't trained Abigail on the use of handguns, but it seemed simple enough. Safety off, point and shoot.

Abigail looked back down the stairway where a fearsome battle raged within the Grotto of Hearts. She walked slowly down the stairs so that she had time to catch her breath and gird herself for whatever she must face. She walked past a turn and three Scourge crawled up the stairs toward her. They looked both human and animal, rotted black with decay. Chunks of grey skull and teeth showed through the dark rot of their faces.

She remembered that Caroline told her she didn't know how Scourge could be killed. *Well, we're about to find out.* She flipped the safety off one of the pistols and fired at the nearest ghoul. The weapon discharged with greater recoil than she'd anticipated. The shot passed over the ghoul's head. The spent shell casing bounced off the wall and plinked down the stairs. Thinking back to her firearms training with the assault rifles, she remembered that the body must become part of the weapons system. Holding the pistol with more strength she sighted the pistol and squeezed the trigger. The bullet hit the ghoul in the forehead and blew the back of its skull out, spewing a black mass behind him. The spent shell casing trailed a plume of smoke over Abigail's shoulder and bounced on the stones somewhere behind her. The creature fell on the stairs, inanimate.

She flipped the safety of the other pistol off, and shot each of the advancing Scourge in the head. They fell to the stairs dead, or whatever passes for death with their kind.

She stepped down to the nearest ghoul and kicked its head to ensure that it no longer posed a threat. Unexpectedly, the head detached from the spine and bounced down the stairs, around the curve and out of sight. She looked at her boot. Black gunk covered the toe and she tried to shake it off, but no matter how hard she kicked the goo clung like oil and wouldn't come clean. She imagined what she looked like in that moment, standing on one leg while shaking the opposite foot and holding a pistol in each hand. *This is ridiculous.*

She put her foot down and walked through the remaining bodies with the pistols pointed at their heads. She expected the ghouls to smell like rotten meat, but instead they had the stench of dozens of humans confined to a small space. They reeked of body odor, sweat, urine, sex, and foul breath all tumbled together. She tried not to breathe.

At the landing a chest high wall of snarling shadows confronted her, with blue-white eyes and canine heads that thrust from the dark. The angels fought somewhere in the background.

She backed up the stairs and wondered what to do. From out of the snarling, snapping jaws of the wraiths, a Scourge emerged. And another. And another. And more. She stepped back up the stairs, aimed for their heads and fired. She stumbled and fell backwards over the bodies of the ghouls she'd previously killed. She edged backwards on her elbows but the floor ran slick with black goo and she could hardly gain traction. Bursts from both pistols slowed the ghouls and downed a few so that she could regain her feet and retreat up the stairs. More ghouls emerged to replace the ones she'd shot.

She continued firing with both weapons until the slide of one pistol locked open on an empty magazine, and then the other. The guns were empty! This is what she'd seen in her nightmare, before she asked Rayna for firearms training. She dropped the weapons and continued backing up the stairs. The width of the entire stairwell now filled with shambling ghouls, all advancing on her.

"What'd they do? Empty Wall Street?" she asked no one in particular.

Rayna stepped beside her and answered her question with a controlled burst of automatic weapons fire from an AK-47. The bullets impacted the ghouls, tearing apart bodies and skulls. The first few waves fell to the stairs, finished.

"Screw Wall Street," Rayna said. She handed Abigail an AR-15 with a bandolier of loaded magazines she carried across her back, and reloaded her own weapon. The women looked at each other and nodded assent.

"Let's do this," Abigail said.

With weapons blasting they advanced down the stairs and massacred the Scourge in their path. Smoke from the weapons filled the stairwell and expended magazines littered the steps. Empty shell casings hit the walls and bounced down the stairs in a tinkling musical they couldn't hear due to the discharge of the weapons. An empty casing went down the back of Abigail's blouse and seared a path down her skin, but she could not stop to remove it. They kept firing, reloaded, and fired some more. Finally the last Scourge fell to the stones. Rayna kicked the head of one of the fallen ghouls and the skull detached from the spine and tumbled down the stairs.

Rayna reacted with surprise as the skull bounced out of sight.

"It happens," Abigail said, as she shrugged her shoulders.

The women checked their weapons and then looked at the mess the battle made of them. Splatters of black goo covered their torsos and plastered their legs up to knee level. The smell was awful. Abigail pulled the back of her blouse out of her jeans and allowed the empty casing to fall to the floor.

"Ouch," Rayna said, and then fluffed the back of her shirt, demonstrating that it hung open at the bottom. She'd apparently had the hot casing experience and dressed accordingly.

A wall of darkness advanced up the stairs. A canine form with snapping fangs and blue-white eyes leapt out of the wall. Abigail tore the beast apart with a short burst. The non-corporeal portions of the wraith continued to climb up the stairs and struggled to become coherent. More canines came out of the wall and were met with sustained fire. Some exploded into bits, others survived and continued to climb the stairs with shattered legs and snouts. The surviving pieces joined together, trying to form a whole creature. Others stuck their heads and forelegs out of the dark wall and clawed to break free of the incorporeal shadows.

The women looked at each other. There were too many wraiths, and they just kept coming.

"Is there a Plan B?" Abigail asked.

"Fight like amazons," Rayna said. They had no other options. When their ammunition ran out it would be hand-to-hand combat to the death.

Thunder rolled up the stairwell and rocked the women on their feet. Something horrific must have happened inside the grotto. The wall of darkness momentarily flattened, and then began to retreat down the stairwell.

"They're leaving!" Abigail exclaimed. "They're leaving!" Thinking for a moment, she looked at Rayna and asked, "Why are they leaving?"

"They're rejoining the fight in the grotto," Rayna answered. "Check your ammo."

Abigail removed the magazine from the rifle and inspected it. "I have half a magazine and the bandolier is empty."

"About the same here. This won't last long," Rayna replied. "Remember the rifle is still a weapon, even when it is unloaded."

"Roger that!" Abigail responded. Rayna grinned at Abigail's use of military vernacular.

At the bottom of the stairs they came upon a scene of incredible destruction. The dome lay in a shambles with automobile-sized stones and smaller rubble strewn across the grotto. The ceiling contained huge gaps and portions of the wall had collapsed to reveal only earth and rock. The heart-shaped planters sat in shattered heaps on the floor, their red blossoms scattered like blood. Dust and smoke hung in the air higher than a man can reach.

Raphael moved among the larger stones, fighting the demons with a long wooden staff. He jabbed and smashed and at first glance appeared to be making progress. On closer scrutiny it could be seen that some of his strikes hit non-corporeal shapes and left only swirling trails in their wake. He felled ghouls with blows to the head, only to have wraiths absorb their essence in an effort to become corporeal. Injured wraiths fell back into the shadows and were reabsorbed.

It was obvious that the demons withdrew from the stairwell to use all of their combined energy against Raphael. The situation looked hopeless. How do you fight an enemy that continually regenerates?

Michael wielded his spear and fought both Urielle and Lucifer. Urielle attacked with the same sword she'd used to cleave Lucifer's dark heart, and Lucifer swung a sword that materialized in his hand only moments before it struck. All of them bled from a multitude of cuts and were covered in dust. Michael appeared to suffer the worst of it.

"Let's help Michael," Rayna said.

"Agreed," Abigail said. She didn't know how to help Raphael, but perhaps something could be done to aid Michael. If you can't solve the problem that's in front of your face, then solve another problem that you can do something about!

"I've got Urielle," Rayna said, and ran to the fight.

Oh, thanks. That left Abigail with Lucifer, and they'd had such a sterling relationship! Could bullets harm angels? She didn't know, but she was about to find out.

Rayna engaged Urielle, emptying the contents of her magazine into the rogue angel. The bullets struck Urielle's skin and clothing, but didn't penetrate. They only served to divert Urielle's attention for a moment so that Michael could focus on Lucifer.

Abigail emptied her magazine into Lucifer's torso. She expected to see the same results as Rayna's assault on Urielle, but he roared in anger as the bullets penetrated his skin. In that moment Michael thrust his spear toward Lucifer's heart. Lucifer rolled with the thrust and the spearhead sliced a gash across his chest. Michael dropped the spear and grabbed Lucifer by the throat. The two of them rolled into a pool of dense smoke. Canine snouts of shadow wraiths rose from the mist with snaps and snarls while the two angels fought in the darkness.

Well, I'm certainly not going in there. Abigail turned to see Rayna and Urielle engaged in hand-to-hand combat. Or rather, it was hand-to-empty rifle combat. Urielle struck at Rayna with open palm blows and side-of-hand strikes. Rayna blocked the blows with her AK-47 and fought back with slashing strokes of the butt and barrel. The battle looked almost even but it was Urielle who did all the advancing. The wood butt of Rayna's rifle hung in shattered chunks with the barrel bent at the opposite end. Rayna could hardly absorb the impact of Urielle's blows without dropping the weapon. She was simply no match for the rogue angel.

Abigail ran forward and thrust the butt of her rifle at Urielle's head. Without breaking stride Urielle swatted it away as though it were no more than a housefly. The weapon flew out of Abigail's hands and landed in rubble a distance away. The blow left Abigail's arms hanging numb and useless.

In the background Michael joined Raphael to fight the wraiths and ghouls. She couldn't see what happened to Lucifer.

Urielle smashed the rifle out of Rayna's hands with a powerful down stroke. The AK-47 clattered to the floor and bounced, its receiver bent from the force of Urielle's blow.

Rayna stood before Urielle, her arms hanging limp at her sides. She looked Urielle straight in the eyes, and said in a calm voice, "Urielle." Without hesitation Urielle struck her chest with an open palm strike that sent Rayna flying off her feet. Rayna's eyes registered both surprise and anguish as she flew backwards.

Urielle held her arm outright, palm flat, shocked by what she'd done. Rayna laid amidst rubble some distance away, holding one hand to her chest. She struggled to breathe and choked on a heavy stream of blood running from her mouth and nose. Urielle's energy appeared to collapse. She had just injured, possibly killed, the one human to whom she could relate the most. Urielle walked to Rayna's side, examined her for a moment, then picked her up and in one jump flew through an opening in the ceiling of the dome.

Michael and Raphael were making progress in their battle with the demons. Dust and smoke intermingled with the shadows of the wraiths and it was difficult to see everything that happened. A dark mist curved around the combatants and rolled toward Abigail across the floor. She had no weapons and her hands were still numb from Urielle's swat. She backed away, watching her steps amidst the rubble on the floor. She didn't want to fall and give the mist a chance to roll over her!

Lucifer strode from the mist and dusted off the arms of his black long-sleeved shirt. Holes in the shirt showed where bullets passed through, but there was no blood. He smiled and said, "Abigail! At last we have time to chat with one another!"

He looked back over his shoulder at the battle between Michael and Raphael and the demons. "Tell me, are you curious about what happens next?" he asked. "Do you have anything that you would like to say, while your mouth still works?" He smiled at the last remark, and looked at Abigail with the entitled sneer of every male who holds a woman in his power and thinks he is her master.

Abigail didn't have much else going for her at the moment but her mouth did in fact still work. She stared Lucifer in the face and asked, "S-s-so, is it okay if I call you Luci?"

He stepped forward and whipped his arm in a backhanded slap that rocketed towards her as fast as a stone from a slingshot. She almost had time to put her arms together for protection before the blow struck and sent her flying. The impact was like being hit by a wrecking ball. Every bone in her body seemed to pop and snap back into place. She hit the floor amongst small stones and rubble. Everything hurt and went black.

Stand Defiant

"Come and get me."

I am broken, and I cannot rise. Abigail struggled to focus through her confusion but found no anchors. She pushed up with her arms and saw the floor slide up, and then down. *I am a screwed unit.* I am in shock...or my brain is not right.

She lay amidst the rubble trying to remember something important. Mists and shapes passed across her field of vision from her sideways view of the world. The floor stayed reliable as long as she didn't try to lift her head, but small rocks and shards of stone poked her skin.

Oh yes, I need to breathe! She inhaled through her nose and exhaled through her mouth. Simple. In, out. In, out. *I can do this.*

A pair of black shapes kicked up contrails in the airborne dust. The shapes grew larger and stopped in front of her face. One of the shapes contained a shiny orb. The orb represented something and she should have known what it meant, but couldn't recall. A force moved her body and her face came closer to the shiny orb. It was a medallion, a shiny medallion on a boot.

Her body rose in the air, pulled by some unseen force. A field of black blocked her vision and then she saw the open lapels of a man's shirt and a chest black with hair. A man lifted her to her feet. How kind, could you give me a wash and a wax with that?

Her body convulsed, a rag doll shaken in the air. The man brought her face to his. *Lucifer*. Lucifer had a fist full of her blouse and with one arm held her dangling in the air. His breath smelled like burnt meat and decay. He tilted his head from side to side as he studied her face.

"Abigail? Abigail? Is that you?" he teased, as though they were long lost friends who'd just met again.

Abigail is not here anymore. Can't I just sleep?

He threw Abigail over his shoulder and carried her across the floor of the grotto and up the circular stairwell to a guest's room. He sat her down in a chair and straightened her body. All she could see was his black shirt.

He lifted Abigail's chin and scolded her, "Abigail! Abigail! Wake up! I have something I want you to see!" He slapped her face sharply with one hand, and then slapped her again. The slaps stung like electrical shocks and snapped her out of the stupor.

He stepped out of her line of sight and there lay Caroline, unconscious in bed. Sedated, she'd slept through the entire attack on adobeDreams and lay defenseless, but unmolested. Lucifer went to the far side of the bed and rested both arms on the mattress. He smiled as he looked down at Caroline, and asked, "Do they not all look like angels while they sleep?

"It's a pity we don't have more time," he said. "But your angelic friends will be here soon. Of course, they're not all your allies, are they?"

He meant Urielle. Urielle wasn't her friend, or mankind's. And then Abigail put the pieces together. Urielle had been working against her the whole time.

It was she who allowed Lucifer into adobeDreams the first time he attacked. Her hesitation before she struck Lucifer with her sword gave him time to react. It was Urielle who divulged the destination of their Taos trip when no one else knew they were coming. Even when she accompanied Rayna to save Abigail in Liberia, it wasn't truly for Abigail's sake, but simply an excuse to slaughter men.

Lucifer laughed.

"You're learning, but alas, too late."

He licked his lips with his thick bull tongue and jerked Caroline upright by the hair. She screamed in pain, her eyes wild as she searched the room in confusion. He turned her head so that she could see his face and she gasped with terror. She struggled to escape but he dropped her face down on the bed and held her with one hand.

"Tell me, Abigail. Do you prefer rib meat, or would you like a leg with that?" he asked.

He's going to rip her to pieces right in front of me, Abigail realized. And that will rip me to pieces, too. Her heart sank and anguish twisted her guts like a taut rope. She tried to move, but couldn't. She looked away and closed her eyes, unwilling to see.

"Now, now, that is cheating," he said. "And I want you to see every moment."

Lucifer walked around the bed and stood behind Abigail. He smelled the side of her neck and hair then grasped her face with both hands and tilted her head up, then stretched her eyes open with his fingers. She tried to close them again but found that she could not.

He pointed her face at the bed. She tried to speak but her mouth made no sound. She tried to beg but had no voice. She could only look at Caroline and weep as Lucifer returned to the far side of the bed.

Caroline trembled on the sheets, held in place by some unseen force. She reached out to Abigail, her face twisted with anguish. Lucifer grabbed her nightshirt from behind and shook her in the air. She screamed as he held her in his grip. He looked at Abigail while he extended his thick tongue, then licked Caroline's neck from shoulder to ear lobe. He dropped her on the bed face down. She tried to crawl forward but he held her ankles and pulled her back.

Lucifer paused and listened, as though he heard something at a distance. "I hate to slay and run, but we're out of time," he said.

That was twice he'd used the word "time." Abigail saw his mouth clearly enunciate the word. Raphael told her that time didn't exist, that it was only an illusion created by changes of state in the ever present now. He'd also said that she possessed the ability to *tune*, to master more of the human experience. Could she use that ability to change state now?

Abigail reached out with her spirit and found the Earth, grounded herself, and dug deep. The life force of the planet rose up through her body and she became one with the power, her body a conduit indistinguishable from the energy that surged through it. She stood up. Or rather, her spirit self stood up, the spirit self she experienced while looking down on the guesthouse in Taos where she and Caroline made love under the stars.

The room disappeared and she faced Lucifer, alone. He looked at her with surprise. His face twisted into a snarl as he realized the transition she'd made, and his fingers flexed like claws. He meant to tear her apart, spirit self or not.

Well, I have had just about enough of this, she decided. She remembered her experience as the Australopithecus ape-girl, her night in the storm, and the unbroken chain of women across the centuries that struggled to survive so that she might be here at this moment.

"Come and get me," she said.

Lucifer's anger surged into his chest and his hands snapped to shoulder level with his fingers outstretched like the tines of steel rakes. He rushed toward her like a lightning bolt exploding from out of a storm.

Rayna pushed Abigail to look for the key joints of every adversary. The first time Lucifer attacked she turned his vanity against him. The creature before her now manifested the masculine rage of an unfettered beast; vanity was irrelevant.

Raphael said that Lucifer's power was the power of man's evil in the world, his heart of darkness. *What if she ripped that dark heart right out of his chest?*

Lucifer's hands converged on her throat and she bent low and thrust her fist up through his scrotum and into his torso. He screamed and shuddered at the sudden impalement. He looked down at her with his mouth open and his eyes wide with fear.

Don't like it when you're the one being penetrated, eh? She ripped her arm up through his body and found his heart. Lucifer's head flew back and he gasped as his body convulsed in the air like a fish impaled on a hook.

Abigail summoned the power of her beast form and merged it with her spirit body. Canine fangs extended from her jaw and inside Lucifer's chest her fingers transformed into claws.

She looked into Lucifer's startled face and said very matter-of-factly, "Now *this* is going to leave a stain."

She twisted her hand and ripped the organ out of his chest, bursting the rib cage open. He threw his head back and screamed as his body fell backward. She held his den of black snakes in her palm and crushed it with her fingers. Black globs splattered the walls and ceiling. Lucifer's body hit the floor and disintegrated into a mass of writhing fragments that scattered like black cockroaches in all directions.

She stood there, back in the room, back in her body, and held her hand in an empty fist. Rivulets of black water ran between her fingers and splattered onto the floor. Lucifer was gone. Caroline lay on the bed with her eyes on Abigail, and wept with relief. It was over.

"You did something with your hair," Caroline said.

"Yes, I did," Abigail chuckled, and then smiled with love in her eyes.

Epilogue

"Is there anything better?"

The little brown-eyed girl stood in the garden of adobeDreams. Puffs of cotton ball clouds brightened the deep blue sky, and bees hummed amidst red coneflowers. The little girl held out her hand and grasped Abigail's fingers.

The child looked even lovelier in the daylight, with her face perfectly framed by two long braids of black hair fastened with silver barrettes. She wore the same black shawl and for the first time Abigail could see that the two flowers woven into the end of the cloth were indeed red poppies. *Caroline's totem.*

The girl raised her head to look at Abigail and squinted as the sun caught her eyes. A few stray hairs grew between the girl's dark brows. *We're going to have to pluck those, as you get older.*

The girl moved her head to avoid the direct sun and looked up. Her brown eyes sparkled in the sunlight and were unmistakable. Those were Caroline's eyes. In some incarnation of adobeDreams magic, Caroline's spirit reached out to Abigail in the form of a young child.

"Hello, Caroline," Abigail said, as warm tears moistened her eyes.

The little girl smiled and said, "Te quiero."

"I love you, too," Abigail said.

Abigail opened her eyes. Morning light filtered in through sheer curtains. Spooned together in bed, Abigail slid her hand down the flank of her lover's body. She slid her fingertips over the dip created by the iliac crest of the other woman's hipbone, then rested her hand on the curve of the woman's belly, just above the pubic mound. The other woman placed her hand on top of Abigail's and squeezed.

"Good morning," the woman said with a sleepy voice, and then added, "Do you smell that bread?" Yes, Abigail did. The aroma of fresh bread and pastries from the corner bakery woke them each morning.

Caroline lifted Abigail's hand and placed it behind her, then pulled back the sheets and stood up. Walking to the balcony she opened both doors and leaned out with her arms stretched across the upper doorframe. Her buttocks and legs were inside the room while her upper body leaned out onto the balcony. Abigail's eyes drank the play of light over every curve and striation. *Thank you, God. She is exquisite!*

Abigail got out of bed and placed a robe over Caroline's shoulders, then wrapped her arms around Caroline's waist. Caroline leaned back and held Abigail's arms, each woman snug in the other's embrace. In the distance jet contrails streaked across a deep blue sky and the Eiffel Tower stood tall.

Abigail smiled. *France! I finally made it to France!* To be young, gay, and in love, is there anything better?

###

About the Author

Robert Burke is a Colorado-based author, photographer, digital artist, and Reiki practitioner.

Author's blog: adobeDreams.blogspot.com

Related photographic products:
www.adobedreams.com

Other photographic products by Robert Burke:
www.earthsmiles.com